TAKE OUT

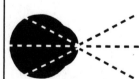

This Large Print Book carries the
Seal of Approval of N.A.V.H.

TAKE OUT

MARGARET MARON

THORNDIKE PRESS
A part of Gale, Cengage Learning

GALE
CENGAGE Learning·

Farmington Hills, Mich • San Francisco • New York • Waterville, Maine
Meriden, Conn • Mason, Ohio • Chicago

Copyright © 2017 by Margaret Maron.
Thorndike Press, a part of Gale, Cengage Learning.

LIBRARY OF CONGRESS CATALOGING-IN-PUBLICATION DATA

Names: Maron, Margaret, author.
Title: Take out / by Maragret Maron.
Description: Large print edition. | Waterville, Maine : Thorndike Press, 2017. |
    Series: Thorndike Press large print mystery
Identifiers: LCCN 2017022668 | ISBN 9781432838706 (hardcover) | ISBN 1432838709
    (hardcover)
Subjects: LCSH: Women detectives—Fiction. | New York (N.Y.)—Fiction. | Mystery
    fiction. | Large type books.
Classification: LCC PS3563.A679 T35 2017b | DDC 813/.54—dc23
LC record available at https://lccn.loc.gov/2017022668

Published in 2017 by arrangement with Grand Central Publishing, a
division of Hachette Book Group, Inc.

Printed in the United States of America
1 2 3 4 5 6 7 21 20 19 18 17

For Joe —
What a trip it's been! I wish we could
do it all, all over again.

CHAPTER 1

When her phone rang that afternoon in early June, Lt. Sigrid Harald, NYPD, was finishing up the paperwork that would close out the file on how and why she and her homicide team had arrested the owner of a tile store in the West Twenties for the murder of his business partner, a murder that would have gone down as an accident if Sigrid hadn't noticed a trivial inconsistency when she questioned the victim's wife. That tiny unnecessary lie was the loose thread that unraveled a complicated plot and led to a confession.

She moved the manila folders that covered her phone and in the process overturned a small bowl of Turkish puzzle rings. The bowl didn't break, but rings scattered across the floor as she lifted the receiver and said, "Lieutenant Harald."

"Sigrid? Oh, good," said a familiar male voice. "You too busy to talk?"

She assured him that he wasn't interrupting anything and waited to hear why he had called. Although he was slightly older and she was an only child, she had come to think of Elliott Buntrock almost as a younger brother in the brief time that they had known each other. She did not make friends easily, but circumstances had thrown them together, circumstances that continued to cast a bittersweet shadow on their friendship.

He was a rising star in the arts, a curator of modern exhibitions at important museums. She was a homicide detective who was carving out a reputation among her peers for solving difficult cases but was otherwise unknown outside the force until their worlds collided. One of the leading artists of the day had fallen in love with her and the three of them wound up in a murder investigation two Christmases ago.

"I know it's short notice, but when I called Gottfried to tell him that the catalog galleys are in, he invited us both to supper tonight. He just sold another picture."

"Let me guess where we'll be eating," Sigrid said dryly. "Tavern on the Green? Lutèce? La Côte Basque?"

"Only tourists go to Tavern on the Green these days." Buntrock, born and bred in the

Midwest, was now a consummate New Yorker who kept his fingers on the social pulse of the city. "He sold a picture, Sigrid. He didn't rob a bank. Anyhow, you ought to take a look at the galleys, too. I told him six o'clock. That okay with you?"

"I'll be there," she said, and hung up the phone to retrieve the puzzle rings that helped her focus when a case presented similar complexities. The most difficult ring, an intricate ten-band version, had stayed intact, but several of the simple four-band rings had come apart and as she manipulated the thin circles, her mind wandered to the catalog copy Buntrock wanted her to vet.

As if she knew enough about modern art to critique a catalog of Oscar Nauman's work.

It was the man she had loved, not his art, and she had made no secret of her preference for the exquisite portraits painted by the Dutch and Flemish of the sixteenth century. Too many women had been dazzled by Oscar Nauman's twentieth-century fame and it amused him that Sigrid was totally indifferent both to his fame and to his abstract paintings.

Intimacy did not come easily for her and in the beginning, she had resisted him instinctively, as if sensing that her life would never again be the same if she allowed him past her defenses. He kept her off balance, showing up unexpectedly, coaxing her into trying new things, turning her well-balanced world upside down until she capitulated so completely that when he died in a car accident out in California, she was helpless with grief. Even worse was when his attorney informed her that Nauman had left behind a hastily drawn will that made her his sole heir, an irony that had not escaped Elliott Buntrock and many of Nauman's associates.

That was a year ago. Time had not made it easier to deal with the repercussions of his death. She still wavered between grief and anger, but she had learned to cope and, with the help of friends like Buntrock, to make decisions about the large estate left in her care.

She slid the last band into its narrow slot and gave it the final twist to lock it into place. Twenty minutes later, she had read over her homicide report, signed it, and routed it for the DA's attention.

Several blocks north of the twin towers, on a street where private homes butt up against commercial buildings, is an unpretentious diner where one can still get a meal that tastes home cooked yet will not empty an artist's wallet if he feels expansive and wants to treat an infrequent guest.

Not that Rudy Gottfried's wallet was exactly empty these days.

"Retro's getting hot again," the old artist said cynically as he added butter to his mashed potatoes and held up the empty saucer for the waiter to bring more. "And I've got a studio full of stuff that didn't sell the first time around."

When Oscar Nauman first came to New York, he had shared a loft with Gottfried and the two men had cut a wide swath through the city's art scene. Gottfried never made it as big as Nauman, but they had stayed friends for forty years, so he was a prime resource for Elliott Buntrock, who was curating an Oscar Nauman retrospective at the Arnheim Museum of Modern Art. Planning had begun before Nauman's death and the show was due to open in the fall. Both artists had spent time in Europe in the days long before email, and Gottfried had saved Nauman's letters, letters that laid out complex theories of line and color that he explored in his work.

Embittered by his experiences with "*helden* curators" who considered the placement of art in a gallery more important than the art itself, Gottfried had been wary of Buntrock when they first met after Nauman's death. Oddly enough, considering how undemonstrative and reserved she usually was, Sigrid Harald was the one who had forged their unlikely friendship. Because of her, the younger man now had Gottfried's trust and cooperation. The only problem was that Gottfried kept dredging up intriguing conversations from the past and Buntrock was torn every time. The catalog was already over budget and behind schedule and to include something new, no matter how pertinent to the show, would mean cutting something too important to leave out.

Tall and thin with bony arms and legs, Buntrock often reminded people of a shore bird — a stilt or ibis, angular and stiff-gaited — and now, as Gottfried described how Nauman became fascinated by Cassinian ovals after attending a mathematics lecture in Zurich and how he had translated them into several of his major pictures, Buntrock looked like a heron regarding a particularly tasty shrimp just out of reach.

"Dammit, Rudy!" he groaned. "Why didn't you tell me about this before?"

The older man shrugged. "Leaky memory. Like a wet sponge. Things keep dripping out that I haven't thought of in years."

Buntrock shook his head in frustration. "When this is over, I'm going to squeeze your brain dry. There's a best-selling memoir sloshing around in there."

"Yeah?" After years of living on the edge of penury, Gottfried's eyes brightened at the possibility of more income.

While the two men conferred over plates of meat loaf, Sigrid gave up on her overcooked broccoli and leaned back in the booth to watch the people who passed by the diner's wide plate-glass windows. Rush hour was long over and daylight was fading, so foot traffic this mild spring evening was sporadic.

According to Gottfried, a world-famous soprano lived in one of the three-story Federal-style row houses across the way and the elderly widow of a Mafia don lived a few doors down in another. The don had been murdered, gunned down in this very street, while Sigrid was still in grade school and Gilbert and Sullivan were the closest she ever got to the opera, so she knew she would not recognize either woman should one of them suddenly appear in the street. Nevertheless, it was amusing to speculate.

Gottfried himself lived and worked in the basement apartment of a house directly opposite. The front of the apartment was dark and cramped with the low ceilings and small rooms deemed sufficient for servants' quarters during the eighteenth century, but the back opened into a large glass solarium that had been tacked on sometime in the last fifty years. North light flooded the space and Gottfried had long ago cleared out the last anemic plants to make room for his riotous abstract paintings, two of which now belonged to Sigrid.

The situation still bewildered her. How, she wondered, could she be so involved with modern art that her off-duty hours would be taken up with meetings like this? Her taste in art leaned toward the precisely mannered portraits of the late Gothic, not the sloppy-looking chaotic works of her own time. She had fashioned herself an orderly life and had risen through the ranks by her ability to solve complex cases with a logic that fitted one fact with another until a pattern was revealed. Almost against her will, though, she had fallen in love with one of the icons of late twentieth-century art, and when Nauman's car plunged off the road last year, she was shocked to learn that he had left her everything — not only his own work but also several works done by his friends, a list that read like a Who's Who of the most important artists of the day.

The Arnheim show was shaping up to be *the* art event of the year. At least three private Midtown galleries would be linked to the show through their holdings, and both Buntrock and her attorney insisted that Sigrid keep herself fully informed. Thus tonight's meeting.

At a diner.

An unlikely setting for stratospheric maneuverings, thought Sigrid. Almost as unlikely as the three of them — a late-thirties homicide detective, an eccentric mid-forties curator in a rainbow-colored Jeff Gordon racing jacket, and an elderly artist who looked more like a stevedore who'd spent his life unloading ships than someone who pushed paint around a canvas.

Nauman had been linked with several beautiful women over the years, from a violently temperamental Austrian artist to a titled Irish redhead who planned charitable events for the city's movers and shakers. Knowing this, few people could understand his attraction to this police officer. Lt. Harald might be the daughter of a noted photojournalist, but she was tall and thin with none of the voluptuous curves of Nauman's earlier women. Her neck was too long, her mouth too wide, her chin too strong. But her wide-set gray eyes changed from slate to silver, depending on her mood, and when they met after one of his colleagues was murdered, Sigrid's prickly nature had intrigued him, especially when she rejected his advances and showed no interest in falling into bed with him.

She was like one of those Chinese puzzle boxes that take patience and perseverance to open and he had patiently persevered until she opened up to him with all her secret compartments laid bare, delighting him with their complexity.

After all these months, time had blunted the worst of her grief, but she still had irrational bursts of anger that his cavalier driving habits had done this to them both.

From the skid marks left on that mountain road in California, the reporting trooper theorized that Nauman had been driving much too fast to make that hairpin turn. What was he doing up in those hills anyhow? As chair of Vanderlyn College's art department, he was supposed to be attending a meeting of the College Art Association in LA where he and Buntrock were featured speakers, not off sightseeing in an unfamiliar car. Yet, while Buntrock met with colleagues at the Getty Museum, Nauman had taken their rental car for a long drive out into the

16

hills, where he lost control and plunged over the edge of a mountain road into one of the canyons.

Damn you, Nauman! Why, why, WHY?

She took a deep breath to gain control of her grief, willing herself back to calmness.

Across the street from the diner and two doors to the left of Gottfried's building, a rather short old woman in a bulky gray cardigan climbed the stoop, one laborious step at a time. She carried a white shopping bag with a red-and-green logo that proclaimed delicacies from Giuseppone di Napoli, a Village institution known for its homemade pasta, its spicy sauces, fresh buffalo cheese, and imported olives. Holding on to the iron railing, she carefully drew one foot up beside the other before attempting the next step.

"Is that the Mafia widow?" Sigrid asked as the woman unlocked the door and disappeared inside.

Gottfried had been watching, too. "Naw. Her housekeeper. And before you ask, that's not Charlotte Randolph either," he said of the woman who approached the doorway to the immediate right of his own door.

"I do know that Charlotte Randolph must be nearly eighty by now," Sigrid said.

Like Sigrid herself, the slender white

woman who climbed the stoop and pushed the doorbell was probably thirty-nine or forty. Wearing form-fitting red tights and a long white tunic fringed at the neck and hips, she must have been hailed from farther down the street, because she turned and waved to a tall black man in a short-sleeved blue shirt. His tie was loosened around his neck and a jacket was slung over his shoulder. He carried a white paper bag in his free hand and took the steps two at a time to join her at the top of the stoop as someone from within opened the door for them.

"That's the niece and stepson," said Gottfried. "They come bearing dinner at least twice a month. She's the granddaughter of La Randolph's sister and he's the son of her third husband."

"Keeping themselves in the will?" Elliott Buntrock asked with an amused lift of one eyebrow.

"Why not? The niece is her closest relative and she's certainly not going to leave it to the Met. Not after the board backed Rudolph Bing when she had that fight with him."

Diverted, Buntrock paused with a forkful of meat loaf in midair. "Surely all those board members are long retired or dead by now?"

"Bing, too, for that matter," Rudy Gott-fried agreed cheerfully. "But Randolph's famous for holding grudges. It was four years before she would sing there again. I hear she's writing her bio. That catfight should be good for at least one chapter."

"Why is it that whenever a woman takes a stand, it's always called a catfight?" Sigrid asked. Her tone was not accusatory and appeared to express only genuine curiosity, but Buntrock grinned and Rudy Gottfried's bulky frame stiffened.

"I don't *always* do anything," he protested. "But what else would you call it? He was bitchy. She slapped his face. Then they clawed each other to shreds. Too bad it happened before the *National Enquirer* hit its stride. These silly little feuds between rock stars are like powder-puff duels compared to that."

He saw the amused glance Buntrock sent Sigrid and gave a sheepish grin. "Okay, yes. I do read the tabloid headlines."

They laughed and as they turned their attention back to the timeline he was amending for the Arnheim catalog, Buntrock said, "So how much do you remember about Nauman's first meeting with Rothko?"

It was a pleasant evening, not yet fully dark,

19

so when supper was over, Sigrid and Bunt-rock walked the few short blocks to Houston Street.

"Did you hear?" he asked. "The new board of trustees at the Breul House fired their incompetent director."

The Breul House was an idiosyncratic historical house where a longtime friend had almost persuaded Nauman to stage his retrospective. A murder had cancelled that venue, to Buntrock's relief, and Sigrid had to smile, remembering that the director was both incompetent and not completely ethical. Something about deaccessioning art works at his former post. She had forgotten the details, but Nauman had introduced her to Buntrock in the course of the investigation and a friendship had developed based on a mutual fondness for Gilbert and Sullivan.

"Have they hired a replacement?" she asked, threading her way between some overflowing garbage pails at the curb and a vegetable stand that encroached on the side-walk.

"As a matter of fact, she interned with me when she was finishing up her doctorate." He paused in front of the cut flowers at the end of the stand. "Dorothy Reddish. *Doctor* Dorothy Reddish. I wrote a glowing recommendation." He lifted two bunches of flowers from their tubs. "Tulips or daisies?"

"You don't need to buy me flowers."

"Need and want are two different things, Sigrid. Which?"

"Tulips, then."

He paid the grocer, who wrapped the stems in tissue paper and handed her the bright yellow blossoms with a broad smile.

They parted at the Houston Street subway, where he would take the Seventh Avenue train uptown to his apartment on West End Avenue, while she kept walking west to her own place near the river with no more thought of divas or dons.

CHAPTER 2

Near the lower end of Sixth Avenue, on a corner where the windowless side of one building pulls back eight feet farther from the other, an opportunistic sycamore tree shelters a long metal park bench anchored in cement. The space isn't big enough to be called a park — no grass, no flowers, but it's a shady place to sit in the summer and with cardboard scraps to cover its slats in winter, the bench makes a warmer bed than the icy sidewalk, sheltered as it is on two sides by brick walls. Despite the city's periodic efforts to rid the homeless from its streets, the bench does seem to invite them. The nearest bus stop is a block away and the storefronts on the other side of the street are not for browsing but strictly utilitarian — an electrician, a shoe repair, a locksmith, and a dry cleaners. Locals seldom use the bench and they don't complain about the street people who do.

Live and let live.

Except when they don't.

That mild June morning, a patrol car on the beat stopped at the corner. When the officer got out to prod the sleeping derelict onto his feet, he discovered that the man was dead with no obvious sign of violence. This was not a first for the young officer, nor even a second. Living on the streets too often meant dying on the streets. Too much rotgut whiskey, too many drugs, or an untreated medical condition, who knew?

Not his problem.

Ordinarily, he would have called it in, waited for the wagon to come take the body off his hands, made a note of it in his daily report, and that would have been that.

What made this death different was finding a second body under a dingy comforter at the far end of the bench.

"I thought it was the first guy's belongings," the officer told Lt. Sigrid Harald when the homicide team arrived. He pointed to the takeout cartons strewn under the bench where ants and yellow jackets were busy with the food scraps. A crumpled bag bore the logo of a nearby Italian restaurant. "It's like he had supper and then slumped down against the armrest and went to sleep, but then when I saw the other one

23

and he was bleeding, too . . ."

Sigrid watched the ME swab identical thin trickles of blood that had oozed from the mouths of the dead men. Both were white and both wore jeans and knit shirts. The first man was at least seventy. His white hair was worn in an abbreviated ponytail secured by a blue rubber band. His short white Santa Claus beard looked hand-trimmed. His green, long-sleeved cotton T-shirt was marginally newer than the faded gray shirt of his companion in death, and he wore thick leather sandals without socks while the other man had on ragged sneakers.

The younger man's graying hair was close-cropped and he appeared to be in his early fifties, but he had the sunken cheeks and ashy skin of an addict, so he could have been much younger.

His immediate examination finished, Dr. Cohen stood and indicated that the detectives could begin searching the bodies.

"Overdose?" Sigrid asked him.

The ME shrugged. "The younger guy's got the physical signs of a crystal meth user, but the other one? He's got a pacemaker. No sign of meth and no tracks on his arms. Time of death for both of them was probably sometime between midnight and six a.m."

"Food poisoning?" she asked.

"Botulism or ptomaine?" He cast a doubtful eye over the two bodies. "Won't know till I open them up. No vomit, though, and it does look as if they had a good final meal, if that Giuseppone bag means anything. I'm not ready to call it a homicide, but it sure as hell would be a real coincidence if their deaths were natural. Not with that blood. I'll take samples, but you know how long it takes to run a tox screen if it's not something common."

To be on the safe side, Sigrid sent several officers to canvass shops and houses in the immediate area, then walked over to Detective Elaine Albee, an attractive blonde in her early thirties, just as Albee pulled a roll of fifties and twenties from the older man's pocket.

"Four hundred eighty," Albee said as she finished counting, and slid the money into an evidence bag.

"No ID?"

"Sorry, Lieutenant. Just a Duane Reade receipt from two days ago — the one on Ninth and Forty-Third — for a bottle of aspirins. Three subway tokens, a five, two ones, and some change in that other pocket. Nothing else except these two keys."

The keys could have been for an apartment door, but there were no identifying names or numbers.

"The small bills were separate from the large ones?" asked Detective Tildon, glancing over at Albee's findings. He had turned out the pockets of the younger man. No ID, but he'd found a flyer for a soup kitchen two blocks down, a small nondescript switchblade with a bone handle, a twenty-dollar bill, and a handful of change. "Four hundred and eighty in that guy's pocket and a twenty here? You suppose that bankroll started out at an even five hundred?"

A few years older than Albee and Lowry, Tillie was Sigrid's most trusted team member even though he occasionally tried her patience with his excessively detailed reports. Nothing was too small to escape his attention.

"You're suggesting our first man shared his wealth?" she asked dubiously. "Why?"

Tillie had no answer to that. In the meantime, Albee's partner, Detective Jim Lowry, had finished with the grocery cart parked behind the bench. It held an umbrella, a half-used roll of paper towels, a box of crackers, and some articles of clothing, but nothing to identify the owner.

"Probably belonged to the methhead," Lowry said, "since he's the one with the blanket."

When their crime scene photographer had taken several instant pictures of the men's faces, Tillie said, "Want us to go talk to the staff at the soup kitchen? See if they knew one of these guys?"

Sigrid nodded and Tillie signaled to Ruben Gonzalez, one of the newer detectives, as a uniformed officer rounded the corner and approached them. Holding on to his arm for support was an elderly white-haired woman who barely topped his elbow and who seemed to move with difficulty. A small group of curious pedestrians had collected behind the yellow tape that marked off the bench. When asked, none volunteered knowledge of the dead men.

"I'm ashamed to say I never look at street people very closely," said one woman.

"Don't beat yourself up," said her friend. "What can one person do? It's the city's problem and City Hall keeps shifting the blame for why we don't have more homeless shelters."

"Lieutenant?" the officer called. "This lady may know one of them."

Sigrid motioned them forward.

"This is Miss Orlano," he said. "She lives just down the block. A guy in the diner says he's seen her come this way with takeout pretty regularly and her employer said she came last night."

Until then, Sigrid had not paid attention to their precise location. Now she looked more closely at the direction from which Miss Orlano had come and recognized the diner where she and Elliott Buntrock had eaten supper with Rudy Gottfried last week. And unless she was mistaken, this was the same woman who had entered the house across the street, the house where Rudy said the Mafia widow lived.

Seen up close, the old woman had a small wrinkled face overshadowed by thick eyebrows of coarse wiry gray hair that almost met over the bridge of her nose. She ignored Sigrid's outstretched hand and shuffled straight over to the bodies still on the bench. Albee pulled back the paper sheets that covered them.

She stood gazing at the first one for so long that Albee gently touched her arm. "Did you know him?"

"That one I see many times," she said with a distinct Italian accent. She gave the older man a cursory glance. "Him? Never."

"But you brought the other man food?" Sigrid asked.

Those bushy eyebrows drew together over a frown and she spoke with obvious reluctance. "Not just him. Most places give too much food for two old women and when there are leftovers, we give to the hungry. If no one is here, I leave it on the bench. Someone always takes it."

Both of the open foam cartons on the ground under the benches bore smears of alfredo sauce, white cheese, and scraps of pasta, but the one under the meth addict seemed to have less of the red sauce than the box lying closer to the other body. Miss Orlano pointed to the first box. "That was ours. Fettuccine alfredo. Not the lasagna."

"Did you eat any of the fettuccine?"

The woman nodded. "And my signora, too."

"You brought it in that Giuseppone bag?"

"Yes."

"What time did you come?"

"About eight-thirty. Before dark."

"But you knew this one?" Sigrid asked, pointing to the speed addict.

"Not to *know*," the woman said. "Just to see. Just to know he was sometimes here."

"So when did you last see him?"

From farther up the block, a fire engine pulled out into the street with lights flashing and siren blasting, so Sigrid had to repeat the question.

Miss Orlano beetled her thick gray eyebrows, then shrugged. "Last week. We had Chinese that day and my signora sent me with the egg rolls we did not eat. Matty —"

She broke off in sudden consternation.

"Who's Matty?" the lieutenant asked.

"One of the bums that's sometimes here."

Sigrid fixed her with skeptical gray eyes. "You sure it's not one of these men?"

Miss Orlano dropped her own eyes.

"You might as well tell us the truth, Miss Orlano. I have a feeling we'll find out anyhow as soon as we run his fingerprints."

The older woman sighed and gestured to the younger man. "He's Matty. Matty Mutone."

"And how do you know him?"

"His mother was a good friend to my signora. He turned into a bum. Broke her heart before she died."

In a mixture of sadness and scorn, she told them how her employer, a Mrs. Benito DelVecchio, had tried to help the young man break free of drugs, but after his last failure, she washed her hands of him and forbade him to come to her house again. "She does not talk to him and she does not give him money, but every week, for his mother's sake, she pretends she's very hungry and then there is too much food to throw away, so I bring it to this bench.

Every Tuesday. Usually, he's here, sometimes not."

"But not last night?"

"No."

With lips clamped tight, she turned to go and would have fallen had Sigrid not reached out to steady her. She signaled to the young uniformed officer who had escorted the old woman here.

"Officer —" She looked at the man's name tag. "Officer James, please see that Miss Orlano gets home safely."

"Yes, ma'am," he said, offering his arm.

"I can walk," she snapped. "I'm no cripple yet."

"I'm sure you can manage on your own," he said cheerfully. "But this sidewalk's uneven and if you fall, they'll have my scalp, so please, ma'am?"

Still grumbling, she took his arm and they moved slowly back down the block.

Giuseppone di Napoli was a popular neighborhood restaurant and when questioned by Detectives Albee and Lowry, the manager rolled his eyes. "Lasagna? Do you know how many of our customers order that? And half of 'em take some home with them." But he thumbed through the receipts from the night before. "Twelve lasagnas served on-site, and four takeouts, two of those on credit cards. Five servings of fettuccine. No takeouts. And nobody got sick either," he added defensively.

Within the hour, Sigrid's team had names and addresses for the two who had used credit cards. One was a woman, who lived two blocks over on Prince Street. The other lived half a block up on Sixth. For once they got lucky. Both customers were home and both still had their takeout boxes. The woman's was in her garbage pail, the elderly man's was in his refrigerator. "One order of Giuseppone's lasagna lasts me three meals," he told them.

They came up empty on the neighborhood canvass, but Sigrid gave orders for officers to come back after five to try finding people who were not at home now.

"Albee, you and Lowry stop by the restaurant later and see if any of last night's waiters can remember who took lasagna or fettuccine home with them."

Martha's Table was the name of the nearby soup kitchen. Its motto was "Works, not words," a sly poke at those sisters in the Gospel of Luke. Two volunteers immediately recognized the instant picture of Matty Mutone that Gonzalez showed them; the other victim's picture drew only shrugs and headshakes.

"But yeah, poor Matty was one of our regulars. Friendly kid," said the woman who was probably no more than forty.

"Kid?"

The woman laughed as she dumped a gallon can of string beans into a serving tray on the steam table. Although the place wouldn't open for at least another hour, a savory odor of beef stew wafted through the large room and people were already lining up on the sidewalk outside.

"He was like a puppy — eager to please."

"You didn't know him from the old days," said the other volunteer, a small black man with a shiny bald head who was stacking loaves of two-day-old bread at the end of the counter. "When I first came here a few years ago, he'd show up every once in a while. He was heavy into meth — twitchy eyes, quick to mouth off about how he was 'connected.' Like anybody believed that. But then he went into rehab, cleaned up his act, got a job, even volunteered here once in a while."

"Yeah?" said the woman. "I didn't know that."

"He crashed and burned a few months ago," said the man as he finished stacking the loaves with the precision of a bricklayer. "Right before Christmas. He went back to using again. Yo-yoed back and forth between wanting to punch somebody out and crying for how things had gone so wrong."

"Matty? C'mon. He never punched anybody out," the woman objected. "He was a puppy dog."

"One that'd been kicked too many times," said the man. He sighed. "Yeah, he was one beat-down little puppy."

"Who were his friends here?" asked Gonzalez.

"Friends?" They shrugged. "He was pretty much a loner."

On the likely chance that this was indeed a homicide, Sigrid signaled to Tillie and they walked down the side street, past Rudy Gottfried's basement apartment, to Number 409, a well-maintained private home. It was period Federal style on the outside, but when Miss Orlano answered the door and showed them into the living room, Sigrid was instantly reminded of her grandmother Lattimore's early twentieth-century home down in North Carolina. Polished mahogany chests and tables held tasteful keepsakes. The chairs were upholstered in harmonizing colors and Oriental rugs lay on the hardwood floors.

All bought with mob money, thought Sigrid.

Like Sigrid's grandmother, Mrs. DelVecchio's wrinkled face held traces of youthful beauty. A tall woman with fair skin and the clear blue eyes of northern Italy, she did not rise when they entered and was clearly accustomed to deference. Seated in a high-backed wing chair like a contessa on a throne, she did not smile in welcome. No sooner had Miss Orlano announced them than she waved aside Sigrid's ID and fixed her with a cold and arrogant eye.

Before Sigrid could express sympathy, the woman gestured for them to be seated.

"Orla has already told me. Where will they take the boy's body and when will it be released?"

"Are you Mr. Mutone's next of kin?"

There was a further tightening of those thin lips. "I will be responsible for his burial."

"We'll still need his next of kin."

"There *is* no other next of kin. Only me. His godmother."

"When did you last see him?"

Mrs. DelVecchio frowned and glanced at the woman who seemed as much her companion as her housekeeper. "In February. He came here talking crazy, begging me for

35

money. I told him no more. Not a penny."

"What about you yourself, Miss Orlano?"

"Yesterday, I went to the bakery up on Houston Street and he was sitting on a bench there, so I gave him a muffin when I came out."

"And last night?"

"I told you. I left fettuccine on the bench."

"Where did he live?"

"On the street. That grocery cart. Everything he owned was in it."

"It was his choice," said Mrs. DelVecchio. "He —"

She paused at the sound of a key turning in the outer door and they watched as a heavyset middle-aged man let himself into the foyer. He was just under six feet tall, his broad flat face was pitted with old acne scars. Without removing his sunglasses, he let the door slam behind him and lumbered into the room.

"Sofia! I came as fast as I could. A fender bender had traffic on the bridge backed up. Are you all right?"

He bent over the seated Mrs. DelVecchio and kissed the thin cheek she offered him.

"Now that you are here, yes," she said. "These are police officers, George."

His glasses finished turning from dark to clear as he straightened to face them and behind the lenses, his brown eyes widened. "Lieutenant Harald, isn't it?"

"I'm sorry," Sigrid said, rising from her chair. "Have we met?"

"Only informally." He held out his hand. "George Edwards. It was at that gawdawful opening for one of Hal DiPietro's artists. Last spring. Right before he was killed. Didn't you handle that investigation?"

Sigrid nodded. "You're an attorney, aren't you?"

"Yes. Sofia — Mrs. DelVecchio — called me as soon as she heard that Matty was found dead next to another body. Something about the fettuccine Orla took him?"

"We don't have a cause of death yet, Mr. Edwards. We're just here to learn more about him. Do you know any of his friends? Where he lived?"

"No. I helped him get back into rehab two or three years ago. When he came out, we got him a room over on West Summer Street, but he gave it up when he started using again. Would rather spend the money on drugs than a bed." Edwards gave them the name of the facility. "They might know something. They were supposed to do follow-ups."

Mrs. DelVecchio gave an impatient wave of her hand.

"If there are no further questions for my clients —"

"Just one for now," said Sigrid. "Miss Orlano, you said that others leave food on that bench, too. Who?"

"Different ones," the housekeeper replied. "The red door woman most often and sometimes the boy from the diner. Maybe others from the street. I do not keep watch."

They stood to go and George Edwards showed them out. At the door, he handed Sigrid his card. "If you need to speak to them again, please call me first."

Back outside, Tillie spotted a red door at the opposite end of the street. There was no professional signage on the front of the otherwise nondescript three-story building, but steps led down to the basement and a homemade board wired to the iron handrail announced that jazz played there nightly from 8:30 till 2:00, Wednesday through Saturday. They crossed, rang the brass bell, and were answered by a tall, loose-jointed woman who wore her brown hair in a single side braid across her shoulder.

She cocked her head in amusement.

"You're not plumbers, are you?"

When they showed her their badges and introduced themselves, the woman frowned.

"Somebody complained again?"

"Complained?" Sigrid asked. "Complained about what?"

"Oh, people are always complaining about something," the woman said smoothly, leaning against the door frame. She wore a red shirt and white capris and the toenails of her bare feet were painted a pale green.

"And you are — ?"

"Janis Jennings. How can I help you?"

"We're investigating two deaths at the end of this block, down on Sixth."

"Oh, is that why all the police cars and people are down there? I was wondering. Who died?"

"We don't have a full identification on both men yet, so maybe you can help us, Miss Jennings," Sigrid said.

"*Mrs.* Jennings," the woman corrected cheerfully. "Just don't ask me where *Mr.* Jennings is. Haven't seen him in four years. He went down to the diner for coffee one morning and never came back."

"Did you file a missing persons report?" Tillie asked.

Mrs. Jennings hooted with laughter and her braid bobbed up and down against her red shirt. "God, no! Good riddance. He took his clothes and our dog and cleaned out our bank account. I wouldn't mind having the dog back, though. She was good company."

Tillie handed her the pictures of the two dead men. "Do you know either of these men?"

"Never saw this guy," she said of the older man. Her face fell at the second picture. "Awww! Poor Matty! Oh, jeez. That's too bad. Did he finally overdose?"

"You know him?"

"Know who he is. He's been hanging around the neighborhood ever since I got here. Liked to brag about being connected."

"Connected?"

"To the Mafia guy who used to live over there." She pointed down the block to Number 409, the DelVecchio house. "Said he was a nephew or something. Said he was keeping an eye on the guy's widow. Protecting her."

"Protecting her from what?" asked Tillie.

Mrs. Jennings shrugged. "Who knows? I thought it was all in his head till somebody at the diner told me that some Mafia guy was gunned down right in front of his house there. I felt sorry for Matty. Gave him a couple of freebies."

"Freebies?" asked Sigrid.

"You know. A free meal, a couple of dollars."

"Did you ever take food to him?"

"If I saw him down at that bench when I came up from the subway." She grinned. "He told me his aunt didn't like him hanging around, so if he was there when I was passing, I'd give him my doggie bag if I had one. A few bucks now and then."

"I take it you don't care for Mrs. DelVecchio?" said Sigrid.

"I don't care for hypocrites. That house wasn't bought with clean money, was it? Drugs, too, probably. Yet she could turn up her nose at poor Matty and complain about —"

"About you?" Sigrid asked when the woman changed her mind about whatever it was that she started to say.

"Me and anybody else on the block that annoyed her. If we left our trash barrels out at the curb too long. If we were having a party or the jazz club got too loud on a Saturday night."

"You didn't happen to see him last night, did you?"

The woman shook her head.

A plumber's van pulled up to the curb. The man behind the wheel rolled down his window and called, "Jennings?"

"You got it, honey," she said happily. "Sorry, Lieutenant, but there's a leak in my

41

washer line."

On their way back to the park bench, while Tillie stopped to ask questions at the diner, Sigrid crossed over to Gottfried's apartment but the artist did not respond to the doorbell.

By now, the bodies had been removed and the beat officer who had called it in was rolling up the yellow tape. The foam food cartons had been bagged and tagged and there was nothing left except Matty Mutone's grocery cart.

"Might as well bring that in, too," Sigrid said. "And get the other guy's clothes from the ME, Albee. Maybe you missed something the first time."

Before heading back to her office, she left orders for the officers who would come back to canvass the neighborhood a second time to see if they could learn who had brought lasagna to that park bench.

CHAPTER 3

While waiting for the medical examiner to determine if they were dealing with two accidental deaths or a double homicide, Sigrid had a clerk pull Matty Mutone's record. It showed several misdemeanors and that he had twice done time for minor drug-related felonies.

With no other pressing cases, Tillie did a search for data on Mrs. DelVecchio and her housekeeper.

"Nothing on Miss Orlano," he reported, "and any mention of Mrs. DelVecchio has to do with her husband's activities. Matty may have bragged about being connected, but his only link to the mob seems to be through her, and everything I found indicates that DelVecchio kept his home life totally separate from his business."

When Albee and Lowry returned to the office after lunch, they had little to show from their latest canvass of the neighborhood. As was common in the SoHo area so close to the river, the street was a mixture of scruffy commercial and pricey residential. Except for the diner and that house with the red door at the end, the buildings on the south side of the street were all warehouses. No windows and nobody there on a regular basis.

"We checked by Giuseppone's again," said Albee, who brushed back a lock of her long blond hair as she laid her notes out on her desk. "One of the waiters remembered that they'd had an extra takeout order for lasagna. The customers ordered it at the table after they'd finished eating and they paid cash, so it didn't show up in the receipts. She said that she'd seen the couple before but she didn't know their names."

"The woman's white. The man's black. Both good-looking, both mid-to-late thirties. She's pretty sure she would recognize them again," said Jim Lowry, popping the top on a can of soda. He took a long, thirsty swallow, then set the can on his desk so that he could flip through his notes. "The guy that runs the cleaners across the street from that bench says he saw Mutone talking to Miss Orlano a time or two. He's open later than the other shops along that block, so

44

he's seen people from the neighborhood drop off food there. A black guy showed up on that bench last fall and was sleeping there pretty regularly till late February or early March, when Mutone claimed the bench for himself and ran the guy off. Nobody has a name for him and he hasn't been seen around there since, but he's why people first began bringing food there."

"We told the patrol in that area to try to come up with a name," said Albee. "And we asked the Jennings woman at the other end of the street if she'd ever talked to him. She says not."

Tillie looked up from his computer screen, a smile on his round, cherubic face. "I forgot to tell you, Lieutenant — Janis Jennings owns her building and it's registered as a single-room occupancy."

Sigrid frowned. "An SRO? It seemed a little upscale for that."

Tillie was looking so pleased with himself that the penny dropped right away.

"Are you saying that her red door isn't just a decorative whim?"

Tillie nodded. "Nothing's been proved and nobody's been charged. But complaints have been made. Mostly by Mrs. DelVecchio. It appears to be very discreet. The ground floor's a common area — shared kitchen and laundry room, dining facilities and lounge. Unlike most SROs, though, each bedroom seems to have a private bath and the rooms are individually rented."

"So the freebie that Matty got?"

Albee rolled her eyes and Lowry grinned. "I doubt if it was a takeout carton of left-overs."

"What about the second man?" Sigrid asked. "Any hits on his prints yet?"

Tillie shook his head.

"The dry cleaner didn't notice him and the other shops close at five."

"We spoke to someone from every house on the street," said Lowry, "and no one recognized his picture. At least no one said they did."

"Oh, and a Rudy Gottfried sends his regards," said Albee. "He lives across from the diner and says he knows you."

Albee tried to mask the open curiosity that everyone in the squad room felt about their boss's personal life. They knew that Oscar Nauman and the lieutenant had been lov-ers, as unlikely as that seemed, because the newspapers had covered his death and aspects of his life and his art in minute detail.

Before the pause grew awkward, they were joined by Detective Sam Hentz. He had accompanied the bodies to the morgue and a faint chemical smell clung to his brown linen sports jacket and to the two large bags that held the dead men's clothes and personal effects.

Tillie immediately reached for one of the bags and began going through the pockets again.

Of all the detectives in Sigrid's command, Hentz had been most resentful of her appointment and they were still somewhat wary of each other.

"Cohen give you the results?" she asked.

"Sorry, Lieutenant." He handed the bag with Matty Mutone's things to Albee. "He said he'd try to have something for us by midmorning."

Sigrid turned back to Lowry and Albee and said, "Did you question Charlotte Randolph?"

"Who?"

"A door or two up from Gottfried."

Sam Hentz paused in turning out the pockets of a pair of pants from the unidentified dead man and looked up with interest. "*The* Charlotte Randolph? She lives there?"

"Who's Charlotte Randolph?" asked Dinah Urbanska, the most junior member of the team. Built like a golden palomino, she was forever dropping coffee mugs, tangling her jacket on doorknobs and arm-rests, and bumping into people and doors. For some quixotic reason, the normally impatient and urbane Hentz had taken the awkward young woman under his wing to mentor and turn her into a proper detective.

"Before you were out of the egg," Hentz told her. "She was one of the greatest sopranos of her time."

"Which was when?" asked Lowry.

"When I was still a kid myself," Hentz admitted. "The Met used to build whole new productions around her. I saw her in *Rosenkavalier* and I've never forgotten it. She was golden."

Elaine Albee was impressed. "You went to the Metropolitan Opera when you were a kid?"

Hentz shrugged. "I have an aunt who loves it. So, did you question Randolph?"

"I questioned an old woman at Number 403," Albee said. "But now that you mention it, she carried herself like she'd been somebody and she did have a nice voice."

"She still is somebody," said Tillie, who had abandoned his inspection of the clothes to search online for Charlotte Randolph's name. "She just signed a big contract to write her autobiography. The publishers're

48

calling it a 'tell-all blockbuster.' Sounds like she's had quite a colorful personal life — a couple of famous singers, a wealthy philanthropist, a New York senator *and* a Connecticut governor."

He swiveled his screen around so that they could see the woman's picture, evidently a publicity photo taken from one of her concert performances. She wore a low-cut period gown with a diamond necklace and earrings. Her blond hair was carefully styled and there was a definite come-hither twinkle in her blue eyes.

"Wow!" said Dinah Urbanska.

"The hair's white now and shorter, but that's her, all right," said Albee. "She said that she sent food down to that bench once in a while, but not Tuesday night. And she didn't recognize either of our guys from the pictures."

"On the other hand," Sigrid said, "according to Rudy Gottfried she has a niece and a stepson who bring her food fairly often. I saw them the other night. The niece is white and the stepson's black."

"That couple from Giuseppone's?" Albee asked Lowry.

"We'll wait for Cohen's report," Sigrid said. "If it *is* poison, we'll ask if they brought her a takeout of lasagna last night."

Across the room, Tillie was giving Matty Mutone's extra pair of pants a closer examination. They were of good quality and had probably started out as the bottom half of an expensive suit. Except for lint and two pennies, the pockets were empty and Tillie was ready to move on until he noticed the small watch pocket almost obscured by the left front pocket. He stuck his finger in and touched metal.

"Lieutenant?" he said. "It's another key. Looks like a car key."

The key went around the room, but no one could say what make of car it was for. "Looks like a standard blank duplicate," said Lowry. "There's a hardware store at my subway stop. I'll check it out."

With nothing more to do till Cohen gave them his findings, Sigrid was pleased to realize she could keep an appointment she'd made earlier in the week. As she passed Sam Hentz's desk on her way out, she couldn't resist saying, "Your opera-loving aunt. That wouldn't be your aunt Lizzie, would it?"

When she took over the department, Sigrid had read through all the personnel files. Because of Hentz's early antagonism, she had taken a second look at his. She seldom paid much attention to clothes in those days, but then Lowry made an envious comment about a well-cut jacket Hentz was wearing, so when she spotted him driving an expensive sports car, she had gone back for a third look, hoping to learn how one of her team could legitimately afford it.

Listed as his next of kin was an aunt, "Lizzie Stopplemeyer." A few clicks on the computer confirmed that Elizabeth Stopplemeyer was the widow of Irving Stopplemeyer, whose face was almost as familiar as that of a certain Kentucky colonel. Stopplemeyer pastries could be found on the shelves of every grocery store east of the Mississippi from Canada to the Gulf of Mexico. When Sigrid asked, Hentz admitted that he was his childless aunt's favorite nephew. Hence the sports car, the beautifully tailored suits, and the silk ties. Relieved not to have a dirty cop on her team, she had not shared Hentz's secret with the others.

Now Hentz gave a wry smile. "What can I say? She thought I might have musical talents."

According to Elliott Buntrock, Hentz's aunt Lizzie was right. He had heard Hentz play at a Village jazz club and had learned that he was a better than average jazz pianist who had put himself through college playing in cocktail bars. Sigrid had a feeling that

51

this was something else Hentz never planned to share.

Well, she could understand that.

"It would be a kick to meet Charlotte Randolph in person, though," said Hentz. "She was the classic showbiz story where the understudy goes on as a complete unknown and comes off a star."

Marcus Livingston's warm brown face lit up in a wide smile and he chuckled when his secretary showed Sigrid in. "I was beginning to think you were blowing me off again," he teased.

Oscar Nauman's attorney had his law office on Madison Avenue and Sigrid was only a few minutes late, but his words recalled the many times she had failed to show up after Nauman's death. Unexpected circumstances had necessitated a new will and Nauman had planned to give it serious thought while out in California. As a stopgap, though, he had signed a simple "everything to Sigrid" will. When Livingston explained that she was now a very wealthy young woman, she had been so unnerved that she couldn't deal with all the complicated decisions that suddenly faced her. Instead, she'd pulled the covers over her head and started sleeping eighteen hours a day.

Eventually Livingston had persuaded her that they could do it together. "Besides," he'd said, "taxes are going to take most of it anyhow."

Not quite true, of course. Not by a long shot, but his calm reassurance persuaded her to make a start. Nauman had agreed to the major retrospective that Elliott Buntrock had proposed, but no papers had been signed, so that had been the first order of business. After that, step by step, she and Livingston had formed a working relationship and she now trusted him completely.

Today's meeting was to sign the final papers for the sale of Nauman's Connecticut house. As chair of the art department at Vanderlyn College, he had rented an impersonal three-room furnished apartment here in the city, but his home and his studio were in Connecticut and that's where he spent his weekends and summers. Livingston's secretary had arranged to have the apartment cleaned out and Sigrid had given up the lease to it without regret, but the house was harder. It wasn't just the memories of their weekends there together, it was his books, his notebooks, his clothes, his unfinished paintings. A thousand items and each item demanded a decision.

In the end, overwhelmed, she had kept nothing except Nauman's pipe and the silverpoint pen he'd used to draw her portrait. Instead, she had turned the keys over to the two people best suited for the job — Elliott Buntrock and Hester Kohn, the current owner of the gallery that had represented Nauman for almost thirty years.

When they first met, Sigrid had been more than a little intimidated by the woman, who exuded so much blatant sexuality.

"So round, so firm, so fully packed," Hentz had murmured when they interviewed Hester after the murder of another gallery owner. "Something my grandfather used to say about women who looked like her," he explained. " 'So round, so firm, so fully packed, so free and easy on the draw,' whatever that meant."

"I'm sure you knew exactly what he meant," Sigrid said dryly.

Hentz had grinned. "Probably not cigarettes," he'd agreed.

Now, to her surprise, Hester joined them in a cloud of musky perfume. Eyes shining with mischief, she gave Sigrid an air kiss, then leaned over to kiss Marcus Livingston on his cheek and give him a glimpse down the front of her low-cut summery dress. No longer intimidated, Sigrid could smile when Livingston said, "Quit trying to make an old man's pulse beat faster, Ms. Kohn."

"When are you going to call me Hester?" She pouted but took a chair next to Sigrid, smoothed her skirt around her shapely legs, and took a thick manila folder from a soft-sided green leather case that looked more like a purse than a briefcase. "Here's the inventory and a check for the things we sold minus our commission. You didn't specify who should get the check, so it's made out to your firm, Marcus, and you two can fight it out. Also a list of the art works that are consigned to Kohn and Munson Gallery, pending your approval, of course. We don't want to flood the market before the Arnheim show."

"And how's that coming?" he asked. "Still on schedule to open in September?"

"That's what Elliott Buntrock says." She turned to Sigrid. "I've heard that Søren Thorvaldsen plans to come over for it."

"Really?" The last she'd heard of Thorvaldsen, a Danish entrepreneur and an avid collector of Nauman's paintings, he was facing some rather serious charges of money laundering. "He's not in prison?"

Hester gave a cynical shrug. "Amazing what a good team of international lawyers can do, present company excepted."

Livingston laughed. "I'm no international lawyer, Ms. Kohn."

"Next he'll be telling us that he's just a country boy from the cotton fields of Columbia Law School," Hester told Sigrid. "I'd love to stay and chat, but I have a client flying in from LA." She reached into her briefcase again and drew out a small sketchbook. "I know you said you didn't want to keep anything, but I thought you might change your mind about this."

Sigrid opened it at random and saw her own eyes looking back at her. She had never posed for Nauman, yet here were her hands, her face, the back of her head in page after page of Nauman's quick, sure pencil strokes.

"When — ?" she whispered. "How — ?" She swallowed back the lump of grief in her throat. Turning another page, she saw herself sitting cross-legged on a couch in Nauman's studio, absorbed in a crossword puzzle in the Sunday *Times.* Only a few penciled lines, but he had caught her concentration. She remembered glancing up to find him looking past her as if his mind were miles away before this sketchbook claimed his attention again.

"Elliott said that Oscar was thinking about line and portraiture, but this is the only example we found," Hester said. "There's one near the back." She reached for the book. "This one of you is quite amazing, isn't it? Too bad he never finished it."

"He finished it," Sigrid said quietly.

"Oh? What happened to it? Where — ?" And then she took a closer look at Sigrid's eyes. "Ah," she said. "How stupid of me. I'm sorry, Sigrid."

She handed the pad to Sigrid, who closed it and laid it next to her purse.

"You okay?" Livingston asked when Hester had gone.

Sigrid nodded.

"May I?"

She handed him the sketchbook and the silence of the office was broken only by the slow turning of the pages.

When he came to the end, he sighed, then gave it back to her without comment before straightening his shoulders and opening the folder on his desk.

"Here's the best offer we've had on the house. Quite a bit over the market value, I'm afraid."

"Afraid?" For a moment, Sigrid was puzzled, then the meaning of his words came to her. "Because it was his?"

Livingston nodded. "Nothing we can do

about it. All the locals up there know who owned it. But for what it's worth, I don't think the buyer plans to exploit the connection. Now, are you absolutely sure this is what you want to do, Sigrid?"

"I could never live there," she said firmly. "And the house is too beautiful to just sit empty. Let someone else enjoy it."

She signed the papers and felt a sudden lifting of her spirits. The last of the hard decisions had finally been made. Hester and Buntrock would see to the art, which might take years to dispose of, but that was okay. Somehow, the art had less personal meaning for her.

"Do you know yet what you'll do with the money?" Livingston asked. "You've talked about scholarships or a foundation to award grants. Any decision?"

"Not yet. Could we leave it open for now?"

"Of course."

"Thanks, Marcus. You've been very patient with all this."

He tried to wave away her thanks, but she persevered even though expressing emotions had always been hard for her. Now she looked at him directly, the cool silver of her eyes meeting the warm topaz of his. "I'm glad you were Nauman's attorney."

"So am I, Sigrid," he said. "So am I."

CHAPTER 4

Next day, they were no nearer an ID for the second dead man. A doctored picture of him had been released to the news media and had run on the local TV channels. So far, no one had come forward to say, "Yes, that's my neighbor, my customer, my ex-wife's uncle."

Jim Lowry's hardware store thought that the unmarked key found in Matty Mutone's watch pocket was for a car or truck, but without a brand name, there was no easy way to tell the make.

Another canvass of the neighborhood had added nothing of significance, but the ME was ready to give them a cause of death. "Both died from internal bleeding, Lieutenant. A pretty heavy dose of warfarin. I've seen it before so it was an easy call."

"Rat poison?" Sigrid asked.

"Well, yes," he said. "But in controlled compounds, warfarin is commonly prescribed to prevent blood clots. Coumadin's the most popular form and I'm guessing that's what this is. I'll run a few more tests to be certain. The meth user probably would've lived if he'd been clean and his internal organs hadn't already been compromised. The older guy may've already been taking it. He had a pacemaker and that's a common drug for heart problems. If so, an overdose added to what he was already on would have pushed him right over the edge. In addition, he'd recently drunk quite a lot of gin. I'm surprised he could walk."

"Which box had the warfarin?"

"We found it in both cartons."

"But which had more? The lasagna or the fettuccine?"

Sigrid could almost hear his shrug over the phone.

"Too much cross-contamination to say for sure. Sorry, Harald."

The men's fingerprints were on both takeout cartons, which further suggested that the two had shared the food. Although their prints overlay each other, the fettuccine box was marginally cleaner, as if it had been wiped.

"If someone wiped that carton, that could be where the Coumadin began, right?"

asked Elaine Albee. "In the DelVecchio house?"

But Sigrid wasn't ready to commit so quickly. "It's a starting point, though." She took out the business card Mrs. DelVecchio's attorney had given her. "I'll give Mr. Edwards a call and you two see if you can find the homeless man that Mutone dispossessed of that bench."

When she finally got past his switchboard, George Edwards gave the heavy sigh of a much put-upon man. "Is this really necessary, Lieutenant?"

"I'm afraid so, Mr. Edwards. Do you know if your client has a heart condition?"

"Is that what killed Matty? Some sort of heart pills?"

"That's what our medical examiner thinks."

Silence from his end, then, "She's eighty-two, Lieutenant, and she has a pacemaker. I don't know what medications she's on, though." He gave another long sigh. "Very well, I'll clear my schedule and try to meet you at the house by noon."

"Bridge or ferry?" Jim Lowry asked Elaine Albee when they had questioned the staff at the soup kitchen again and learned that the man they sought, a man called Lunk, was now living in a halfway house on Staten Island.

Elaine had looked up the address. The halfway house was only a few blocks from the ferry landing and it was a beautiful spring day, so they wouldn't really need a car.

"Ferry," she said.

He grinned. "I'll buy you lunch. Sauerkraut or onions?"

"Big spender," she teased, happy that their relationship had eased into something smoother now that they had gotten over that rough patch. He had come on so strongly when they were first partnered that she had instinctively backed off, knowing the dangers of hooking up with a co-worker. She'd had no intention of short-circuiting her career for a quick fling. Besides, he wasn't her type — too confident, too handsome, too sure that she would fall into his arms and into his bed.

She had clamped down so hard on his overtures that when Dotty Vargas, a forthright brunette from the Bronx and one of their crime scene officers, started flirting with him last year, he had responded. Elaine had told herself that she wasn't jealous, that there was nothing to be jealous about. He wasn't her personal property. But Vargas went through men quicker than a hay fever sufferer goes through Kleenex and Jim had grown up on a Pennsylvania apple farm, which, in her eyes, made him a babe in New York's woods. She'd kept her mouth shut, though, and to her relief, the flirtation seemed to have died a natural death with no wounded feelings on either side.

Hot dogs were perfect for lunching on the ferry and they found a place near the stern and out of the wind where they could comfortably watch the buildings of Manhattan recede in the distance. A nearby group of tourists with several children were also munching on hot dogs and the tang of sauerkraut and onions mingled with the smell of salt water. Soon the children were tossing the ends of their buns over the railing and raucous seagulls dived for them, their white wings flashing in the late morning sun as they passed the Statue of Liberty.

At the halfway house, a grandmotherly white woman pushed back the glass panel that separated her cubicle from the lobby. "May I help you?"

Her brow furrowed when they showed her their badges and asked to speak to someone named Lunk.

"Lunk? Lunk?" She leaned forward to call to some men standing by the front door.

"Any of you guys know somebody named Lunk?"

"Yeah," said one of them. "I think his last name's Church."

A few clicks of her computer and the woman said, "Here he is. Of course. Laurence Church. According to his schedule, he's probably up on the roof weeding our vegetable garden."

They found him gazing out over the bay with a trowel in his hand. A stocky black man with hunched shoulders, he gave them a gap-toothed smile as they approached and gestured with his trowel to the row of planter boxes. Two of the boxes looked like leafy salad bowls; the rest contained ten-inch-high bright green plants.

"Ain't this something? Born on a farm in Alabama and here I am raising lettuce and tomatoes again. On a rooftop in New York City."

"Mr. Church?" asked Lowry. "Lunk Church?"

"Laurence Church," he said. "I'm Laurence now. Laurence with a U. Done left Lunk behind over yonder. Along with the whiskey bottles and sleeping on cardboard."

"Actually, that's what we want to ask you about," said Albee. "Did you know a Matty Mutone?"

"Who?"

Lowry showed him a picture of the dead man that had been doctored to look as if still alive, with open eyes.

Church shook his head. "Ain't nobody I know."

"You sure? We heard you used to bed down on a bench near that soup kitchen on the lower end of Sixth Avenue till he kicked you off."

"He kicked *me* off?"

"That's what we were told."

Church turned back to the picture and studied it more closely. "Oh yeah, I sorta remember him now. Skinny little white dude. Started hanging around there 'bout the time I heard they had a place for me here. No way he kicked me off. I was ready to split. Got me a real bed here. And they found me some part-time yard work around the neighborhood. Couldn't wait to get off the farm when I was a kid. Now I wish I could get back on one."

"You and Matty talk much?"

Reluctantly, Church brought his attention back to the picture. "Naw. He was strung out on something. I might've let booze mess me up, but I never did no drugs. I got asthma, so I can't smoke and I've always hated needles. How come you asking about him anyhow?"

"He's dead. Looks like someone gave him some poisoned food."

"No shit?"

"He ever say who he might've pissed off?"

"Naw. Like I said, I only saw him — what? Two times? Three?"

"People bring food while you were sleeping there?"

"Sometimes."

"When Matty was there?"

"Oh yeah. Some old woman brought us Italian right before I left. He said she knew his mother."

"She give you food, too?"

Church shrugged. "He passed out before he could eat it all, and I didn't eat all day, so I finished it off. Guess I was lucky, huh?"

"Lucky?"

"That it didn't have poison in it that night."

In midmorning, Sigrid gathered up several folders and went down the hall to brief her boss. One file held Matty Mutone's record, another the new one they'd begun upon his death. Yet another was a bulky brown expansion envelope held together by the thick cord that had long ago replaced the original elastic string. These were the files on Benito

DelVecchio, which she had not yet read. The papers inside were dog-eared and beginning to yellow. Several were chipped along the edges.

Last year, things had still been awkward between them, but most of that had dissipated since she first learned of Captain McKinnon's history with her parents. Until then, she had wondered if he resented her assignment to his command. She hadn't known that he and her father had been roommates and partners when they both made detective, nor that McKinnon and her mother had been lovers. Now she knew that her father had been as handsome and charismatic as a tall blond Viking and had probably cheated on her mother from the beginning, but when Leif Harald caught a bullet from a low-level mobster, a guilt-stricken Anne had blamed McKinnon and cut him out of her life.

Somehow Sigrid's grief and near breakdown after Nauman's death had brought Anne and McKinnon back together again. Night before last, her mother had let slip that she and McKinnon planned to marry when he retired at the end of the year.

"Don't tell him I told you," Anne said.

As if.

She and McKinnon had kept each other

at arm's length after he and Anne began seeing each other. No way would either of them want it gossiped about in the department or have to endure snickers about Mac becoming her stepfather.

Built like an overgrown teddy bear, Captain McKinnon still ran things on a "trust 'em or bust 'em" basis and could appear sleepy-eyed and easygoing until faced with incompetence. That's when those sleepy brown eyes would sharpen and underlings became abruptly aware that the muscles on his large frame had not softened.

Now he listened intently as Sigrid briefed him on the two men found dead at the end of the street where Benito DelVecchio, a Mafia don, had been killed. "You okay with this?"

"Okay?" she asked.

From her puzzled look, he realized that she had not made the connection.

"Benito DelVecchio," he said. "Aka Benny Olds?"

"What?"

"*Vecchio* means old in Italian."

Several years ago, once she had joined the force and had access to its records, Sigrid had read the official reports of Leif Harald's death in the line of duty, but she had concentrated on her father's shooter, not on the shooter's connections to the mob. There had been mention that he was part of the Benny Olds organization and she had let herself be distracted by the nickname and how he passed out Oldsmobiles like Christmas bonuses. Even though McKinnon might have mentioned the don's real name when he told her how Leif had been shot, it had not registered deeply enough for her to recognize it again.

McKinnon reached for Matty Mutone's folder and gave it a quick scan. "Doesn't look as if this guy was ever really in the life, does it?"

"No," Sigrid said, dismayed by the anger and sadness that suddenly enveloped her as she considered the ramifications of how this case connected to her father's death. "When I read the records, there was nothing to show that Olds's shooters were ever found or charged. Why?"

"We heard it was the Gambinos, but no names surfaced and back then, nobody looked very hard to find a killer's killer." McKinnon gave a weary sigh. "Benny Olds was a career criminal and one of the important bosses, Sigrid, but he didn't put out a hit on your dad. Gianni Gold was just a bagman, one of many foot soldiers. He shouldn't even have been carrying a gun, but it made him feel big and he popped off when Leif laughed at him. Disrespected him."

"What about George Edwards?"

"Who?" he asked absently, paging through the don's bulging folder, pausing at a report here, thumbing through old black-and-white pictures there.

"Mrs. DelVecchio's attorney. He showed up at the house when we went to question her. She must have called him as soon as she heard that her godson's body had been found."

McKinnon shook his head. "Never heard of him. I think she cut all ties to Benny's associates after he was killed. Her people came from northern Italy, so she wasn't one of those Sicilian matriarchs."

"No?" Sigrid thought about the woman's regal air and expectation of deference.

He turned over a small three-by-five photo that had slipped down into one of the dividers.

"Benny always had an eye for blondes."

Sigrid reached for the picture. "Is that Mrs. DelVecchio?"

Even with that dated hairdo, she had been a knockout. Her hair was just a little too blond, though, as if it had been helped along by a good hairdresser. Cuddled next to her handsome husband, she looked straight into the camera while he gazed down at her with an indulgent smile.

"Don't suppose she still looks like that," said McKinnon. "Did she get fat and matronly?"

"Actually, no. Thinner, if anything, and her hair's white now. I guess they stayed married?"

"Good little Catholic girl? Oh yes. He had lots of women, but she must have turned a blind eye to them. Besides, they never lasted. Benny was old-school that way — kept the two parts of his life well separated. She was his wife, the mother of his daughter, and he kept her out of the criminal part of his life. Never let it touch them."

"Except for the dirty money."

"Most money is," he said with a cynical smile.

There was a tap on his open door and a uniformed officer said, "Lieutenant? There's a George Edwards downstairs to see you."

"Really? Show him up to my office," she said, and shrugged when McKinnon gave her a quizzical look. "We were supposed to meet at the DelVecchio house."

"As long as I was coming into town, I thought we could clear the air before you speak to Sofia again," said the attorney, settling heavily into the chair across from her, with his elbows on the wooden armrests.

Despite the acne scars and wary eyes, there was something appealing about his smile. He probably did very well with juries, Sigrid thought. "You don't practice here in town?" she asked.

"Riverhead."

"I'm surprised Mrs. DelVecchio wouldn't want her lawyer nearer to hand."

"Because of her husband's reputation?" An amused smile spread across the attorney's broad pockmarked face. "He died years ago, Lieutenant. Besides, my practice is mostly wills and trusts."

"Yet you came running as soon as you heard Matty Mutone was dead."

"Sofia's his godmother and I'm her son-in-law. Of course I came."

"You, but not her daughter?"

All amusement faded from the man's face. "What exactly is it that you need to know about Matty?"

"What was his relationship to Mrs. DelVecchio?"

"It wasn't much of a relationship these days. Orla said she told you how Sofia still saw that he had a good meal once a week?"

Sigrid nodded.

"His mother was Benny's cousin and she introduced him to Sofia. Matty was a sweet kid. Weak, but sweet. He and my wife used to be close till he got into drugs. He was like a brother to her when they were growing up. Then he started using. Sofia tried everything. Paid for rehab. We got him a part-time job and a place to live. She even let him drive her for a couple of years. We thought he'd finally kicked it for good, but back in December, he started using again and dived straight to the bottom. Became unreliable. At that point, Sofia pretty much washed her hands of him. She felt sorry for him but there's been no real contact with him since —" He hesitated as if catching himself. "No contact since December, so I hope it won't be necessary to bother her about this again."

Sigrid handed him the key Tillie had found. "This was in one of his pockets. Did he have a car?"

"Not that I ever heard."

"Would this key fit Mrs. DelVecchio's car?"

"I doubt it. He handed those keys over to me when Sofia told me to fire him."

"What about Miss Orlano?"

"Orla? What about her?"

"How did she feel about Matty?"

73

Edwards leaned back in the chair and tented his fingers as he considered her question. "She's absolutely devoted to Sofia and she knows how much it hurt her when Matty started using again, so she's not exactly mourning his death. Why?"

"I don't have to spell it out for you, Mr. Edwards. I told you. Matty Mutone died from an overdose of a blood thinner."

"Your medical examiner's positive it wasn't speed? What do they call it? Crystal meth?"

"He thinks Coumadin. So you can see why we need to question the people who provided his last meal."

"Coumadin?" The attorney collapsed his tented fingers. "I know several people who take Coumadin for their heart. I doubt if it's hard to come by."

"Granted. All the same, there was Coumadin in the pasta Mrs. DelVecchio sent down to him."

"But there were *two* men dead on that bench, right? And Orla said there were two takeout cartons. Who was the other guy? Where'd he get *his* food?"

"We haven't identified him yet." She handed Edwards a picture of the older dead man. "Recognize him?"

Edwards studied the second man's face

74

for a long moment. "Sorry. Never saw him before."

"It's too soon to know precisely what happened on that bench, but there's a possibility that the men seemed to have shared their food."

"Yeah?"

"If indeed it *is* poison and if it started out in the takeout Miss Orlano gave him and neither she nor Mrs. DelVecchio put it there, then maybe it was originally meant for one or both of those women. Did they order the fettuccine from the restaurant? Who delivered it? We'll want to know who had access to it — visitors or workmen, maybe?"

"That's ridiculous," Edwards said.

"Nevertheless . . ."

He stood up and flexed his shoulders to shoot the cuffs of his white shirt. "Very well. I'll meet you over at the house, but I'm asking you, Lieutenant. Please don't upset my mother-in-law. She's an old woman with a bad heart. She's been through a lot and she's not as strong as she looks."

"We'll make it as brief as we can," Sigrid said.

CHAPTER 5

"Coumadin?" Mrs. DelVecchio paused in thought, then finished wiping the ink from her fingertips and handed the cloth back to her companion as Detective Hentz stowed the prints of both women in a file folder. "Matty died from Coumadin?"

"It's a blood thinner," her son-in-law said helpfully.

"Yes, yes, I do know what it is, George." Her tone was impatient. "My doctor prescribed it when I got my pacemaker, but it was so tedious to have to keep going for the blood tests every five or six weeks. Now I take . . ." She snapped her fingers. "What is it I take, Orla?"

Miss Orlano dutifully supplied the name of a nationally advertised drug.

"That's right. Now I only have to be tested twice a year."

"How long ago did you stop using it?" Sigrid asked

The old woman frowned. "Six months ago?"

Her companion nodded.

"In December. I told my doctor I could no longer come to his office so often and he changed the prescription."

"Do you still have some of it on hand?"

"Do we, Orla?"

Miss Orlano's thick eyebrows drew together over the bridge of her nose like two fuzzy gray caterpillars in a staring match. "You did not tell me to throw the bottle away."

"I didn't tell you to keep it either," snapped Mrs. DelVecchio. "Go get it, please."

The woman turned and stumped her way laboriously through the archway to the stairs, where she seated herself in a chair lift that carried her up to the second floor.

Edwards watched her go. "I thought you were going to get someone to help out," he said.

"Do you think I haven't tried? She fights me at every turn."

Edwards shook his head. "I'll ask Laura to reason with her."

"If she wouldn't listen to Aria, she certainly won't listen to Laura."

"Who else lives here besides you and Miss

Orlano?" asked Sigrid.

"We've tried to keep live-in help," Edwards answered, "but you see the situation. The best we can do is a weekly cleaning service."

Mrs. DelVecchio gave a wintry smile. "Poor George. Always having to deal with stubborn women. Yes, Lieutenant. There's only Orla and me in this big house now."

"And Sal," her son-in-law reminded her.

"And Sal," she agreed.

Sigrid looked up from her notes. "Who's Sal?"

"My Alberich," said Mrs. DelVecchio. "He lives downstairs in the basement apartment. He shovels the snow, tidies the back garden, keeps the cars running, and does all the heavy lifting Orla can no longer manage, which is why she thinks we can do without someone else underfoot all day." She cast a jaundiced eye at her son-in-law. "He's also supposed to be our bodyguard."

Through the open doors to the central hall, they saw Miss Orlano descend in the electric chair lift, then shuffle back to them, carrying a small orange plastic bottle.

Mrs. DelVecchio held out her hand, but the other woman shook her head.

"The bottle's not there. You must have thrown it away. This is your new stuff."

"Where was the old bottle kept?" asked Sigrid.

"In the medicine chest in my bathroom, of course."

"When did you last see it?"

With a graceful shrug of her thin shoulders, Mrs. DelVecchio said, "Probably the day I took my last dose of it back in December. I thought I put the bottle up on the top shelf when I started taking the new medicine, but I must have thrown it away."

"Let's go back to Tuesday night and your fettuccine," said Sigrid. "Did someone bring it to you or — ?"

"Sal," said Miss Orlano. "I called downstairs and he went around for it."

"Did he eat any of it?"

"Certainly not." Mrs. DelVecchio looked offended at the idea of sharing a dish with a handyman.

"So only the three of you touched the fettuccine box?"

"Only Sal and me," said the housekeeper. "He met me in the kitchen and left the box on the table. I fixed our plates and carried them into the dining room."

Of course, thought Sigrid, her face expressionless. *No serving herself from a plebian takeout box in the kitchen for Mrs. DelVecchio.*

A sense of fairness reminded her that her proper Southern grandmother would never allow a takeout box on her own table either and she abruptly realized that she was letting her father's death color her objectivity.

She took a deep breath and kept her voice civil. "Does this mean your bodyguard has access to the house and can come and go as he wishes?"

"There are steps from the back of his apartment up to the kitchen," Miss Orlano said.

Mrs. DelVecchio's lips curved in a wry smile. "A bodyguard is useless if he can't get to you quickly when you need him, Lieutenant."

"May we assume that there are back stairs from the kitchen to the second floor?"

"You may, but Sal never goes beyond the kitchen unless he's asked to do something. If you're suggesting he went upstairs and rummaged through my medicine cabinet for pills to put in our food, no."

George Edwards stirred in his chair.

"Yes, George, I know it didn't get into the food by itself, but *Sal*?"

"It really is very unlikely, Lieutenant Harald," he said.

Sigrid turned back to the housekeeper. "And when you finished eating?"

"I sent her down to that bench with what we hadn't touched," said Mrs. DelVecchio.

"Please let Miss Orlano tell us."

"I *did* tell you," the other woman said. "Nobody was there, so I left the box on the bench and came back here."

"We'll need one of your current pills for elimination purposes."

Mrs. DelVecchio started to object, then wearily motioned to Miss Orlano, who gave the bottle to Hentz, who tipped a pill into an evidence bag as Sigrid closed her notebook.

"Where can we find Mr. Alberich? We'll want his fingerprints, too."

Miss Orlano looked puzzled. "Who?"

"Your bodyguard."

Mrs. DelVecchio's laugh held patronizing scorn. "Sal? His name is Salvador. Pete Salvador."

Sigrid glanced at Hentz, who studiously avoided her eyes and seemed intent on putting away his own notes.

"George will go with you," said Mrs. DelVecchio.

It was a dismissal. And despite Sigrid's attempt at professional objectivity, it felt rather like entitled royalty directing the end of an audience with the peasants.

■ ■ ■ ■

"We'll have lunch now, Orla," said Mrs. DelVecchio when they were alone. "Is there enough minestrone for George, too?"

"I can stretch it with a salad," replied her companion. "I'll get Sal to give us some herbs."

She tried not to seem stiff-jointed as she hoisted herself out of the chair and made for the kitchen. There, she took the leftover soup from the refrigerator and put the pot on the stove over a low flame, then opened the glass door and stepped out onto the back deck. Sal knelt on a bright green rubber pad to weed a border of trailing thyme.

"Yeah?" he said when she called to him in a low voice.

"We need parsley and thyme and some of those green onion tops," she told him. "And the police are coming to ask you questions about Matty."

"Me? Why?"

"They'll ask you when you saw him last and what he said."

"So?"

"You haven't seen him in over a week. That's what you tell them."

"But —"

"Unless you want me to tell our signora about how you — ?"

He made a short chopping gesture with the side of his hand. "*Basta!* I did not see him, okay?"

"*Bene.*" She scowled as the side door to the garage opened and hurried back inside before the soup burned.

Outside, while Sigrid and Hentz waited on the sidewalk, George Edwards walked down the basement steps to the door under the front stoop. When no one answered the bell, he led them to a narrow door beside garage doors that closed off what was probably once an open alley between 409 and 411.

"I think it began life as a stable," Edwards said as he unlocked the door and gestured them into a space that held two cars end to end. The first was a late-model Toyota sedan. At the far end, a heavy canvas tarp covered a longer, bigger automobile and Hentz lifted a corner to reveal a gleaming chrome grill.

"Is that an Oldsmobile from the fifties?"

"Nineteen fifty-four," Edwards said over his shoulder. "It was my father-in-law's. A real classic, I'm told."

"Still run?"

"Oh yes. Sal drives the girls through

83

Central Park a few times a year."

"So Benny Olds really did have a thing for Oldsmobiles," Hentz said.

"That's what they say. Before my time. I never met him."

At the rear of the garage was a workbench with tools neatly hung on a pegboard. On either side of the workbench were open shelves. The left section held bottles and cans for car maintenance: motor oil, brake fluid, and windshield washer. The right side seemed devoted to gardening supplies — insecticides and fertilizers. A small electric tiller was tucked under the workbench beside a push mower.

Edwards opened a side door and they stepped into a surprisingly deep formal garden that reminded Sigrid of British travelogues. A wide curved bed of colorful perennials bloomed along the back and side walls, a clipped boxwood hedge rimmed the back deck, and a tree covered with white blossoms shaded one corner of the deck. The center of the garden had been paved with closely fitted flagstones that held a teak garden bench and an artful koi pond with pink water lilies.

Across the garden, a skinny man with stooped shoulders seemed to be in a spirited conversation with Miss Orlano, who had come out onto the rear deck. He wore green coveralls and could not have been more than an inch or two over five feet. As soon as the housekeeper saw them, she went back inside, but the man's wrinkled face broke into a smile and he moved briskly toward them, waving his trowel in greeting as he crossed the flagstones and skirted the koi pond. "Hey, Mr. George."

His face was creased with wrinkles and tanned from the sun and his shaggy hair was more white than brown. "Damn shame about Matty, huh?"

"Yeah, pretty bad, Sal. I guess Orla told you the police are looking into his death. They want to ask you some questions."

"Yeah?"

Sigrid introduced herself and Hentz. "Do you remember when you last saw him?"

"I dunno. Maybe a week? Ten days? He stopped me a couple of blocks up on Sixth. Wanted me to try and get her to forgive him and let him come back. I told him it was never gonna happen."

"Her? Mrs. DelVecchio?"

The man nodded.

"Forgive him for what?"

"For using drugs again," George Edwards answered when the handyman hesitated. "It's okay, Sal. They know."

85

"Yeah," Salvador agreed. "She couldn't rely on him no more."

"Rely on him for what?"

"He didn't show up on time when he was supposed to drive them somewhere."

"He drove for Mrs. DelVecchio? Not you?"

"I banged up my arm summer before last." He pointed to a climbing rose that covered the garage wall in fragrant white blossoms. "Fell off the ladder pruning back the Lady Banks roses. Broke my arm in two places. Matty needed a job, so she hired him to drive her and the girls when they came into town."

"The girls?"

"My wife and daughter," Edwards explained.

Salvador flexed his right arm vigorously. "It's fine now."

"How did you get along with him?" Hentz asked.

The man shrugged. "Okay. We didn't have much to do with each other. He was good with cars. Liked to wax them, keep them clean. Never put a dent in them, anyhow. And he kept the herb beds weeded when he was around."

They showed him the key they'd found in Matty's pocket.

"Not one of our cars," he said.

"Are you familiar with Coumadin?" Sigrid asked.

"What's that? An herb?"

"No, it's a blood thinner. Prescribed for heart conditions."

"Never heard of it and my heart's just fine."

"Mrs. Orlano said you picked up supper for them?"

"Yeah."

"We're going to need your fingerprints," Hentz said, undoing the clasp on the expansion envelope that held the necessary form and ink pad.

"Huh?" The man drew back defensively. "Why? What do you need mine for?"

"It's only for elimination purposes," Hentz said.

When the man continued to balk, Edwards said, "Don't worry, Sal. They don't care about stuff that happened twenty-five years ago."

Hentz led the reluctant Salvador over to the bench beside the central fishpond and Sigrid raised a questioning eyebrow to Edwards, who smiled.

"He snatched a couple of purses back when he was a bicycle messenger. Couldn't resist the temptation when women crossed

87

in front of him dangling their handbags by the handle. His criminal career was cut short when a woman's husband chased after him. He crashed into a Sabrett's wagon and the husband nearly beat him to a pulp. I don't know how they met, but right before he was killed, Benny hired him to drive Sofia and Aria, my wife. I guess you know about that?"

"That he was shot down in front of the house? Yes."

"Aria didn't see it happen, but she was here in the house and ran out to the street when she heard the shots. She was only a teenager. Had nightmares about it for years. Natural, I suppose."

"Yes," said Sigrid. At least Benny Olds's daughter had clear memories of him. She herself could barely remember her own father.

According to Mac, Olds had been a loving and protective father, so yes, seeing his body bloody and torn apart by bullets would surely be the stuff of nightmares.

By now, Sam Hentz was finished with Salvador and the two detectives followed George Edwards back through the garage to the street.

After Edwards left them to reenter the

house through the front door, Sigrid turned to Hentz and said, "So who or what was Alberich that so amused you and Mrs. DelVecchio?"

"Sorry, Lieutenant. He was the dwarf in Wagner's *Ring* cycle who lived in a cave and stole the Rheingold. I'm afraid that Salvador looks a little like the way Alberich is often described, and since he lives in the basement . . ."

"Opera again? I should have known." She glanced at her watch. "Well, you wanted to meet her, so let's go see if Charlotte Randolph's remembered anything."

CHAPTER 6

To Sam Hentz's disappointment, no one answered the doorbell at Number 403.

"The Jennings woman said she gave Matty a freebie," Sigrid said, "so why don't you go question her again, while I see if my friend knew him or has anything useful to say about the neighborhood."

Rudy Gottfried seemed surprised to find Sigrid at his door, but immediately invited her in and led her through a series of dark, low-ceiling basement rooms to his studio, a bright and spacious solarium at the back that was cluttered with easels, a rack of canvases, and paint-spattered chairs and small tables. He wore a denim chef's apron with a bib that covered his short-sleeved shirt, but there was a smear of red paint on his chin.

This was the first time she'd been here since shortly after Nauman's death, and the sharp smell of fresh turpentine and earthy pigments hit her senses like a palpable blow, with wave after wave of a grief so acute that she had to reach out to a sturdy wooden easel to steady herself. Nauman's clothes, his hair, his very skin, had been so permeated with these strong, clean, almost medicinal smells that she moved blindly to the far end of the studio where she could keep her back to Gottfried and pretend to be interested in the view while she regained control.

The glass curved out into a neglected backyard that was only a few inches below the windowsill. Weeds rimmed a cracked square of concrete that held a couple of plastic chairs and a rusty metal picnic table. They were shaded by a single pathetic tree not yet in full leaf. Some sort of wild vine had died on the ugly concrete wall at the rear and left behind a tracery of dried leaves and stems. No flowers, no fountain, and certainly no water lilies floating serenely on a pristine fishpond. With her hands flat on the dusty window ledge, she leaned forward to look for yellow roses atop the wall that enclosed Mrs. DelVecchio's lush garden, but from this position, three feet below ground level, her view was blocked by a thick privet hedge and a tall wooden fence beyond that. If Charlotte Randolph had a garden, it was hidden behind by a tall concrete wall on the other side of Gottfried's yard.

He joined her at the windows, which were badly in need of washing. "Good thing I was never interested in painting landscapes. I tend to forget how dreary this view is. I sometimes sit out there to read the morning paper and have my coffee. Maybe I ought to get a couple of flower pots or something."

"I just came from Mrs. DelVecchio's garden," Sigrid said now that her emotions were back in check. "Were you ever in it?"

He nodded. "Now that's a garden Monet would have been right at home in. She hosted a meeting of the block association there a couple of years ago. Wanted us to sign a petition to close down a place," Gottfried said.

"The one with a red door?"

"You know about that?"

"Mrs. Jennings said that Mrs. DelVecchio had complained about her, but that's no concern of mine. I'm here about the two men who died around the corner on Sixth. Did you hear about it?"

"Wednesday morning? Yeah. Some of your people came by. Cute little blonde."

"Did you know either of them?"

"Just the one they called Matty. Not that I

really knew him. He used to drive for the don's widow and he gave me a lift uptown once when he was on his way to pick her up last fall. Friendly guy. Told me his whole life story in the time it took to drive up to Forty-Fourth. How his mother was the don's cousin and how the daughter was like a sister."

"Any talk about him in the neighborhood?"

"Not really. At the diner I'd heard that they were related and that the widow fired him when he started using drugs again. He didn't mention drugs to me, but then why would he?"

"Did you know he was still hanging around that bench on Sixth and that she sent food down for him every week?"

"Yeah, I heard that at the diner, too." Gottfried shook his head in amusement. "I just realized that if I didn't eat there once a week, I'd never know a thing about what goes on around here. But the widow's not the only one. Other people leave food there, too. Janis Jennings, Charlotte Randolph, Nick Finmore."

"Who's Nick Finmore?"

"Kid that waits tables at the diner. He takes stale bread down to the bench and feeds the pigeons there. Used to feed them in front of the diner, but it pissed off the owner. People didn't like walking through the droppings."

"You ever leave food there?"

Gottfried grinned and patted his rotund belly. "Does this look like I ever had left-overs?"

"What about the second man?"

Gottfried shook his head. "Your blonde showed me his picture, but I never saw him before. Was it poison?"

"The ME thinks so. Warfarin."

"Rat poison?" He gave a sour laugh. "Well, they did die outside, didn't they? Isn't that how rat poison's supposed to work?"

Moving over to a table littered with books and papers, he opened a drawer and handed her several old black-and-white photographs. "I found these the other night. Think Buntrock might be interested to see what Oscar was painting back then? You can't really see the details, but I'm pretty sure that's the first picture Kohn and Munson ever sold for him."

And there was Nauman, young and intense, standing in front of an easel with a pipe clenched in his teeth, a paintbrush in his hand, his face half turned away as if totally oblivious to the camera. He wore a thick wool jacket and gloves that had the fingers cut off.

"That was our place over in Chelsea. The boiler kept breaking and the radiators never gave any heat."

"Is that you?" She recognized Nauman, but the man standing beside him had his back to the camera. He was almost as slim, but a little shorter, with a bushy head of hair, a thicker neck, and broader shoulders.

"Yeah, that's me. Before I started to pack on the pounds."

"Who's that?" Sigrid asked when she came to a picture of Nauman, Gottfried, and a woman who had wrapped herself in a blanket from head to toe and sat atop a table with her knees drawn up as if she were freezing.

"Lila Nagy. You know about her?"

"The name's familiar. She and Nauman were together when he first came to New York, weren't they?"

"Yeah."

Sigrid passed to the next picture, taken on what must have been a warmer day, because the blanket was gone and Nauman had his arm around her slender waist. Sigrid could not help but notice that the woman did not lean into his embrace. Nor was she smiling. Long, dark hair and bold eyes stared directly into the camera.

"She was quite beautiful, wasn't she?"

"Sexy as hell, but too intense and crazy as a loon," said Gottfried. "He ever tell you how she did a van Gogh on him? Tried to cut off his ear?"

"*What?* No! Why?"

"She was an artist, too, but not half as good as she wanted to be. She was jealous of Oscar. Thought it came too easy for him, that he needed to suffer for his art."

Their time together had been so short, Sigrid thought. Too short for sharing all their stories. She had seen the scar behind his ear, of course, had even run her fingers along that thin white line but hadn't asked about it because he had turned his head to her and once their lips met, she forgot about that nearly invisible scar.

"Was she trying to kill him?"

"Not really. Just wanted to drive home a point. I mean it, the woman was crazy. Still is, I suppose."

"She's alive?"

"So far as I know. When I heard how Oscar went off a curve up in the hills from LA, I asked Buntrock if that's why he was there."

Sigrid stared at him in bewilderment. "I don't understand."

"Oscar wasn't the only person she attacked. After they broke up, she stalked him and tried to stab the woman he was seeing after her. They put out a warrant on her, but she left the state before she could be arrested. Next thing we heard, she'd moved to an art colony out near Sacramento where she stabbed a teenage girl to death. I don't know that Oscar kept up with her, but the last I heard, she was serving life in a prison out there for the criminally insane."

"And that prison is out in the hills from LA?"

Gottfried nodded. "Oscar visited her once when he was there — maybe twenty, twenty-five years ago? They'd cut her hair and she'd gained a lot of weight. He almost didn't recognize her and she didn't know him at all. Sad. Still, I wondered if maybe that's where he went that day."

Sigrid looked down at the pictures in her hand.

Lila Nagy.

Dark flowing hair.

Eyes that challenged the camera.

She had known there were other women before her. Beautiful women according to the snippets of gossip she'd heard. She had never been jealous, but looking at this picture, knowing that this woman might have been the last person Nauman spoke to before his death? Yes, she had to admit that she was jealous.

CHAPTER 7

The woman who opened the red door at the end of the block did not look like what Sam Hentz's aunt Lizzie would call a woman of the evening. She was almost as tall as he with iron-gray hair pinned back from her face by blue plastic barrettes. No perfumed hair or makeup and no sexy clothes. Instead, she wore white sneakers, khaki shorts, and a denim apron that covered the message on her T-shirt. The cloth in her hand smelled strongly of furniture polish.

She looked at the badge Hentz held up and rolled her eyes. "Oh, Christ! Don't you people have anything better to do?"

"Ma'am?"

"What part of 'not a whorehouse' do you not understand?"

"Something wrong, Frances?" asked a woman's voice from the head of the stairs above.

"Just another fucking policeman here to hassle you."

From the room beyond, a gentle voice said, "Language, Frances."

Peering over her shoulder, Hentz saw an elderly woman of Asian descent, who sat in a high-backed chair as she knitted something in fuzzy pink wool.

"I'll handle this, Frances," said the first woman as she reached the foot of the stairs and came forward. "Besides, I think the dryer's ready to be unloaded."

The one called Frances ceded her place at the door. "Did Cookie's pajama bottoms turn up?"

"I don't think so. Check the hampers and start another load." She turned to Hentz. "May I help you, Officer?"

He held out his ID again. "Detective Hentz, ma'am. And I'm not interested in what goes on here. I've come about the two deaths down at the other end of this block on Tuesday night. Are you Ms. Jennings?"

"Janis Jennings, yes. Do come in, Detective."

As she stood aside to let him enter, a man of late middle age hesitated at the bottom of the steps. "Mrs. Li? I'm Eustace Boyle."

"One minute, Detective." She turned and called to the elderly woman, "Mrs. Li? A

Mr. Boyle for you."

The woman stowed her knitting in a basket beside the chair and reached for her cane. "Right on time." She beamed. "My room's on the second floor, but luckily we have an elevator."

Boyle and Mrs. Li both had to be in their seventies and both walked with pronounced limps as they passed down the hall and around the corner. A moment later Hentz heard an elevator door open. He was bemused. What was this? A cathouse for the geriatric set?

He followed Ms. Jennings into a living room that was more like a hotel lounge. Somehow she didn't really fit his picture of a brothel keeper either, despite a good figure and a long single braid of thick brown hair.

"As I told your Lieutenant Harald, I knew Matty only casually and I never saw the other man."

"I was hoping to talk to the woman who serviced him. Maybe he said something to her about who would want him out of the way. Or why."

"That would be Peg Overhold, but she's out of town right now. Her mother's sick and she's gone up to help out for a few days. She's due back the first of next week."

"Was she the only one who gave him a

freebie?"

"No, as your lieutenant must have told you, I did, too. I felt sorry for him, so I gave him food, as well, and the occasional five dollars."

"Did you talk?"

She gave him a puzzled look. "Of course we talked. You can't spend time with someone without talking. What do you think?"

Actually, Hentz didn't know what he thought. Hookers must have to put up with a lot of scumbags and it was not his place to judge, but Janis Jennings seemed so fresh and clean that it was hard to imagine her with someone like Matty Mutone. Those discolored teeth? That sour skin? His street-soiled clothes?

"Was he in trouble? Fearful of anyone?"

She shook her head and her braid swayed with the motion. "Not fearful, just very, very sad. Someone he loved had died and he couldn't talk about her without crying. That's why I asked Peg to take him if she had the time. She's such a natural empath."

"When did she last see him?"

"I really couldn't say. I don't keep up with the bookings."

Again Hentz was puzzled. He'd never worked Vice, but it was his understanding that brothel owners took a percentage of a working girl's take.

"But then how do you know how much they owe you?"

"How much they owe *me*?" For a moment, Jennings's face mirrored Hentz's puzzlement, then she started laughing.

On the second floor of a building in Midtown, the assistant seated at the desk just inside Kohn and Munson Gallery smiled apologetically at the tall white man in jeans and a navy sports jacket who had just pulled open the glass door. "I'm sorry, sir, but we'll be closing in a few minutes."

"That's okay," he said. "I'm not here to look at the exhibit. I'd like to see Ms. Kohn."

B'Nita Parsons gave a quick glance down at the calendar on her computer screen and saw only Elliott Buntrock's name. "She's in a meeting right now. Did you have an appointment?"

"No, but I think she'll talk to me."

A moment later, Hester Kohn looked up as her assistant tapped at her office door and entered without waiting for an answer.

"Sorry, Hester, Mr. Buntrock, but there's a man here to see you."

"Tell him to come back, B'Nita. We're busy right now."

"I really think you should see him. Both of you. He says he's Oscar Nauman's son."

CHAPTER 8

"What?" Buntrock came to his feet so abruptly that his chair tipped over and papers went flying as he scrambled to catch them.

"He's *who*?" asked Hester Kohn. "Like hell he is!"

"Don't shoot the messenger," said B'Nita Parsons, holding up her hands. "Shall I show him in?"

Hester could only nod mutely as Buntrock retrieved his papers and righted the chair.

The man who entered appeared to be in his early forties. He was as tall as Oscar Nauman and his hair was going white; otherwise, Hester saw no resemblance to the artist she had known since she was a child playing under her father's desk in this very office. His shoulders were broader, his neck much thicker, but yes, his eyes were blue and returned their appraising stares with an unsmiling appraisal of his own.

To break the awkward silence, Buntrock stretched out his hand. "Elliott Buntrock. This is Ms. Kohn, and you are — ?"

The stranger gave an embarrassed shrug. "Actually, I'm not quite sure what to tell you. My passport says Vincent Haas. My birth certificate says Vincent Nauman."

His spoke with a slight accent.

"Sind Sie Deutscher?" asked Buntrock, who was semi-fluent in several languages.

"Not German, no. Austrian . . . well, actually, I'm an American. Born in California, but brought up in Austria. Please. May I explain?"

"By all means," said Hester Kohn. She gestured for him to take the other chair across from her desk, an asymmetrical slab of sea-green glass. The heady scent of her gardenia perfume elicited an appreciative smile from the stranger.

"My birth mother was Lila Nagy," he said, laying a manila envelope on the irregular corner of the desk that jutted out toward him. He looked from Hester to Elliott. "I see that the name is familiar to you, Mr. Buntrock."

Elliott, who labored under the delusion that he had a poker face, nodded.

Hester looked at him inquiringly.

"Rudy Gottfried said she and Nauman

met soon after he came to New York," Elliott said. "Back when he and Oscar shared a studio downtown."

"Then perhaps you knew that when she left him, she went to California?"

"I really don't know any of the details. Just that they were lovers and that she tried to cut off his ear and —"

Hester was startled. "She did *what*?"

"And," said Elliott, "I think she tried to attack the woman he started seeing after they broke up."

"Yes, this too is what I have been told. After that incident, she fled to California and gave birth to me there." He took a document from the envelope and slid it across the green glass surface of the desk. "As you see, Oscar Nauman of New York City is listed as my father."

Hester scanned the paper and passed it on to Elliott. "Back then, she could have named anybody. This birth certificate doesn't make it so."

"True," he agreed. "But why would she lie all those years ago? I only know what she told my mother. My adoptive mother."

"Let him finish, Hester," said Elliott, and she subsided back into her chair.

"Thank you," said Vincent Haas. "You know that Lila Nagy is in a prison for the criminally insane?"

Clearly, Hester did not, but again, Elliott nodded.

"I was told that even as a child, she would go into uncontrollable rages. In the end, she killed a young woman and this time, they sent her to prison. Her sister — my adoptive mother — flew over for the trial and took me back to Austria with her. I wasn't even three, so I have no memory of that time. Some of her paintings hung on the walls of our house and they talked about her talent and her beauty, but I was never told that Lila was my mother. Instead, I was brought up as the son of Anja and Klaus Haas."

Hester frowned, but did not speak.

"My father died about two years ago, my mother this past January. Among her papers was a letter to me and this birth certificate. The letter told me Lila's history — where she was and the awful thing she had done — and that I was Lila's son by a famous artist. She said that she wrote to him after my father died and told him about me, but she never heard back from him."

"Oh, dear God," Hester murmured. "Anja Haas! That's why the name sounds familiar. A registered letter came for Oscar the day he left for California. From an Anja Haas.

It had an Austrian return address and it was marked *urgent, private,* and *personal.* I remember that I took those words at face value because they were heavily underlined, so I put it in a new envelope the same day and overnighted it to his hotel. When we heard that he'd died, it went right out of my mind, but you were there, Elliott. Did he get it?"

"If he did, he didn't mention it to me."

"So he never knew," Vincent Haas said sadly. "When first I read my mother's letter, I hoped it might mean that I had a brother or sister, but I searched online and it didn't say he ever married or had children."

"No," Hester said.

"Maybe if he'd lived," Elliott murmured.

Hester lifted a skeptical eyebrow. "You think? Can you see Sigrid in an apron? Or changing diapers?"

"All the same —"

Vincent Haas stirred in his chair. "Is there anyone who would know about his brothers or sisters?"

"Maybe," said Hester. "I never heard any mention of relatives. In fact, I think he was an only child, but my father's partner is still alive. If anyone would know, surely it would be Jacob."

Haas's face brightened. "Is he here in the

109

city? Can I see him?"

"I don't think so." She looked at Buntrock. "Maybe Sigrid could arrange it?"

Buntrock frowned. "Do we really want to bring her into it now?"

"Who is this Sigrid?" Haas asked.

Ignoring his question, Hester said, "Tell me, Mr. Haas. What exactly is it that you want? Are you planning to put in a claim against Oscar Nauman's estate?"

Haas shrugged. "Why not? Is that so strange? He was my father. I'm his son. Doesn't that give me certain rights?"

Hester Kohn turned to her computer screen and clicked several times, and lights blinked on the printer behind her. A moment later, she handed Vincent Haas the printout.

"That's the name and address of Oscar Nauman's attorney." She stood up and her voice was cold. "He's the one you should talk to. Not us."

"Please!" he protested. "Money is not the important thing."

"No?" She touched a button on her desk phone. "Mrs. Parsons will show you out."

When they were alone, Hester reached for her phone. "I'd better give Marcus Livingston a heads-up."

Buntrock was pacing her office like an agitated shore bird whose catch had just been snatched away by an opportunistic gull. "God knows what this is going to mean for the Arnheim retrospective."

"And somebody needs to tell Sigrid," she said.

CHAPTER 9

When Sigrid got back to her office, she stepped out of the elevator without looking and collided with a uniformed officer, who dropped the sheaf of papers he was carrying. As they both apologized, she stooped to help him pick up the pages and saw that they were photocopied pictures of the older dead man that had been doctored to show him with open eyes. Across the top in bold black letters was "DO YOU KNOW THIS MAN?"

"Detective Tildon's asked me to pass these out along Tenth Avenue," he explained.

In the squad room, Sigrid asked Tillie, "Why Tenth Avenue? Did someone recognize him?"

"Not yet, but if I'm right, we could know who he is by Monday." He flourished a plastic bag. "Remember this blue rubber band from the guy's ponytail?"

Sigrid didn't, but she was used to the way

Tillie noticed details the rest of them often missed and now that she looked at it more closely, she saw that white letters were printed on the band — *C.J. Smith Farms* — *PLU 4080.*

"What does that mean?"

"This rubber band started life around a bunch of asparagus from a farm in New Jersey," he said happily. "PLU stands for price look-up, and 4080 is the code number for asparagus. This rubber band looks new, so our victim probably acquired it fairly recently. And you know that Duane Reade receipt that was in his pocket?"

Sigrid nodded.

"It was from the store on Ninth and Forty-Third. I called C.J. Smith Farms and they said they sell asparagus to a market that's just around the corner. I figure that if we distribute the guy's picture within a three-block circle around the drugstore and the market, we might get lucky."

"Good thinking," Sigrid said.

Albee and Lowry described how they had located the homeless man who had slept on that bench for most of the winter until Matty Mutone claimed it for himself.

"His name's Laurence Church," said Lowry. "And Mutone didn't chase him away. He left of his own accord for a halfway house over on Staten Island. Doesn't sound like there was any bad blood between them. In fact, he probably wouldn't have remembered Mutone at all except that some old lady — probably the Orlano woman — brought Italian food down there the last night before he left for Staten Island and Mutone said that she'd been a friend of his mother."

"So it looks like we've pretty much covered the block except for your friend Gottfried," said Elaine Albee.

"I talked to him today," Sigrid said, looking over her notes. "He told me that one of the people who occasionally left food there was a Nick Finmore from the diner. Anybody talk to him?"

Dinah Urbanska raised her hand like a schoolgirl. "That was Sam and me, Lieutenant. We spoke to him on Wednesday. He said he hadn't seen Mutone in a couple of weeks, though."

She nodded at Lt. Hentz, who had just joined them.

"What about the other one?" Sigrid asked.

"We showed him the picture. He thought our guy was there Tuesday afternoon, but he couldn't be positive. Right, Sam?"

"Right," said Hentz as he dropped his notepad on his desk and sat down. "He remembered the ponytail. Said if it was the same man, he ordered coffee, nothing else, then took a table by the window and seemed to be waiting for someone."

"Who?"

"He couldn't say. They got busy then and next time he looked, the guy was gone."

"Try the diner again," said Sigrid. "It seems to be information central for that block. Maybe someone else noticed if he left with anybody. In the meantime, did you learn anything about Mutone from the Jennings woman?"

Hentz laughed. "Oh yes. That's quite a business she's got there." As Dinah Urbanska managed to set a full mug of coffee on the corner of his desk without spilling it, he thanked her, then continued his report. "Her ladies get eighty dollars an hour for their services or four hundred for all night."

There were snickers around the squad room and Sigrid frowned. "Is somebody on the take? Why hasn't she been shut down?"

"Because she's not selling sex, Lieutenant. She's selling cuddles. It's a cuddles-for-hire place."

"Cuddles?"

"Oh, I read about that," Urbanska said. "It's so sad, isn't it?"

"Sad?" asked Elaine Albee.

Urbanska nodded. "Imagine if you didn't have anybody in your life who would touch you or hug you. Lonely people. Ugly people."

"Elderly men who've lost their wives and women who don't have any relatives. Or the disabled," said Hentz. "They pay to have someone lie down beside them and just cuddle. Hug them, stroke their arms, smooth their hair. Physical human touch."

Lowry looked at them in disbelief. "They pay? Just to get hugged?"

"What else do they get for their eighty bucks?" asked Detective Gonzalez with a cynical leer.

"Nothing," Hentz said flatly. "Both people are fully dressed and the clients have to sign a paper that they will not try to have sex."

"And there's a market for that?" asked Albee.

"Yep."

"You're right, Dinah," Albee said. "That *is* sad."

Tillie shook his head. "Was that the 'freebie' Janis Jennings gave Mutone?"

Hentz nodded. "She felt sorry for him. They keep extra clothes on hand and if it's needed, the clients take a shower first and change into clean pajamas. She gave him a session back in the winter, but it made him so emotional that she passed him over to one of her other residents the next time she felt charitable."

"Residents?" asked Sigrid.

"All women and all currently single. They seem to range in age from late twenties to late seventies. It really is an SRO," said Hentz. "With a waiting list. They pay her a monthly rent and they get a single room and bath, kitchen privileges, and the use of the common rooms on the first floor. She doesn't handle their bookings, but she will take phone messages if they don't want to give out their private numbers. Besides, some of them have regular jobs."

"Did you speak to the other woman who did Mutone?" asked Sigrid. She knew she sounded condescending, but damned if she was going to say *cuddled.*

"She left for the weekend," he said, "but she's due back on Monday."

"Monday it is, then," said Sigrid, who was ready to call it a day.

Sigrid was neither a jogger nor a yoga enthusiast and exercise machines bored her. Nevertheless, instead of heading straight home, she yielded to the siren call of the gym she had joined several years ago because of its Olympic-size pool. She had discovered the value of swimming back in boarding school and now it was both workout and yoga, a way to blank her mind and give herself up to the sensual pleasures of the water.

In the locker room, she changed into a one-piece white suit, then sluiced off in the shower. As soon as she entered the large tiled space with its clean, uncluttered surfaces and strong smell of chlorine, she felt herself relaxing. As usual on any afternoon, this close to quitting time for so many of Manhattan's office workers, the marked lanes were all occupied and she waited till a space opened up in a lane that had only one swimmer. He seemed to be setting a comfortable pace, so she slid into the water several lengths behind him, stroking steadily, arm over arm.

Just when she felt she could go no longer, her lungs seemed to open deeper. It was as if she had slipped into overdrive and an out-of-body euphoria took over. Now she could let surface thoughts skim across her mind, could let herself think about Nauman's sketchbook and all those quick studies he'd made of her while she was unaware. She could consider loneliness and how people would pay to have someone hold them, which led inexorably to memories of Nauman and how it had felt to lie in his arms and feel the steady rise and fall of his chest as he slept. He slept so quietly that more than once she had reached out in the darkness to reassure herself that he still breathed. Given their age difference, logic had warned her that she would probably outlive him by several years. At the time, though, she had pushed logic aside, and when the inevitable came so much sooner than anyone would have predicted, logic was cold comfort.

"You were not his first," Buntrock had told her after Nauman's death. "But he said you were his last."

She had turned away, not wanting him to see her raw emotions. "Don't," she'd said, but Buntrock had persisted. "He did not want to be your last, Sigrid."

Unthinkable then, but here in the water, she could finally consider the possibility of another love, as unlikely as it still seemed.

She wondered if Buntrock would know if Lila Nagy was the reason Nauman had driven out into the hills above LA and if so, why he hadn't mentioned it.

After another twenty minutes, a third swimmer entered her lane, so she cut short her cool-down period and was soon on her way home to the house she shared with Roman Tramegra on Hawker Street, a block or so east of the Hudson.

It belonged to his godmother's sister and when a series of circumstances forced Sigrid to find a new apartment, Roman had convinced her to give sharing this house a try. It had worked out much better than she'd hoped.

In the beginning, she had fallen into the stereotypical trap and assumed that an unmarried man in his early fifties was gay. But he had never brought anyone home and she eventually decided that, while he loved gossip and societal intrigue, he was one of those rare free spirits with absolutely no interest in sex.

Although he had never said, she gathered that Roman possessed a modest trust fund, which he augmented by writing and selling short articles for a wide variety of small magazines. He had been enchanted to learn that Sigrid was a homicide detective, and had immediately set about writing a mystery novel. To her surprise, the book actually found an editor and he was currently working on a sequel. The thrill of being published, together with the tax write-offs for research and travel, more than compensated for the publisher's small advances.

Roman could be exasperating with his adventurous approach to cooking, his magpie curiosity, his speculations as to who was doing what with whom, and his endless questions about police procedure. For the most part, though, he respected the boundaries she set and they had settled into a comfortable relationship. He was enough older that it was rather like living with an eccentric uncle, an uncle whose eccentricities occasionally caused her to look at her cases from a different angle.

Seen from the narrow street, Number 42 1/2 could have been a run-down industrial site. The dirty gray concrete wall was too high to see anything except the upper stories of an old factory, so there was no way for casual passersby to realize that the wall concealed a single-story dwelling that had been added for the factory's foreman sometime in the 1930s. Set in that wall was a dilapidated wooden door that left flakes of green paint on Sigrid's shoes when she unlocked it. Roman had convinced her to leave it as it was.

"We don't want anyone thinking there's a reason to scale the wall," he'd said when she suggested a fresh coat of paint.

As she stepped inside and let the door latch behind her, she found Roman deadheading some yellow flowers that had bloomed last week. Their courtyard was less than half the size of Mrs. DelVecchio's garden and it lacked both a pool and the manicured formal flower beds, but it did have some tall flowering bushes, and a white marble replica of a Greek god stood in one corner beneath a Japanese cherry tree.

A nude replica.

A well-endowed nude replica.

"Tante Caroline thought he looked like her first husband," Roman had said. "A nice man, but he came from the south of France and he hated New York winters."

As a result, whenever it snowed, Roman always felt as if he ought to throw a blanket over those bare muscular shoulders. Today, bathed in June's warm afternoon sunshine, the god had a wreath of flowers in his sculpted hair and Sigrid thought he looked faintly embarrassed.

"I've been wanting to show you something," Roman said, leading her toward the thickest bush that grew in the corner of the L where the maid's quarters that he occupied joined the larger side formed by the living room and two bedrooms.

As he gently parted the leaves, a small brown bird shot out of the bush.

"See?" he said.

There near the ground was a nest of twigs

and grass. It held four speckled eggs.

"I think it's a white-throated sparrow. But sparrows are so hard to identify."

"Why is one of those eggs so much bigger?" asked Sigrid, who had almost no knowledge of wildlife.

"I rescued it from some wretched boys who found a nest in the park and tore it down. They said it was a red bird. Probably a cardinal or tanager, and being boys, they smashed the other eggs to see what was inside. I managed to talk them out of this one. It's been in the sparrow's nest for two days now, so I think she's accepted it. Maybe I can get an article out of it like the one I wrote on cowbirds. They lay their eggs in other birds' nests, you know, and sometimes the baby cowbird will push out the legitimate nestlings so that —"

"Is that for me?" Sigrid asked, pointing to a padded envelope on the garden table. Given a chance to lecture, Roman could run on for hours, but he never seemed to mind being interrupted.

"It's from Anne," he said in his deep sonorous bass. "Addressed to both of us, so I took the liberty of opening it. Your mother is an absolute angel! She's sent us passes for Saturday."

"Passes? Passes for what?"

"BookExpo. Didn't she tell you?"

"What's BookExpo?"

"Christmas and birthdays with tons of free books for presents."

Then Sigrid remembered that Anne had invited her back in March to join her at the Javits Center for the huge annual book fair that would see the launch of the book she had written about her near-death experience in Somalia. Part memoir, part coffee table book, it was illustrated by the graphic and heart-rending photos she had taken, one of which had won her a second Pulitzer.

"Mac can't come that weekend," she'd said, "so why don't you? My publisher wants me to speak at a breakfast. Billy Collins is supposed to be signing after lunch, so you can score a free book and get him to autograph it. I'll get an extra pass for Roman."

Free books? A chance to meet one of her favorite poets in person? "I'm in," she'd said happily, then promptly forgot all about it.

"Anne's so fortunate," Roman said now as he read the name of her publisher on their passes. A large, soft man with thinning hair, his accent was a cross between cinematic British and cultured Midwest spoken in a deep bass voice. "True class."

He fitted the passes into the plastic holders that Anne had included and handed Sigrid one of the lanyards. "Of course she's a star and I'm a midlist nobody, but my editor brushed me off when I asked them to give me a signing time. It wouldn't have had to be in the official autographing area. I would have been quite happy to sign at their booth but they declined. Wouldn't even give me a pass."

As they talked, Sigrid became aware of an appetizing smell that drifted from an open window, reminding her how long it had been since lunchtime.

"Something smells good," she said, opening the door.

"Only boring chicken pot pies, I'm afraid."

As far as Sigrid was concerned, "boring" was preferable to some of Roman's more exotic leaps of culinary fantasy.

Unfortunately, she was not to taste it that evening. Before Roman could take the pot pies from the oven, the phone rang and she smiled upon hearing Buntrock's voice. "I haven't had a chance to go over the catalog proofs yet, Elliott, but . . . what? Marcus Livingston? No, he hasn't called. Why?"

Thirty minutes later, Sigrid slid into a booth in the diner across the street from Rudy Gottfried's studio. Buntrock had avoided telling her why this meeting was so urgent.

"What's happened, Elliott? Is the Arnheim still trying to make us to pay for the extra insurance? Rudy?"

The older man seemed distinctly disturbed. "I swear I didn't know, Sigrid, honest."

"Didn't know what?"

"That Oscar may have had a son," Buntrock said bluntly.

"What?"

"He came to the gallery today while Hester and I were finalizing the picture selections." He quickly described how Vincent Haas had arrived claiming to be Nauman's son. "And he had this with him."

He handed Sigrid a copy of the birth certificate that Haas had given Hester. She quickly scanned it and her gray eyes were stormy when she turned to face Gottfried. "Is this for real, Rudy?"

"Damned if I know. I was just as surprised as you when Buntrock called."

"But you and Nauman shared that loft with her. She had Nauman's baby? How could he not know? How could *you* not know if she was living there?"

"Because she never said. The dates are right for when she and Oscar broke up and she split for California. If this birth certifi-

126

cate is legit, he was born about six months after she moved out of the loft. I helped her pack up her things, but she didn't say a word about being pregnant. Not to me anyhow."

More upset than she wanted to admit, Sigrid took a long, deep drink from the glass of water a waiter had brought her when she sat down. "Did Nauman know?"

"Maybe," said Buntrock, and told her about the letter from Austria that Hester had forwarded to their hotel in LA. "That could have been where he went that day."

Finally, Sigrid thought. *A real reason for him to drive out from LA alone, because surely he would have tried to question her about a child no matter how crazy she was.*

"You guys ready?" asked the waiter, who had brought over a basket of warm rolls.

When he had taken their orders, Sigrid leaned forward. "What does Marcus say?"

"He plans to backtrack on this, see if he can locate any of Oscar's relatives."

"Relatives? Why?"

"DNA," Buntrock said. "Unless you kept something like a hairbrush?"

"Only his pipe," she said sadly, "and it won't be of any use. Marcus's secretary cleaned and waxed it before she brought it to me."

Mrs. Bayles had meant well, but in preserving the wooden bowl and plastic stem, she had polished away most of the fragrant tobacco smell that had been as much a part of Nauman as the turpentine and oil paints of his studio.

"According to Livingston, when he drew up Oscar's preliminary will, he was under the impression that there were no close relatives."

"Does this mean that you don't think he's Nauman's son?"

"Doesn't matter what *we* think, Sigrid. Livingston wants more proof than this birth certificate if Vincent Haas plans to put in a claim against Oscar's estate."

"Is that what he's going to do?"

"I'm afraid so."

Sigrid leaned back in the booth and took a deep breath to steady herself. "I should meet him."

Buntrock frowned. "Do you think that's wise?"

"Maybe not, but I need to see him for myself."

"Except for his white hair, he looks almost nothing like Oscar."

"I don't care, Elliott. If he *is* who he says he is, he's entitled to make a claim. To all of it, if that's what he wants."

"Oh, I imagine he'll want," Gottfried said with a cynical face.

"I hope you won't do anything rash until we know for sure," said Buntrock.

"Don't worry. Marcus won't let me," Sigrid said, smiling for the first time. "Does this man have any artistic leanings?"

"Not that he's mentioned," said Buntrock. "His parents — his adoptive parents — were lawyers and he himself is a statistician. A bean counter. He'll be looking at the balance sheet, figuring up how much the works will bring."

"He won't be the first," Sigrid said quietly.

As the waiter set their plates in front of them, he gave Sigrid a sheepish grin. "I meant to call you, Lieutenant, but I couldn't find the card you gave me."

"Oh?"

"Yeah, one of our customers? He's the locksmith down at the end of the street, across from where those bodies were. We were talking about it yesterday and he said that he'd got called out after hours the evening before . . . Tuesday evening, right? When he went by the shop to get his tools, he saw an old guy with a beard sitting on the bench and he was talking to a man with a takeout box."

"Did he know the man?"

The waiter shrugged. "Said he might've seen him around the neighborhood. Didn't know his name, though. Guess I should've called you, huh?"

CHAPTER 10

"No ID on our second victim," Tillie said as Sigrid came out of her office with a cup of black coffee on Friday morning. "But we may be close. A news vendor in the area recognized the picture but didn't know his name or anything about him except that he buys *Variety* every week."

"*Variety?*" said Hentz. "Ninth and Forty-Third? That's right in the Theater District."

"Which could mean he's connected with show business," Elaine Albee said, "but that's not going to help us without a name."

"We'll get it," Tillie said confidently. "Just a matter of time."

"Till then, we concentrate on Matty Mutone," Sigrid said. "Hentz, call Mrs. Jennings. Find out when that Overhold woman's due back. And I want to talk to Charlotte Randolph."

"Randolph told us that she didn't recognize either man," said Jim Lowry as he came back to his desk with two steaming mugs of coffee and handed one to Albee.

"But those were the first pictures we took of them," she reminded him. "Maybe it will jog her memory to see ones with their eyes open."

The morning briefing continued with a report from Gonzalez and Jackson, the two newest members of their team.

"We should finish up the paperwork on that domestic stabbing tomorrow," said Jackson. "The DA will knock it down to manslaughter if he'll confess."

"And will he?" Sigrid asked.

Gonzalez handed her a picture of two frightened children. "The boy's five, the girl's seven. They saw him do it. He doesn't want to put them on the witness stand. His sister says she'll take them in."

"Poor kids," Dinah Urbanska said softly.

Three days since those bodies had been found, yet they still had no identity for the second body. Sigrid knew she should update Captain McKinnon on their meager progress, but it was difficult to concentrate on the case while still reeling from the news that Nauman might have had a son. Had he known? Had he visited his old mistress? Had a coherent talk with her? Learned about their son? Frustrated, she pushed back from her desk and fished a puzzle ring out of the bowl that held her collection. Fitting the circlets into a unified band usually helped her to focus, but not today.

She frowned when her phone interrupted the alternate scenarios she was piecing together in her head and she was not happy to hear Marcus Livingston's voice on the line.

"I understand Buntrock told you about Vincent Haas?"

"Yes."

Livingston waited for her to say more. The silence stretched between them until the attorney said, "Hester Kohn sent him to me. He just left."

"Is he Nauman's son, Marcus?"

"I honestly can't say. He has a birth certificate, but that alone doesn't prove anything to me. He doesn't particularly look like Oscar and he has nothing more than the letter his mother left. His adoptive mother."

"Did you know about Lila Nagy?"

"Never heard her name till Buntrock called. Oscar didn't mention her to me and I'm sure he would have if he'd known there was a child. I gather that Rudy Gottfried confirms that the dates are right?"

"Yes," Sigrid said, back to monosyllables again.

"Let me reassure you that even if he proves to be who he says he is, Sigrid, he has no real claim on Oscar's estate. I've never had one of my wills successfully contested."

"There's always a first, Marcus. Does he plan to contest?"

"Probably. It's a lot of money. He says that isn't his primary concern."

"But it's probably his secondary?"

"Exactly."

"If he really is Nauman's son, though . . ."

"Let's wait about crossing that bridge. A pity my Mrs. Bayles is so efficient. She tells me the cleaning crew removed all his personal effects months ago. I don't suppose you — ?"

"No."

After hanging up the phone, Livingston called for Oscar Nauman's file, but he didn't immediately see what he was looking for.

"I clipped it to his death certificate," said his secretary. "Shall I call them and see what I can find out?"

Getting the information he wanted would probably mean listening to hours of execrable elevator music broken by a chirpy "Please continue to hold. Your call is very important to us."

"Thank you, Mrs. Bayles," he said. "That would be most helpful."

The manager of the market on Tenth Avenue studied the flyer the policeman had handed him and shook his head. "Sorry, I don't know him. What's he done?"

"Died," said the officer. "With no ID on him."

"Yeah? Too bad. I'll stick this on our board over there by the door. Maybe someone will recognize him."

"He bought a bottle of aspirin over a week ago?" asked the clerk at the Duane Reade on Ninth Avenue. He gestured out at the crowded store. "And you expect me to remember him? Give me a break."

"You were right, Charlotte," Grace Landers said. "Mom did have some pictures that Grandma took when you went to Rome to have those polyps removed, but you may not be able to use any of them. I'm afraid they're not very flattering."

Charlotte Randolph watched her sister's granddaughter unzip a flat leather envelope and dump several dozen snapshots on the glass-topped table. It had been her sister's first trip abroad and she had snapped roll after roll of film with her Brownie camera. St. Peter's, the Colosseum, the Trevi Fountain, the Spanish Steps. And even through Charlotte had expressly forbidden Daisy to take pictures of her, there she was — more than forty years younger and caught in candid shots that were embarrassingly awful.

"Mom says that's when Grandma started putting on the pounds."

"I'm afraid we both did," said Charlotte, grimacing at a particularly unattractive view of her round face and pudgy waistline. "All that pasta. Took me six months to get back to singing shape."

"Too bad she didn't follow your example," said Grace, who did not carry an extra ounce on her slender body.

"She didn't have the same incentive," Charlotte said complacently. "But it was good of her to come with me and keep me from overdoing. When I was in rehab, my voice therapist said that the extra weight would help keep my vocal cords flexible while I recovered. It was the first time I'd had a real rest since joining the Met and a side benefit was that I came back fluent in

Italian, which was a huge help for some of my roles."

As Charlotte sorted through the scattered pictures, separating the purely tourist shots from those that might make it into the book, she paused and said, "Could you make us a cup of tea, darling? Just talking about my vocal cords has dried them out."

"Of course."

The real kitchen was downstairs in the basement, but here on the first floor where she entertained, mirrored panels concealed a butler's pantry that had a wet bar, hot plate, a microwave oven, and everything needed for making hot or cold drinks.

As Grace disappeared behind the mirrors, Charlotte Randolph quickly plucked four of the most unflattering pictures from the pile and tucked them into the pocket of her robe.

More loose ends to be tidied away.

If this book made as big a splash as her editor predicted, she would once again be in the public eye, and who knew where reporters would go poking?

"You've papered that neighborhood with flyers?" McKinnon asked when they met late that afternoon. "And it's on television, right?"

"Yes, sir," Sigrid said.

"Then I don't see what else you can do to ID him till someone comes forward." He noticed the dark rings under her eyes. "You okay?"

"Just frustrated," she said with a wan smile.

"It'll come," he said. "It always does, doesn't it?"

Except when it doesn't, Sigrid thought as she walked back to her own office. On the other hand, she and her team had only one unsolved case on their book, a young woman found burned in a dumpster. Her nude body had been spread-eagled over several cardboard boxes that were soaked in gasoline, then set on fire. By the time she was found, her body was so badly charred that there was almost nothing left to help identify her aside from the fact that she'd had perfect teeth without even a single filling. Caucasian, average height, blue eyes, brown hair, approximately 125 pounds.

"Probably new to the city," Tillie said, when no missing person report came close to matching what they could say about her. She could have been from anywhere.

Surely someone could put a name to their second victim.

"WholeLife Research," said a pleasant voice

on the other end of the call.

"Dr. Gustav Bohr, please," said Mrs. Bayles.

"May I ask who's calling?"

"Marcus Livingston's law office."

"And this is in reference to — ?"

"Mr. Livingston arranged a donation to your institution last year. Dr. Bohr was his contact there."

"Organs or whole body?"

"Whole body."

"One moment, please."

The taped music had barely begun to play when a male voice said, "Dr. Bohr here."

Mrs. Bayle pressed the intercom button on her desk. "Dr. Bohr's on line two, Mr. Livingston."

In his office, her employer took a deep breath and said, "Dr. Bohr, this is Marcus Livingston. I hope you can help me."

It took several minutes to explain precisely what it was he wanted and why.

There was a moment of silence and then the doctor said, "This is highly irregular, Mr. Livingston. The remains would have been cremated within six weeks."

"I understand, sir, but I was hoping some of the tissues might still be available."

"That is, of course, a possibility. But locating them?" Another pause. "Let me make

139

some inquiries. It might take some time, but give me your number and I'll get back to you."

At midnight, Janis Jennings put aside the book she was reading and walked out to the common room that served as a lounge for her tenants. It was empty and the rest of the house was quiet. Only one of her tenants was booked to have a client spend the night with her — a widower who still grieved for the wife he'd lost last year. She switched off all the lights except for one dim bulb in the entryway. As she started to throw the deadbolt on the front door, a key turned in the lock and a woman entered, pulling a small roller bag. Late thirties, her auburn hair was skinned back from her strong face and she was casually dressed in jeans and a beige linen jacket.

"Peg?"

"Whoa!" the woman said. "You startled me. I thought everyone would be in bed."

"You're back early," her landlady said. "How's your mother?"

"Fine now, knock wood. It wasn't a full-blown stroke. What the doctor called a love pat from God. No aftereffects, thank goodness, so I called Mrs. Kirkland and told her she could come tomorrow after all."

She turned the deadbolt and moved past Jennings toward the stairs. "Anything happen while I was gone?"

"I'm afraid so. Remember Matty Mutone? He was found dead Wednesday morning."

"Oh no! What happened? Overdose?"

"I'm not sure, but I gather they're treating it as a suspicious death. The police were here and they want to talk to you. They'll be back on Monday to hear if Matty told you anything that would help them. If he had any enemies or anything."

"I'll talk to them," Peg Overhold said, "though it probably won't help them much. His witchy godmother didn't want him back in her life, but it's not like he thought she'd kill him or anything."

"You sure about that?"

They both laughed and said good night.

CHAPTER 11

Anne said her breakfast panel for BookExpo had sold out weeks earlier, so Sigrid would have slept in on Saturday morning except that Roman wanted to get to the convention center as soon as the doors opened. "Before all the day's tchotchkes are gone," he said. "Tote bags. The best books. The good candy."

The main exhibition hall was already jammed with people: buyers for bookstores all across the country, agents and editors there to look at trends and perhaps discover underappreciated authors who might be poached from their current agents and publishers, librarians, specialty retail and museum store staff members, scouts for foreign publishers and numerous other book industry people. Overhead hung brightly colored banners touting publishing imprints, logos, and replicas of book covers.

They walked past booths piled high with

glossy new books, high-tech booths that featured the latest in electronic gadgets, smaller booths waiting to take orders for binding a favorite book with tooled leather, regional and university presses with esoteric subjects. And every booth seemed to have a basket or glass bowl filled with candy or advertising badges and ballpoint pens.

Roman scored a couple of sturdy canvas tote bags from the Dorling-Kindersley booth. "We should pace ourselves," he warned, dropping two bite-size chocolate bars into his bag, but by the time they had threaded their way through the crowds, his bag was more than half full of free books. "I may have to get another bag," he admitted sheepishly as he reached for a glossy picture book on herb gardens.

She herself had succumbed to a collection of Robert Pinsky's poems and a new biography of Hans Holbein.

Anne's multinational publisher had several imprints. Instead of a booth, their space was more like a series of salesrooms under banners of their blue-and-white logo. A company sales rep directed them to where Anne sat at a counter in front of a blow-up of her *Pictures from Mogadishu* book jacket. Aided by a boyish red-haired publicist who had opened the books to the title page for her, she had signed and given away more than fifty copies in the autograph area downstairs immediately after her panel, but now she signed an advance copy for a sturdy-looking woman whose thick white hair was cut in a short pixie with stylish bangs. The woman wore a white shell under a short-sleeved jacket of light blue cotton with a matching A-line skirt. A large, flat gold locket hung from a slender chain around her neck.

Anne smiled as Sigrid and Roman approached and said, "Come meet the owner of your grandmother's favorite bookstore. Nancy, this is my daughter, Sigrid."

Nancy Olson held out her hand. "And this is Sarah Goddin, our store manager," she said of the slender brown-haired woman who had a youthful sprinkling of freckles across her nose. "We've just talked your mother into adding us to her tour."

"You have a store in Cotton Grove?" Sigrid asked.

"In Raleigh," the woman said with a smile so wide that her blue eyes almost disappeared into thin crinkles.

Sigrid introduced Roman, whereupon Olson made him her vassal forever by saying, "Roman Tramegra? Didn't you write *Frosty Death*? One of our local book clubs chose it for their January read and it did real well in our store."

Before Roman could kiss the hem of her blue skirt, she turned back to Anne. "Sorry to run, but we're trying to nail down a commitment for Charlotte Randolph."

"Has her book been published?" Sigrid asked.

"No, it's not due out till next spring, but I want to make sure her publicist puts us on her tour. If she's halfway honest about the life she's led, it's bound to make the *Times*'s bestseller list. I can't wait to read it."

"Wasn't there something odd about how she got her first big break?" asked Anne, who was not an opera buff.

"With her voice, she would eventually have sung title roles anyhow," said Olson, who clearly *was* a fan. "But yes, all the planets lined up to let her step into the role of Mimi that night and gave her career that huge legendary jump start. Especially since an important critic happened to be there that night and wrote a rave review."

Before Sigrid could ask for more details, Nancy Olson hefted her own canvas tote bag. With a wave of her hand and a promise to be in touch before Anne's tour, she and her store manager hurried off.

"I've been hearing about Quail Ridge Books for years," Anne said, "but I bet

Mother's the real reason she invited me to come." She reached for Sigrid's bag. "Are you having fun? What did you get? Holbein?" She frowned. "Nothing modern?"

Sigrid shrugged. "You're the one who exposed me to him."

"I also exposed you to modern art, but it didn't take, did it?"

Abruptly, Oscar Nauman's name hung in the air between them.

Unspoken.

Anne looked stricken. "Oh, Siga, honey, I'm so sorry."

"Stop it, Mother. You can say his name. Nauman knew I liked the Northern Renaissance better than his things and he didn't take it personally. I'm well aware how ironic it is that he left all his pictures to me."

Anne patted her arm in mute apology, glanced at her watch, and said to the redhaired publicist who had been helping her, "Am I through here, Jamie?"

"You are," he said. "Now go have fun."

They had a leisurely lunch in the food court, then browsed in and out of various booths. Roman filled a second tote bag and, to Anne's amusement, Sigrid added a book on makeup techniques to her own bag. An interest in cosmetics had come to her late and she still wasn't totally confident with

146

eyeliner. At the Little, Brown booth, Anne talked the sales rep into giving her the newest Michael Connelly thriller.

"For Mac," she said. "His birthday's next week and I was wondering what to get him. Don't tell."

"Don't worry," Sigrid said dryly.

By the time they got to the autographing area, the line for Billy Collins was so long that Anne immediately begged off. Roman professed himself too tired to wait with those heavy bags and Sigrid reluctantly admitted that having the poet's signature on the title page of a book wouldn't add very much to her enjoyment of his work.

"Write him a letter," Roman said. "I've answered all four of the letters my readers have sent me, so perhaps you'll wind up with his autograph anyhow."

Out on the sidewalk, Anne headed for a crosstown bus while Roman flagged down a cab for the short ride down to Hawker Street. "My treat," he said magisterially as he gratefully deposited his tote bags on the seat between them.

Over on the Lower East Side, Denny Kapps dialed a number the local precinct had given him when he got out of prison last Saturday.

"Robbery detail," said a bored voice.

"This is Denny Kapps. K-A-P-P-S. I'm calling to see if you've found my car yet?"

Once again he had to give the make, model, and license number and once again the bored voice said, "Sorry, sir. By now it's probably been stripped down to the chassis and sold for scrap. I suggest you talk to your insurance agent."

"I don't care what you say, Nonna. I'm moving in with you this week," said Laura Edwards.

"Don't be absurd, Laura." Erect of spine and stern of face, Sofia DelVecchio tried to stare her granddaughter down. Her glare seemed to have lost its power, though.

Her daughter had always wilted beneath that glare, but her granddaughter's lips curved in laughter. "The only absurd one at this breakfast table is you, Nonna. You and Orla. You need younger help in the house and if you won't hire someone, then you're stuck with me."

"Who needs someone younger?" sputtered the woman who was both housekeeper and companion to her grandmother. "I've taken care of your nonna since the day she brought your mother home from the hospital and I won't have anyone else do it."

"Oh, do be quiet, Orla," said Mrs. DelVecchio. She turned back to the girl at the end of the table. "You have another year of school. You can't quit now."

"I'm not quitting. I'll transfer to NYU and finish there. The drama department at Tisch has already accepted me for the fall semester."

"Drama? Not law? That's absurd."

"I know. It's crazy, but I've got to try, Nonna. Dad thinks I could be a great trial lawyer, but arguing cases in front of a jury would just be a substitute for real drama. When I was on stage in my school plays — in front of an audience, hearing them laugh or making them hold their breath — I felt more alive than anywhere else. Mom understood, why can't you and Dad? I want to live here in town, maybe take some voice lessons and go to some auditions this summer just to get my feet wet."

"An actress?" she faltered.

Yet, even as she said it, Sofia realized with blinding clarity that of course she would want to be on stage. She was made for it. That beautiful face, that long blond hair, those flashing eyes. A slender body that curved in all the right places.

Her own hair had been a light brown back then, but her face and body had been that entrancing when she first met Benito. He was older and already a made man. She knew what he was, what he did; but when his beautiful brown eyes lit up at the sight of her, when his smile melted her heart, when he swore to her fearful parents that she would live like a contessa and that the dark side of his world would never touch her, how could she resist?

And for the first few years, it was all that he had promised. The dresses. The jewelry. The way the maître d's bowed to her as if she really was a contessa when they swept into nightclubs with his entourage for an evening of dancing.

"He won't be faithful," they had warned her.

"I don't care!" she had said. But when it happened, she did care. She had stormed and raged, even threatened to leave him.

"No, you won't," he'd said, and there had been such an icy hardness in his voice that for the first time she realized that she did indeed have a tiger by the tail.

"Have a baby," said her mother.

"A baby will keep him at home," agreed the aunts.

God knows she had tried. Then, when she was resigned to her barren fate, the miracle had happened. Aria. And he was so grateful to her that once again she felt like a con-tessa.

Now Benito was gone. Aria, too. But she still had Laura.

"An actress?" Orla protested.

"Yes, an actress," Laura said firmly, "so you can just freshen up Mother's old room for me, Orla. New curtains, I think, and please get rid of those ratty towels in the guest bathroom."

"Ratty towels?" Sofia DelVecchio was in-dignant.

"Ratty," Laura said. "They're frayed on the edges."

"Frayed?" Her grandmother turned on Orla. "Frayed? Are you as blind as you are crippled?"

Miss Orlano's bushy gray eyebrows bee-tled furiously and her eyes filled with tears. Wordlessly, she rose from her chair, gathered up their breakfast plates, and carried them out of the dining room with as much dignity as she could manage, trying not to hobble.

"There now," said Mrs. DelVecchio. "See what you made me do?"

"*Made* you do? Don't lay this one on me, Nonna. Anything you've ever done, you've done because you wanted to."

Chapter 12

Janis Jennings opened her red door Monday morning and said, "Hello again. Lieutenant Harod, right?"

"Harald," Sigrid said. "And I believe you've met Detective Hentz? We'd like to ask you more questions about Matty Mutone."

"Oh, sure." She stepped back to let them in. Today, her bare feet had blue nail polish that matched her blue denim shirt. "They said at the diner that he'd been poisoned."

"That's right."

"And you haven't found who did it?"

"No, no arrests yet."

They were ushered into a large comfortable room that could have been the lobby of a good hotel. Oriental rugs covered the hardwood floor and defined two separate seating areas with couches and arm chairs. The sheer window curtains gave privacy, yet still allowed the morning sun to light up the room. A vase of fresh daisies stood on a side table and soft music issued from concealed speakers. In front of the tall windows stood a mahogany card table with four straight chairs that would do nicely for an interview. Sigrid chose to sit in the one with its back to the windows so that light fell on Janis Jennings's face when she joined them. Her long brown hair hung loosely on her sturdy shoulders. Her only jewelry was a small gold cross that dangled from a thin chain.

"Can I get you anything? Coffee? Water?"

"We're fine," Sigrid said. "Could you tell us again, in more detail, about your dealings with Matty Mutone? How you met, what you know about him?"

"It was back in January. I'd seen him around the neighborhood but I didn't know who he was at first till they told me at the diner. They said he was connected with the DelVecchio woman. That he used to be her driver for a while until she fired him for using drugs. Evidently he used to be heavy into meth. Then she and her daughter got him into rehab and things were fine till this past winter when he started using again. I guess he hit the skids and went straight down the tubes and that's when they gave up on him. Forbade him to come to the house."

Jennings leaned back in the chair with her strong hands clasped together on the table in front of her. "I suppose that's what drew me to him. Stray dogs and anybody Sofia DelVecchio's down on. She's absolutely convinced that I'm running a whorehouse and she's done everything she could to run me off. Unfortunately for her, this side of the street is zoned for business and it's completely legal for me to register my building as an SRO and to have a jazz club in the basement."

She gave an amused smile. "I'm not wedded to this neighborhood, though. I could open up anywhere, so I told her lawyer she could have this place for four million."

"I'm guessing she didn't want it at that price," said Hentz.

"You're right about that. Anyhow, I first met Matty when I was bringing home some egg rolls for lunch. It was right around New Year's and colder than an ice cube sandwich. He was on the bench, wrapped in a blanket, and he was crying like his heart had broken into a million pieces. Really sobbing. I gave him some money and my egg rolls."

While she talked, Jennings gathered up

154

her thick brown hair and braided it into a single plait. She fished a rubber band from the pocket of her white shorts to secure the end and tossed the braid over her shoulder.

"He was there again two days later and he still looked so woebegone that I knew he needed some hugs. I brought him back here with me, cleaned him up, and cuddled him for over two hours. He cried some more and said there was no one left to hug him ever again. He was really pitiful. I tried to get him to talk to me, tell me why his life had gone off the tracks, but he wouldn't open up. That's when I asked Peg to take him on. I think she saw him twice, but you'll have to ask her. Shall I tell her you're here?"

"Please," said Sigrid, and watched as Jennings walked over to the staircase and opened an inconspicuous panel that hid an intercom system.

They heard her say, "Peg? The police are here. Can you come down?"

The speaker crackled and a woman's voice said, "Be right there."

Minutes later, Peg Overhold joined them in the lounge. Early forties, her auburn hair was lightly threaded with gray at the temples and there was something motherly about her smile.

Janis Jennings made the introductions,

then left them.

"You want to hear about Matty?" she asked.

They nodded.

She cleared her throat. "I guess Janis told you how she got me to give him a session?"

"We'd like to hear it fresh from you, please."

"Janis has a heart as big as Texas and she felt sorry for the kid." Peg Overhold had a laugh that bubbled up from her chest. "Kid? Ha! He was probably at least as old as us, but there was something about him that made you think of your kid brother. Like he never finished growing up or something. Anyhow, Janis found him crying on the bench down there and she brought him home with her and gave him a free session. Next time she saw him, he seemed just as miserable, so she asked if I'd take him. I sort of have a knack for getting people to talk to me about what's hurting them."

She cleared her throat again. "Sorry. Airplanes trigger my allergies."

A bowl of individually wrapped hard candies sat on one of the side tables and she got up to get a couple. "Anybody else want one?"

Sigrid and Hentz both shook their heads and waited till she had removed the cellophane and popped one into her mouth. The smell of peppermint wreathed her.

"So you cuddled him?" Hentz asked with a straight face.

"He was a smelly mess," said Overhold, grimacing in memory. "But money was tight for me after Christmas and I was behind in my rent, so Janis said she'd knock some of it off if I'd do it. We keep changes of clean clothes here. He took a shower, washed his hair, and put on a pair of our pajamas and we lay down next to each other on my bed. We don't kiss and we certainly don't have sex, but I hugged him, smoothed his arm, stroked his cheek. He was so damn grateful. Kept thanking me. He cried all through most of our first session. His cousin had died back in December. He adored her and he said that she was the only one who loved him. That the only reason Mrs. DelVecchio had hired him to drive for her was because his cousin asked her to. After the cousin died, he was out of a job and that's when he started using again."

Sigrid was frowning. "How did his cousin die?"

"A car accident. He didn't tell me any details the first time, but I gave him another session about a week later and that's when he really opened up."

She unwrapped a second mint. "He said his cousin was in town to see a play and go Christmas shopping but there was something wrong with the car, so she had to take a cab. She had finished shopping and was crossing the street when a car knocked her down and ran over her. Hit-and-run. Matty was so distraught when he heard about it that he blamed himself for the accident. He said if he'd been driving her, she would still be alive. That's when he went back on meth and that's when Mrs. DelVecchio fired him. He thought she blamed him, too. Her and her housekeeper both. He told me that the housekeeper might bring food to him, but she acted like she wanted to spit on him. That's when he started crying again, poor guy."

"Did he tell you his cousin's name?"

"Aria."

Surprised, Sigrid glanced at Hentz and saw that he, too, had picked up on the name of George Edwards's wife.

"His cousin was Mrs. DelVecchio's daughter?"

The woman nodded.

"Did he mention any enemies, anybody he was having problems with?"

"No, just how much he missed his cousin."

"What about friends, other relatives?"

"If he'd had friends or loving relatives, Lieutenant, he wouldn't have needed my services." Before they could ask more questions, the doorbell rang and Peg Overhold jumped up to answer it. "If that's my client, I'll have to stop now."

"We're finished for now," Sigrid said. "Thank you for your help."

She and Hentz followed her out to the foyer, where Overhold opened the door for a tiny frail woman who stood on the top step.

"Come in, luv," Overhold said, and put her arm around the stooped shoulders to guide her in.

Out on the sidewalk, Sigrid looked at Hentz. "George Edwards said that neither he nor his mother-in-law had spoken to Matty since December. I suppose this is why."

As they walked away, they heard Peg Overhold call to them from the top of the stoop.

"I almost forgot," she said as she came down to meet them. "The last time Matty was here, I had our cleaning woman put his clothes through the laundry. She found this picture when she emptied his pockets and I didn't see it till after he was gone. I kept meaning to give it back to him and just never did."

She handed Sigrid a three-by-four clear plastic sleeve that held a snapshot of Matty in younger, happier times. He sat on the hood of an Oldsmobile beside a very pretty blond teenager. Both were laughing. Sigrid turned it over. On the back, in pencil, was a scrawled inscription: *Me and Aria — Fourth of July.*

"Poor Matty," Overhold said. "His bitchy godmother wouldn't even let him come to the funeral."

At the newsstand on West Forty-Fourth, one of the vendor's regular customers looked at the flyer tacked on the side frame and said, "That looks like Jack Bloss. What's he done?"

"Who's Jack Bloss?" asked the vendor.

"Used to live in my building till they raised the rent last time. And how the hell the city's gonna hold on to people like us, living on a fixed income, when they let landlords gouge us and —"

"Yeah, yeah," said the vendor who'd heard it all before. On his cell phone, he punched in the number listed at the bottom of the flyer. "So where was he living now?"

CHAPTER 13

The woman who opened the door to Number 403 fit Sigrid's stereotypic image of a Wagnerian Valkyrie. Tall and stoutly built, she wore a dark red dress with a square neckline, and it flowed from her broad shoulders to her knees with no hint of a waist. Her blond hair was worn in a braided coronet and her creamy complexion glowed with vigorous health. All she needed, thought Hentz, was a shield and a helmet.

She carefully read the ID badges that Sigrid and Hentz held up, then shook her head. "I'm so sorry, but this is a very inconvenient time. Miss Randolph cannot possibly see you now. She's working."

"Working?" asked Hentz. "We understood that she's retired."

"Working on her book," the woman said. "Once she's in the flow of memory, she hates to be interrupted."

"And you are?" Sigrid said.

161

"Marian Schmidt, Miss Randolph's personal assistant."

"Do you live here, Ms. Schmidt?"

She frowned. "Why do you ask?"

"Were you here last Tuesday evening?"

"Please, Lieutenant — Herald, is it?" She squinted at Sigrid's ID.

"Harald."

"Sorry. Harald. I really must ask what this is about, Lieutenant."

"What this is about," Hentz said sternly, "is a murder investigation."

"Those two men on the bench around the corner?"

"Right. So we need to speak to Miss Randolph. Now."

"I could tell her you're here, but if you interrupt her now, she may be too annoyed to speak to you. Could you possibly come back after lunch? If I tell her to expect you and give her time to decompress, as it were, she'll be in a much better mood to cooperate, believe me."

They looked at their watches. 11:40. Rather than push it, Sigrid said, "Twelve-thirty?"

"One o'clock would be better."

"Tell Miss Randolph to expect us at twelve-forty-five," Sigrid said.

"Very well," Ms. Schmidt said. She did

not sound happy about it.

As they walked back toward the car, Hentz said, "Lunch? Maybe see the waiter who saw our second victim?"

The diner across the street made decent tuna salad sandwiches on thinly sliced sourdough toast but they were told that Nick Finmore wouldn't be in till 1:30. As they ate, Sigrid asked Hentz to tell her about the legendary Charlotte Randolph.

"The way I heard it," he said, taking a bite of his dill pickle, "is that she knew the staging of that production because she was a member of the chorus. I think she had one solo line to sing, but that was it, so it was the classic footlight fairy tale."

Sigrid repeated the words of that Raleigh bookseller. "She said all the planets lined up to let her sing that night."

"She's right. Operas are hugely expensive to put on, so they don't take any chances if they can help it. It's a belt-*and*-suspenders mentality."

"More than one understudy, you mean?"

"Except they're not called understudies. They're 'covers.' Someone in the second tier of singers who's already made a name for herself, knows the role, and is no more than fifteen minutes away. That's what should have happened with Charlotte Randolph. I forget the details, but for some reason, the first cover wasn't available, so when the soprano broke her leg or something just minutes before the curtain was to go up, they didn't have a choice. Randolph went on in her place and corny as it sounds, a star was born."

"Lucky," said Sigrid.

"Should make one hell of a book," Hentz agreed.

"Opera keeps popping up, doesn't it?"

"How do you mean?"

"Well, Mrs. DelVecchio calls her handyman Alberich, so she must know opera, right? And Charlotte Randolph made a career of it. They're neighbors. I wonder if they're friends?"

Before Hentz could answer, Sigrid's phone buzzed. When she answered, Tillie's excited voice came through loud and clear. "We've finally got a name, Lieutenant! Jack Bloss. No details yet."

They rang the bell at Number 403 at precisely 12:45 and this time, the PA was more welcoming.

"Come in, come in! Miss Randolph is expecting you."

Mrs. DelVecchio's Federal-style house had

been furnished in turn-of-the-century mahogany and walnut. The interior of Miss Randolph's Federal-style house was mid-century modern with lacings of operatic bling. Load-bearing walls had been replaced with fluted columns that supported the weight of the house and opened up the ground floor from the front entry to tall windows at the back. Except for a classic grand piano that dominated the far end of the room, the furnishings were a symphony of white and shiny chrome. The two couches and several chairs were upholstered in white and the visible frames were either chrome or white plastic. Occasional tables were topped in circles or squares of heavy glass. Suspended from the ten-foot ceiling were a half-dozen chandeliers of varying sizes. Like smaller versions of the chandeliers at the Met, the spiky crystal starbursts hung at different levels. A couple of iconic Eames lounge chairs sat before a white brick fireplace.

The hardwood floors were stained a rich ebony to echo the piano, and white rugs defined the different areas. A large round rug near the middle of this first floor held a circular chrome-and-glass table that could seat eight. The staircase had chrome railings and it, too, was carpeted in white. Mirrored folding screens blocked off one corner of the room.

What kept the black-and-white space from feeling as cold and sterile as a hospital were the colorful abstract paintings that hung on every wall and the pots of greenery massed around the room. In one corner of the window wall, a nine-foot tree with lacy leaves towered above some spiky plants that looked like green knife blades to Sigrid, who cheerfully confessed to black thumbs when it came to houseplants. Clusters of brightly patterned foliage in shades of red, pink, and yellow filled a large planter in the other corner. Sigrid's housemate grew plants on their window ledges, so she did know that the pots of red flowers were geraniums. Moreover she recognized the miniature bush with fragrant white blossoms because gardenias grew around Grandmother Lattimore's house down in North Carolina.

The whole setting was appropriate for cocktail parties, large dinners, or small chamber concerts.

After the Wagnerian references and meeting Randolph's personal assistant, Sigrid expected an imposing operatic diva. Instead, Charlotte Randolph was short, small-boned and elegant in a simple white djellaba trimmed in silver embroidery at the neck and cuffs. The glass-topped dining table where she sat was strewn with letters, photographs, playbills, and programs. A space large enough to hold a silver tray had been cleared in front of her and she gestured to two adjacent chairs.

"I hope you'll join me," she said in a clear, melodious voice. "My housekeeper makes wonderful little sandwiches. Are you sure you won't stay, Marian?"

Ms. Schmidt shook her head. "Thanks, Charlotte, but they'll want to talk to you privately."

When the outer door closed behind her, Miss Randolph lifted the teapot and said, "Milk, Lieutenant, or as it comes?"

"Neither, thank you. We just had lunch. We're here to —"

"Marian told me. It's about the men that died around the corner. I understand. But there's no reason we can't share a cup of tea while you ask me your questions. Now, then," she said with a coaxing smile. "Milk or lemon?"

Sigrid sighed. "Lemon, please. No sugar."

Time had been kind to the woman. She had to be nearing eighty and while she was no longer the slender beauty pictured in that publicity photo that Tillie had shown them, those few extra pounds had smoothed away many of the wrinkles women of her age usually had. Her naturally blond hair was completely white now and softly curled around her still-lovely face. When she smiled at Hentz, a dimple flashed in her right cheek. She poured tea for him, too, before offering them the plate of dainty sandwiches.

"The circles are watercress and the little squares are cucumber. The triangles are salmon and dill. I prefer savories to sweets this time of day. Push those pictures out of the way if you need more space."

As Hentz started to follow her instructions, he paused to examine the pen-and-ink drawing on top of the nearest pile. "Wow! Is this an original Al Hirschfeld?"

The soprano nodded. "I really should get that framed. Such a clever artist. He drew me at least four times. That was when I sang Desdemona."

"Three Ninas? I only see two."

Sigrid looked across at the caricature of Charlotte Randolph in courtly dress and carrying a lace-edged handkerchief. The artist's style was instantly familiar to anyone who grew up reading show business reviews in the *New York Times*. As a child who loved puzzles, Sigrid had been delighted when Anne explained that the number beside

Hirschfeld's signature indicated how many times he'd hidden the name of his daughter Nina in his drawings. The straight lines of the capitalized letters were so easy to camouflage amid hair, feathers, draperies, and furs that it sometimes took her several minutes to find them all.

"I see two of them in your hair," said Hentz, "and I thought the other one was in the lace on your handkerchief, but —"

"Not the lace," Sigrid said. "It's the front folds of her dress."

Miss Randolph smiled as she bit into a cucumber sandwich. "Brava, Lieutenant."

At a nod from Sigrid, Hentz opened the folder with the pictures of the two dead men.

Miss Randolph made a pouty face. "Must we do this while I'm eating? I told your people last week that I didn't know those men."

"My officers said that you occasionally sent food down to them."

"I did. I do. I don't like food piling up in my refrigerator, so when my housekeeper leaves, she takes any extras down there. My housekeeper, Lieutenant. Not me."

"And did she do that last Tuesday?"

"No, she's only here Monday, Wednesday, and Friday, although she or Marian will

169

help out if I need someone on the weekend."

"You live alone? No companion?"

"As long as I stay healthy, I don't need anyone here at night. Marian's usually here from ten till four and Selma comes on alternate days to clean and do a little cooking. But what do my living arrangements have to do with your investigation?"

"Probably nothing. But please look at these pictures again. Does the name Jack Bloss mean anything to you?"

"Jack Bloss? Was *he* one of those men? Where are my glasses?"

She poked through the clutter of paper on the table, then crossed the room to a side table, where she picked up a pair of rimless reading glasses and put them on.

Sigrid handed her the doctored photograph of the second dead man.

"Ah," Miss Randolph said, sadness in her tone. "His eyes are open here. Makes all the difference in the world, doesn't it? They say that eyes are the windows to the soul. So true. He didn't have a beard when I knew him, but yes, that's Jack Bloss."

"He was here?"

She nodded.

"How did you know him?"

"It was years ago." The soprano's voice softened and deepened with nostalgia. "He worked backstage on the lighting crew at the Met for a while, then moved on to Broadway. Lovely man. Very handsome." She looked down at the picture. "Of course, he had a full head of brown hair back then and a smile that could melt your heart."

"Did he melt your heart?" Hentz asked.

She dimpled. "You'll have to read my book, Detective. In fact, that's how we reconnected. I'm not sure how he found my number, but he phoned on Tuesday morning. He'd heard that I was writing my bio and he asked my assistant if he could bring over the program from that night. It had the insert that explained how I was to go on in Marta Constanza's place. Of course I said yes as soon as Marian told me. That pile on the end." She gestured to papers on the other side of Hentz. "I think that's where Marian put it. Such a surprise to see it after all these years. Inserts usually get thrown away quicker than the programs themselves."

Hentz found the insert and handed it to Sigrid. "What time was that?"

"Marian told him six o'clock and he was here on the dot."

"Did you give him food?" Sigrid asked.

"Food?"

"You said you didn't send any food down

171

to that bench on Tuesday, but on Wednesday morning, there was a takeout box for lasagna that we can't account for. Do you know anything about that?"

Randolph looked embarrassed. "You're going to think I'm an awful snob, Lieutenant. I had made reservations at the Red Chameleon, but when he turned up here in those clothes? Looking like a tramp? It was clear that he had come down in the world, so I insisted that he take some money in return for bringing me that program. I let him think that the insert made it rare and collectible. We had a few martinis and talked about old times for maybe another hour, then I'm afraid I lied some more and said friends were picking me up for a dinner engagement. He said he'd skipped lunch and had thought I might give him dinner. The children had brought me lasagna the night before and it was still in the refrigerator untouched. I said I hoped he wouldn't be insulted and he assured me he wasn't. Then he took it and left, a bit unsteady on his feet, I'm afraid. He was the one who had mixed the drinks and I wasn't too steady on my own feet after two or three of them. I wonder if that's why he stopped at that bench?"

"The children?"

"My sister's granddaughter and my third husband's son. Or was Ray the fourth?" Her rueful laugh was so contagious that even Sigrid smiled. "No, I'm positive he was third. Cameron was fourth."

"Their names, please?"

"Grace Landers and Ferguson . . ." She frowned. "Do you know, I can't remember Ferguson's first name. I've always just called him Ferguson. When you get to be my age, you start losing nouns. Names especially. Would you hand me my address book, please? It's that fat red one."

Moments later, she looked up in triumph. "Abner! Abner Ferguson. Such an ugly name, Abner. No wonder I keep forgetting it."

She read out their contact information for Hentz to jot down, then said, "No one's told me how Jack died. Was he shot? Stabbed?"

"No, he was poisoned," Sigrid told her.

"*Poisoned!* How?"

"He shared your lasagna with the other man and both died."

"There was poison in my lasagna? How did it get there?"

"That's what we're trying to ascertain," said Hentz.

She looked up at them, her blue eyes wide with puzzlement. "So if I had eaten it — ?"

173

"Who else had access to it?"

"The restaurant, of course," she said slowly. "My niece and stepson. Marian, perhaps, but not Selma. She wasn't here Tuesday night. But it's absurd to think that Ferguson or Grace would — No! I can't believe it."

"We'll be contacting them, but in the meantime, we'll need your fingerprints, too. For elimination purposes."

Charlotte Randolph sat in silent thought as Hentz took her prints. When he was finished and she had wiped her fingers clean, she said, "The other man who died? Who was he? Where did his food come from?"

"The DelVecchio house," Sigrid said. "Do you know Mrs. DelVecchio?"

"We've been neighbors for more than forty years, so of course I've met her. Her daughter, too."

"What about her husband?"

"Benito DelVecchio? Oh yes, I met him several times. He could be quite charming. And of course, he loved opera. Almost a cliché, isn't it? An Italian gangster with season tickets to the Met? He used to come down and ask me to sign his programs." That dimple flashed again in her cheek as she confided, "I don't think his wife approved."

"Do you take any medication for your heart, Miss Randolph?"

"How did you know? Or do you just assume every old woman has a heart condition?"

"It's not uncommon," Hentz said in a tone that implied that she would never be old in his eyes. "Coumadin?"

She gave a graceful shrug. "I've taken it for almost ten years. For my a-fib. Is that what killed him? But how?"

"That's what we're trying to find out. Would you show us your bottle?"

"My bottle?" Her blue eyes widened. "Are you accusing my niece or my stepson of trying to poison me?"

"It's just standard procedure," said Hentz, but Charlotte Randolph shook her head and she seemed distressed and apologetic as she rose from her chair.

"I'm so sorry, Lieutenant Harald, but I must ask you both to leave. I really don't think I should talk to you anymore without my attorney here."

When they were gone, Charlotte went up to her bedroom on the next floor where she unlocked the top drawer of a tall chest and pushed aside several bundles of love letters, each tied with a different colored ribbon. Red for the senator, blue for the governor, green for the millionaire who had wanted to marry her and take her to Wisconsin, black for the tenor who would have left his very rich wife for her. Briefly she wondered if men still sent love letters on paper through the post office or was it all now as ephemeral as electronic bytes that disappeared with the click of a button? She had touched on her husbands and most of the men in her book, tastefully and discreetly with just enough details to spice up their chapters in her life. Only one lover had been kept shrouded in secrecy.

But now that Jack was dead?

Underneath the bundled letters was a flat metal box, its tiny key kept hidden behind the mirror of her dressing table. She unlocked the box, lifted the lid, and chose a letter at random.

Like all the others in this box, it began *"Cara mia . . ."*

As long as they were in the neighborhood, Sigrid and Hentz tried the diner again. This time, the waiter who had seen Jack Bloss last Tuesday afternoon was there, but he had nothing new to add, although it did match Charlotte Randolph's account of when Bloss had arrived at her house.

"Like I said, he came in around five-fifteen, five-thirty, ordered a cup of coffee and sat at that table by the window for at least a half hour. Next time I looked over, he was gone. Left his money on the table. Me and the counterman were the only ones working the front and he didn't see the guy leave neither."

As they headed back to the station, Sigrid said, "If Tillie's turned up an address for Bloss, maybe those keys will work, so get a search warrant and check it out."

Up on Madison Avenue, the intercom on Marcus Livingston's desk buzzed and Mrs. Bayles's disembodied voice said, "Dr. Bohr's on line one."

Her employer laid aside the dull brief he'd been reading and picked up the receiver. "Dr. Bohr? Marcus Livingston here. Any success?"

"You got lucky, Mr. Livingston. I've located some tissue at a lab in Rochester. Another three days and it would have been incinerated. They're expressing it to my lab and I should have it tomorrow morning, so if you'll send along the person you're trying to match, I'll take a swab and get right on it."

"How long before we know the results?"

"No more than seventy-two hours. In fact, if they're nowhere near a match, it'll be even quicker. In any event, I'll put a rush on it."

"Thank you, Doctor. I'm very grateful."

A dry chuckle came across the line. "Let's hope you feel the same when you get my bill."

They agreed on a time and the address and Livingston gave the information to Mrs. Bayles, who immediately called Vincent Haas at his East Side hotel.

CHAPTER 14

Sam Hentz and Dinah Urbanska arrived at the address Tillie had given them to find that Jack Bloss's apartment was on the fourth floor.

No elevator.

One of the two keys they'd taken from the victim's pocket opened the street door and as he followed Urbanska up the stairs, Hentz wondered how an old man with a pacemaker had made it up and down so many steps every day. The rookie detective was barely breathing hard but pride alone kept Hentz from huffing and puffing as he joined her on the final landing.

Gonna have to hit the gym harder, he told himself as he turned the victim's second key in the lock of apartment 4-C.

A kitchenette lay directly in front of the door with a living room to the left and a bedroom and bath to the right. The only windows were two in the living room that looked out onto the hodgepodge of narrow storefronts that cluttered Tenth Avenue. Hanging between the windows was a birdcage. The apartment was furnished in what Hentz thought of as "old single male" — utilitarian and comfortable enough, but with little to soften the edges.

"Oh no!" said Urbanska, who had gone straight to the birdcage. "It's dead, Sam."

She gazed mournfully at the body of a blue parakeet that lay motionless on the floor of the cage. "The seed cup's empty and the water bottle's dry. Poor little thing! They can't go without food and water for more than two or three days and if Bloss didn't fill them up before he left here Tuesday . . ."

"Too bad," said Hentz, but his eyes were busily taking inventory of the apartment.

The kitchenette was essentially a single counter with a cooktop, sink, and microwave and it held a bare minimum of equipment — two saucepans and a skillet, a toaster, some mismatched china, and a few pieces of tableware. The refrigerator was empty except for seltzer, a bottle of vodka with perhaps two shots left, a head of lettuce, a plastic container of deli olives, salad dressing, and a desiccated lime with one slice missing. In the cupboard were a can of tomato soup, two cans of sardines, a box of egg noodles, a jar of instant coffee, and some packets of saltines.

"No wonder he stopped to eat that takeout Charlotte Randolph gave him," said Hentz, looking over Urbanska's shoulder at the bare shelves.

A dirty coffee mug sat in the sink, but everything else was clean and tidy.

"He drank his coffee black and I don't see any sugar," Urbanska said. "He could have really been hungry."

In the bedroom, a sofa bed with a double mattress appeared to be permanently open and a small TV sat atop the dresser. A Fresnel light aimed at the ceiling served as a bedside lamp and when Urbanska walked over to turn it on, her foot tangled in an extension cord and almost pulled the television off the dresser. Only Hentz's quick reflexes saved it from crashing to the floor.

"Oh, jeepers!" she cried. "I'm sorry, Sam."

Accustomed to her clumsiness, he just smiled and switched on the light, which bounced off the white ceiling and lit up the windowless room.

"Start with the dresser," Hentz said, and while she began on the dead man's socks and underwear, he stepped into the bathroom.

181

The medicine cabinet held the usual assortment of over-the-counter grooming aids and pain remedies and an orange plastic bottle of prescription pills.

"Coumadin," he said, dropping it into an evidence bag.

A pair of scissors lay in the sink along with some stray gray hairs.

"Looks as if he might have trimmed his beard before he left," said Urbanska.

"Probably wanted to look nice for his old girlfriend," Hentz said.

"Charlotte Randolph?"

"Yeah. She all but told the lieutenant and me that she and Bloss might've had a roll or two in the hay back when they were younger."

"They had an affair, yet she didn't recognize his picture?"

"Not the first one Albee showed her. His eyes were closed in that one and she said the beard threw her off. Also that it'd been years since they last met."

"Did you believe her?"

Hentz shrugged. *"What lips my lips have kissed and where and why . . ."*

"Huh?"

"Just saying that Randolph might have had so many lovers in her day that she couldn't keep them all straight."

They went through the pockets of all the clothes in the closet, finding nothing but a few coins, then moved on to the living room, where again, everything was tidy with nothing apparently out of place. Instead of a couch, there were two lounge chairs with a step table between them that held several library books — a biography of Arthur Miller and two Stephen King novels among them. Salt and pepper shakers and a placemat on the coffee table in front of the chairs suggested that this was probably where Bloss ate his meals.

A waist-high bookcase covered most of the wall beneath the windows. The last two or three issues of *Variety* were neatly piled next to a wicker basket that held parakeet supplies. The wider shelves below were filled with scrapbooks, stacked one upon another, two or three deep and each labeled with the name of a play. Some of the titles were familiar, but for every hit, there were six or eight run-of-the-mill shows that didn't break even and had faded into obscurity.

Probably the record of his life, thought Hentz.

A gap near the bottom must have held the scrapbook that now lay atop a desk at the end of the bookcase. This one was labeled "Metropolitan Opera."

While Urbanska started on the desk drawers, Hentz took the scrapbook to a clear spot under the windows. Affixed to the open page was a program for *La Bohème* from almost fifty years ago. According to the cast list, Mimi was sung by Marta Constanza and she had signed the program, as had the tenor and some other cast members. On the opposite page was a review clipped from one of the New York papers. The headline was "*Mi chiamano* Charlotte Randolph" and it praised the unexpected brilliance of a beautiful young newcomer who stepped in at the last minute when Miss Constanza took a fall backstage and cut a gash in her face that required several stitches and an overnight stay at St. Luke's Hospital.

Charlotte Randolph said that Jack Bloss had worked on that production as part of the lighting crew but his name did not appear in any of the technical credits.

Hentz turned past several pages of autographed Met programs till he came to a clipping from *Variety*, dated a few months later. It noted that Charlotte Randolph would be singing Berta in *The Barber of Seville.* Not the lead soprano, but still quite a step up from the chorus.

Stuck deep in the groove where two pages met were torn pieces of a black-and-white snapshot. They had been crumpled at one point, then smoothed out again. Hentz fit the pieces together. The young woman had blond hair and dimples. The man with his arms around her was smooth-shaven.

Charlotte Randolph and a beardless Jack Bloss.

He put the pieces back as he'd found them.

"You finding anything useful?" he asked Urbanska.

"Looks like he was divorced twenty years ago and the wife got half his pension in the settlement, but what was keeping his cupboard bare is that these bank statements show monthly automatic payments to a nursing home out in Suffolk County."

An hour later, Hentz and Urbanska finished reporting what they'd learned at Jack Bloss's apartment.

"We called that nursing home in Suffolk County," Hentz said. "They wouldn't tell us much, just that his son had been a patient there for several years. We asked if he was allowed visitors and the nurse said yes, but that he wouldn't be able to help us. He's been comatose since the first day he was admitted."

"There was a picture of a young man on

185

his dresser," said Urbanska. "Sitting on a motorcycle. That might have been him. It was the only personal picture in the bedroom."

"Lots of Bloss in his scrapbooks, though," said Hentz. "With actors and directors and fellow crew members. And this."

He opened the scrapbook they'd brought back and handed Sigrid the torn pieces of the photograph he'd found, the picture of Bloss and Charlotte Randolph. As Hentz had done earlier, she put them together on a sheet of paper, this time with double-sided tape to hold the pieces in place.

"Which one of them tore it up, do you suppose?" asked Detective Albee, passing the paper on to Jim Lowry. "Or first balled it up?"

Hentz shook his head. "Doesn't really matter, does it? He's the one kept all the pieces."

"She probably did have a fling with him, either before or after she got her big break," said Sigrid. "But even if it ended in anger, is that a motive for poisoning him now, all these years later? Did you find any indication that they were in touch recently?"

"No, and the man was a real archivist when it came to the shows he worked on," said Hentz. "Every item in these scrapbooks is labeled and dated and so are the photographs. All except for this one."

He slid the composite into a plastic sleeve and labeled it as he spoke.

"We brought back his files," said Urbanska, pointing to five manila folders on the desk behind her. "Those are mostly business records, receipts, and his son's medical records. He doesn't seem to have kept much personal correspondence and I didn't find anything from Randolph."

"What about a cell phone?" asked Tillie. "We didn't find one on him."

"I doubt if he owned one. I did a quick look at his bills. Nothing for a cell phone. Just a landline and no messages on the answering system."

"Go back through all files and the scrapbooks again," Sigrid said. "See if anything jumps out."

Her own eyes were snagged by that first review and she turned the scrapbook page toward Hentz, who had become her de facto opera authority. "What does that headline mean?"

"*Mi chiamano Charlotte Randolph?* In English, it would be 'They call me Charlotte Randolph.' It's a play on the opera's most popular song. When the man asks what her name is, the woman says *Mi chia-*

mano Mimi — 'They call me Mimi.' I guess the critic that wrote this meant that she owned the role."

"Did critics review every performance back then?"

"No," he said slowly. "No, they didn't. And this guy was a pretty big deal in his day. He would have reviewed the opening night performance, not subsequent ones."

Remembering that bookseller from North Carolina, Sigrid said, "So all the planets really did line up for Charlotte Randolph that night, didn't they?"

He nodded. "Makes you wonder, doesn't it?"

Elaine Albee's blue eyes widened. "You think Jack Bloss could have caused the star's accident so his girlfriend could go on?"

Hentz frowned. "He might've caused the accident, but how could a no-name stage hand get a critic like Franklin McCall back to the Met?"

They batted around unlikely scenarios till Hentz said, "This is starting to sound like *All About Eve.*"

Sigrid smiled at the reference. "With Charlotte Randolph in the Anne Baxter role?"

Young Urbanska was looking blank.

"I'll lend you the video," Hentz said.

Glancing at the wall clock above their whiteboard, Sigrid decided to call it a day. "Albee, you and Lowry question Randolph's niece and stepson tomorrow. They had access to the lasagna and it wouldn't be the first time someone tried to hurry up an inheritance. Tillie, see if you can locate Bloss's ex-wife." Turning back to Hentz, she said, "We ought to talk to Randolph again and Mrs. DelVecchio as well. See if she blames Mutone for her daughter's hit-and-run and why."

CHAPTER 15

Sigrid sat bolt upright in her bed Tuesday morning. Between all the complications of the case and the possibility that Nauman had fathered a son who had a moral claim on his estate if not a legal one, she had forgotten all about what the waiter in the diner had told her. As soon as the sun had been up long enough to suppose Hentz was up as well, she called him, apologized if she had awakened him, and asked if he could locate the locksmith whose shop was across the street from that bench where two men had died.

"You're up early," Roman Tramegra said, surprised to enter the kitchen and find Sigrid reading the paper. His green paisley dressing gown was open to reveal purple pajamas and he quickly tightened the belt to close the front as he padded over to the coffee maker.

She was not a morning person and normally slept as late as possible. Today, she was already dressed for work in dark slacks, fitted red jacket, and a white knit tee, with a colorful silk scarf loosely looped around her neck.

So different from when they first met, he thought approvingly.

Until Oscar Nauman erupted into her life, she had worn her long dark hair pulled back into a no-nonsense bun at the nape of her slender neck and most of her clothes were either black or beige and strictly utilitarian. Because of him, she had cut her hair, learned to use makeup, made time for weekly manicures, and purged her closet of everything beige. She would never be as beautiful as her mother or her Southern cousins, but neither would those wide gray eyes and quiet air of self-containment let her be ignored.

"Our eggs hatched yesterday morning," he announced.

"Really? Does one of them have red feathers?"

"No, they're all just little dark fuzz balls."

"That sparrow's in for quite a surprise, isn't she?"

"Oh, they'll look enough like her that she probably won't notice once it starts fledging. By the time it gets red feathers, it'll be able to fend for itself."

He was smiling until he took a second look at her eyes and saw the dark circles beneath them.

"A rough night, my dear?"

"A lot on my mind."

She had spent yet another restless night thinking about this Vincent Haas and what it might have meant to Nauman to learn he'd fathered a son with Lila Nagy. If he had read the letter from Austria that Hester had forwarded to him, had he been pleased or angry? Would he have accepted a middle-aged son or refused to know him?

"Do say it's a complicated case," Roman pleaded as he poured himself a second cup of coffee and topped off her cup. "I need another plot twist for my new book. It's sagging in the middle and I always feel it's cheating to throw in another killing just to hoist things up."

She set aside the paper. Although she wasn't ready to tell anyone about Vincent Haas, Roman was looking so eager that she gave him a thumbnail sketch of the two murders under investigation.

He had written scenarios for a neighborhood dance company and was a walking encyclopedia of gossipy stage lore, so he was entranced to hear that Sigrid's case involved the famous Charlotte Randolph. "Maybe she put a tripwire over the stairs leading up to the star's dressing room and the stage hand saw her. Then when he heard she was writing her memoirs, maybe he tried to blackmail her. That's such a legendary story that she certainly wouldn't want the world to know that her lucky break wasn't an accident."

"So she sent him off with poisoned lasagna in a box from her own refrigerator?"

"Why not? Opera is full of blood and gore, tenors and bassos stabbing each other, sopranos throwing themselves off parapets. And poison is the classic choice for women, isn't it?" He added two cubes of sugar to his coffee and stirred it thoughtfully. "It probably wouldn't occur to her that he'd sit down the first place he could and start eating. That's something I'm sure she would never do. If he'd made it out of that neighborhood, you might never have connected the two of them."

"Possibly," she admitted as her phone rang. It was Hentz, returning her earlier call. He had located the locksmith and was on his way to meet the man there.

As she carried her cup over to the sink, Roman's face suddenly brightened. "I know! Instead of another murder, maybe I can put one of the characters into a coma until it's time to reveal the killer's name."

Sigrid smiled. "That should work."

Hentz was waiting for her outside the locksmith's shop when she arrived twenty minutes later. While they waited for the owner to arrive, Hentz said, "Did I tell you I have a copy of Franklin McCall's biography?"

"Who?"

"The critic that reviewed Charlotte Randolph's performance. Franklin McCall. I looked her up in the index."

"And?

"And he patted himself on the back for being the first to notice her."

"Did he say how he happened to be there that particular night for a repeat?"

"Actually, he did. He called it a fortuitous accident. A friend of his had an extra ticket that night and he thought McCall hadn't been fair to the tenor in the first review, so he asked him to come along and give the guy another chance. Ironically, the tenor was completely ignored in his second review and — Ah, you must be our locksmith," he said to the man who hurried up to them on foot.

"Sorry," the man said. "I had a lady with

a baby locked out of her apartment on Prince Street. She left a spare key for her deadbolt with a neighbor, but the neighbor's out of town."

He unlocked his own door and held it open for them to enter the dingy shop that was cluttered with tools, racks of key blanks, and several locks in various stages of disassembly. "Excuse the mess, but I don't get a lot of walk-ins. Most of my work's off-premise. Like today. I gotta go change the locks on a bunch of mailboxes a few blocks up from here, so this won't take long, will it?"

They assured him it wouldn't.

"You want to hear about those guys I saw last Tuesday evening, right?"

"Right," said Hentz.

"There's really not a lot I can tell you. I'd already closed up for the day and was on my way to go get something to eat when a man called, wanting me to come change the locks so his soon-to-be ex-girlfriend couldn't get in and strip the place. I came back here to pick up a new deadbolt and I saw these two men across the street at the bench. One guy was sitting there eating out of a takeout box and the other one was standing on the side talking to him."

"What time was that?"

"Around seven-thirty, maybe eight."

"Can you describe them?"

"Well, the guy on the bench looked like an old hippie — a beard and white hair in a ponytail. I never saw the face of the other one. Dark hair, maybe going gray? And a lot of it." He rubbed the bald spot on the top of his head with a rueful smile. "You don't really notice hair till you start to lose it."

"Tall, short? Fat, skinny?"

"Not tall. In fact, he was real short. Couldn't have been much over five feet. And sort of thin. He had on like a uniform. Coveralls, anyhow. Dark green or black. I couldn't say. The only reason I even noticed them was because they both had takeout boxes and I was pretty hungry. They said at the diner two guys died. Those two?"

"Your old hippie was one of them," said Hentz. "The other was someone different. Did you see anyone join them or what the short guy did?"

"Sorry." As he talked, the locksmith had been opening and closing long three-by-five-inch drawers beneath the counter at the rear of the shop. "I really need to label these things," he said, slamming one shut in frustration. Irritation turned to smiles as he looked into another drawer. "Ah, here they are!"

He fished out a handful of small locks in individual plastic bags and put them in his tool bag. "If we're done here — ?"

Sigrid thanked him for his help and handed him her card. "If you see that short man again or if you think of anything else you forgot to mention, please call me."

Back out on the sidewalk, Hentz said, "You thinking the same thing I am?"

"Mrs. DelVecchio's Alberich?"

"Yeah."

At Number 409, they walked down three steps to the basement door beneath the stoop and rang the bell. When Hentz's second ring received no answer, they went up to the main door and this time, the door opened a crack and the housekeeper's wrinkled face peered up at him.

"Yes?"

He held out his badge. "Detective Hentz, ma'am."

Before he could say more, her thick gray eyebrows drew together tightly. "Signora DelVecchio is still asleep. You cannot see her now."

"It's Mr. Salvador we want to question, Miss Orlano," Sigrid said. "He doesn't answer his bell. Is he here?"

The thick oak door opened wider and her voice dropped to a whisper. "Come through, but be quiet. She likes to sleep till ten."

That was something Sigrid could appreciate, but she said nothing.

Miss Orlano led them down the long dark hall, past the staircase to a bright and surprisingly modern kitchen. Sigrid rather expected to see appliances from the forties or fifties. Instead, everything was up to date.

When the housekeeper had closed the swinging door to the hallway, she spoke in a normal voice. "He's out in the garden."

"Actually, Miss Orlano, we have a question for you, too," said Sigrid. "Why did you lie about seeing Matty last Tuesday?"

Miss Orlano glared at them, her eyebrows beetling furiously. "Lie? Who says I lied?"

"It wasn't you who took him the fettuccine, was it? It was Mr. Salvador. We have a witness who saw him there at the bench."

Her belligerent wrinkled face crumpled so abruptly, it was like watching air escape from a child's balloon. "Please, Lieutenant. Don't tell the signora."

"Why not?" Sigrid asked. "Why would she care which one of you took it?"

"Look at me, Lieutenant! *Look* at me!"

She held her hands out to them. They

were gnarled and arthritic.

"I am old and everything hurts. To walk, to vacuum, to make the beds. But if I am no use, if I cannot do what she asks, what happens to me? I have no family. What will I do? Where will I go?"

"Surely Mrs. DelVecchio wouldn't turn you out onto the street," said Sigrid. "Haven't you been with her for years?"

The old woman nodded tearfully and her accent had become more pronounced. "Forty-two, almost forty-three years. Since the first day they brought Aria home from the hospital. The cook had quit. The house-maid went back to Chicago. I was supposed to be the baby's nursemaid but there was only me and she wouldn't take the breast, only the bottle, so I was up and down those stairs all night. I was young and strong though, and so was my signora. Together we did everything the first week until Signor Benito hired more help. Someone to clean, someone to cook. I was not trained as a cook, but every week, I made cannelloni for Signor Benito. And sometimes my *fegati della Romano*! He said it tasted like his own mother used to make."

"*Fegati?*" Sigrid asked.

"Chicken livers sautéed in butter with fresh basil and served on buttered toast."

It sounded like something Roman would like but Sigrid resisted the temptation to ask for the recipe.

"While he was alive and Aria was little, I only cooked special things he liked, but after he died and Aria was married, it was just the signora and me."

"You take care of this whole big house and cook, too?" asked Sigrid.

"We have a cleaning service every week and Sal helps."

"Like taking food down to that bench in your place?"

"Please! You won't tell her, will you?"

"Not if we don't have to."

"Lieutenant?"

Hentz pointed toward the window and Sigrid saw the handyman open the garage door and go inside.

Grimacing with pain as she stood, Miss Orlano opened the back door onto the deck.

"When you finish, leave through the garage so she doesn't see you."

CHAPTER 16

Thin to the point of anorexia, Mary Bloss had platinum hair permed into short fluffy curls. From a few feet away, her expert makeup made her look no more than fifty rather than the seventy-one the DMV had in its records. Up close, she still could have passed for sixty. She wore a snug knit top patterned in pale yellow stripes and she was a talker. The officer who showed her up to Homicide seemed grateful to hand her over to Tillie and she switched from uniform to plainclothes without missing a beat.

"— because even if they are two for the price of one, if you only need one, what are you going to do with two giant-size tubes of toothpaste? And don't get me started on the way they size things. You know what I mean?"

"Yes, ma'am," Tillie said, opening the door to the interview room where Dinah Urbanska joined them.

"I mean it's not like we have medicine cabinets the size of steamer trunks, is it?"

"Mrs. Bloss?" Tillie had to say it twice and the second time rather loudly before she paused.

"You needn't shout, Sergeant. I may be getting old, but my hearing's fine, I assure you. My mother was hard of hearing by the time she was my age, but everything's still clear as a bell for me. Now my dad —"

"Mrs. Bloss, *please*!"

She frowned but subsided, taking one of the chairs at the table and plopping her bright yellow plastic handbag on the floor beside her.

"You were married to Jack Bloss, right?"

"That's right. Is that what this is about? Is he trying to pressure me into — ? Well, you can tell him that I won't. I can't. And that's final!"

"Can't what, ma'am?" asked Urbanska.

"Can't live on less than I'm getting now. I'm sorry but it's his fault our son's a vegetable. I told him not to help Jacky buy that motorcycle, but oh no! What did I know? I told them both it was too danger-ous. And what happened? Six days after he got it, he spun out on the FDR and has been in a coma ever since."

"When did you last speak to your husband, Mrs. Bloss?"

"He's not my husband. We've been divorced for years."

"And you haven't spoken to him since then?"

"Of course I have. Back in April. Tax time. The hospital's going to increase the cost of Jacky's care again and he wanted me to help pay part of it, but like I told him, what are they going to do? Throw Jacky out on the street? Besides, he doesn't need to be in that fancy nursing home. I'm sure there are cheaper places that do just as good a job and yes, it might mean moving him upstate, but there's no reason Jack has to visit so often. It's not like Jacky knows either one of us. Last time I was there, it was what? Three years? Four? And he hadn't changed a bit. He just lies there, getting thinner. Tubes going in and coming out. Nobody home. I've begged Jack to pull the plug, let him go, but he won't. He just won't. I know it sounds cold for a mother to say this, but I've accepted it. My son died the day his head hit that guardrail. It is what it is, though, and like my friend Sadie says, I had to move on or stay stuck in grief, so I told him not to come begging me to take less of his pension. The judge gave it to me fair and square and I earned it. Twelve years I put up with him and his philandering. There wasn't a single show he ever worked on that he didn't screw at least one of —"

Urbanska reached across the table and took Mrs. Bloss's hands in hers. "I'm afraid we have some bad news, ma'am."

"Bad news? About Jacky?"

"Not your son, ma'am. It's your husband. Your ex-husband. He died last Wednesday morning."

"Died? What happened? His heart?"

"We think he was poisoned, Mrs. Bloss, and we were hoping you could tell us if he had any enemies, anyone he'd had trouble with?"

"Poisoned? Jack? Enemies? No! Not Jack. Jack walks on water. Everybody loves him. At least they used to. I don't really know him anymore. We had tons of friends back then, but all our friends took his side and once the divorce went through and we settled on what to do about Jacky and who was going to be responsible — Oh, God! That means it's back on me, doesn't it?"

"Unless he left a will. Did he have any other relatives? We'll need someone to make a positive identification."

"You mean go down to the morgue like in all those crime shows on TV where they slide a body out of a drawer and lift up a sheet? No. Uh-uh. Not me. Let Fern do it."

"Fern?"

"His sister. They were thick as thieves. She was my friend first, if you can believe it. Introduced me to Jack, then dropped me like a hot potato when we got married. She'll tell you what you need to know. Just don't believe everything she says about me."

She reached into her purse and pulled out an address book, which she opened and pointed to an address. "Fern Woods. Moved to Suffolk County when she retired so she can visit Jacky every week and make sure he's being taken care of and not getting bedsores like that first place we had him."

Urbanska copied down the contact information and handed it back. Mrs. Bloss dropped the little book back into her yellow purse, zipped it closed, and stood to go. "Is that all?"

"Just one thing more, Mrs. Bloss. Charlotte Randolph. Did you know her?"

"Who?"

"The opera singer."

"Oh yeah. The la-dee-dah Met."

"Did he talk much about her?"

"Charlotte Randolph? I think he may have met her, but he'd moved down to Broadway by the time we got together. I never worked there."

"You were in show business, too?" asked Urbanska.

"Not on stage," Mrs. Bloss said with a feigned show of modesty, "although I did a little summer stock and the director said I had talent. No, I worked as a dresser, Off-Broadway."

She named a couple of actresses that neither Tillie nor Dinah Urbanska had ever heard of and was telling them the plots of her favorite show — "Sixteen costume changes including a mermaid tail" — as they eased her out the door.

The garage door at Number 409 was open and Sigrid and Hentz walked in without knocking.

Perched on a high swivel stool, Salvador was bent over a rusty push mover that lay upside down on the workbench at the end of the garage. He had taken off one of the wheels so that he could smear some sort of thick gunk on the blades. After every two or three backward rotations, he smeared on more, then tested the edges with his finger.

"That thing looks like an antique," Hentz said. "First push mower I've seen since I was a kid. My uncle had one."

"Better than a gas mower for that little bit of grass out there," Salvador answered with a cheerful smile. "This thing's older than me and it'll still be cutting grass after I'm gone if it gets a little TLC and some of this lapping compound every few years. They used to build things to last."

He wiped the blades clean and reached for the wheel assembly. "I guess you've got more questions about Matty?"

"That's right," Sigrid said. "More specifically, your meeting with him Tuesday evening."

"I told you. The last time I spoke to Matty was at least two weeks ago."

"But you were the one who took him the fettuccine, weren't you?"

Salvador slid the wheel onto its shaft and began tightening the nuts with a wrench he'd taken from the top pocket of his coveralls. "Orla tell you that?"

Sigrid nodded. "Someone saw you with a takeout box in your hand talking to Jack Bloss that evening."

"That the guy's name? He didn't say."

"Had you seen him before?"

"No, just the once."

"What did you talk about?"

"Nothing much. The weather. I think he'd been drinking or something because he seemed a little unsteady with his fork. He was eating lasagna. Said it wasn't his favorite, but he'd skipped lunch and was hungry."

"Did he say where he'd gotten it?"

"No. I thought maybe he'd found it there on the bench. There's a soup kitchen down the block but people will leave food on the bench in case somebody needs a meal when it's not open, although to be honest, he didn't look like somebody who'd been sleeping rough. His clothes were too clean. I told him I had fettuccine for a friend. He didn't know Matty, but he said he'd give it to him if he came, so I handed it over and left. But when I looked back, he was opening the box."

"You didn't see Matty at all?"

"Nope."

He finished with the wheel and set the lawnmower right side up on the floor. The handle came almost up to the short man's chest.

"Why did you lie about it when we first asked you?"

"Orla and me, we cover for each other."

"What does that mean?"

"Look, Lieutenant, this is a good place to work. The pay's good and the work's not hard. Mrs. D, she doesn't ask for a lot, but what she does ask for, she expects to get. Between you and me, I don't think she would've cared if Orla'd said 'Let Sal take it,' but for some reason, Orla's scared to do that. Besides, you don't want to cross the old lady. She gets something bad about you in her head and that's it. You're out. No second chances."

"Like what she did with Matty?"

"Exactly like that."

"Because of her daughter's death?"

Sal shrugged but Sigrid persisted.

"We've heard that Matty thought Mrs. DelVecchio blamed him for that, and that he blamed himself even more. What actually happened, Mr. Salvador? How did Aria Edwards die?"

He sighed and swiveled the stool around to face them.

"When I first came, Miss Aria was still a teenager. Long blond hair, beautiful face. She could have been a movie star or a model. And such a sweet voice. When she laughed —" He shook his head ruefully. "You wanted to play the fool just to make her laugh."

He turned back to the workbench and began tidying it up as he spoke. The tools were slotted back in their spaces, then he capped the sharpening compound and put it on a shelf over the counter.

"Matty's mother was still alive then and they were over here a lot. He and Miss Aria were like brother and sister. I always thought he wanted to be more than that to her, but she wasn't interested. They both went off to college, but then she met Mr. George and that was the end of school for her. For Matty, too. He mooned around like a sick puppy. Couldn't keep a job. And when she married Mr. George and moved out to Long Island, he went off the deep end. Started using drugs. His mother died and he was in and out of jail."

It was the usual story that Sigrid and Hentz had heard dozens of times.

"Miss Aria kept thinking she could make him turn his life around. Finally she and Mr. George got him into a rehab place that seemed to work. When I broke my arm last summer, he was clean and started working here part-time. Two weeks before Christmas, Miss Aria came into town to spend a few days with Mrs. D and Orla and to do some Christmas shopping. Matty dropped her off that morning as soon as the stores opened and he was supposed to pick her up after lunch, only something went wrong with the catalytic converter and he had to get it towed, so he couldn't go meet her. It was crappy weather — a little rain, a little snow. She had her arms full of packages and maybe she slipped, who knows? Orla said there were witnesses that said she stepped off the curb just as a white car pulled up and knocked her down and then ran over her. Crushed her skull, then drove away."

"Anyone get the license?" asked Hentz, who had walked over to look at the gardening supplies at the far end of the work counter.

"No. They couldn't agree if it was a Toyota or a Honda or even if it was a man or woman driving. Just that it was dirty and pretty dinged up."

"Must have been rough on the family," said Sigrid.

"Yeah. Mrs. D took it bad, but Orla was even worse. She was here when Miss Aria was born. Loved her like she was her own daughter. And Matty was out of his head. Blamed himself for not being there to pick her up as he'd promised. He went back to using so heavy that he'd probably have been dead in another month or two anyhow."

"Did Mrs. DelVecchio blame him, too?"

"Not really. You'd think she would, but she didn't. She knew how much he loved Miss Aria. If she blamed him for anything, it was for going back to drugs when he knew how bad it would have hurt Miss Aria to see him throwing his life away. That's why she quit having anything to do with him except for seeing that he got at least one good meal a week."

"Lieutenant?" Hentz said. He pointed to an orange-and-yellow box on one of the shelves. It pictured a rat on the front and printed above the rat were the words *Warfarin Rat Bait.*

"You have a problem with rats here, Mr. Salvador?"

"Not anymore. The city did some work on the sewers back in March and I saw a rat in the cabinet under my sink. Orla said she'd seen droppings in the kitchen, too, so I put out some of that stuff. No more droppings and no more rats."

"You do know that warfarin was what poisoned Matty and the other man, don't you?"

"Huh? No! I thought it was heart pills."

"Heart pills that are made with warfarin," said Hentz.

"Now, wait a minute! You think that *I* poisoned Matty?"

"No," said Sigrid, "but it would be helpful if you can tell us if any of the baits are missing."

He took the box and looked inside. "I forget how many I used, but this seems right."

"Mind if we take one?" Hentz asked, pulling a plastic bag from his pocket.

Sal looked uneasy but offered no objection.

CHAPTER 17

Charlotte Randolph pushed back from the glass-topped table strewn with the letters and photographs and press clippings that documented her public life. "I'm sorry, Marian. I just can't seem to concentrate today."

"That's okay," her assistant said cheerfully. "We're ahead of schedule. If you like, I could finish putting those interviews in chronological order."

"No, take the rest of the day off. Go check out that shoe sale. You've earned it. I'll try to get my thoughts in order."

"You've been sitting so long lately, you could probably use a good massage. Want me to call your therapist? See if she can come over?"

"No. Maybe I'll call her after lunch. You go."

But when Marian Schmidt had gathered up her things and gone off with a shoe ad from the morning paper, Charlotte continued to sit at the table, lost in memory.

The police interview had unsettled her more than she wanted to admit. When he was here on Tuesday, Jack swore he hadn't told anyone but she found herself remembering that old warning: "Two people can keep a secret if one of them be dead."

Well, Jack was dead, but how many other secrets were hidden in the papers spread out before her?

And how many of those secrets would she take to her own grave?

She squared her small shoulders decisively. Maybe it was time to find out.

Founded in 1897, Vanderlyn College occupied a leafy green space overlooking the East River that was two blocks wide by eight blocks long. Unlike other institutions of higher learning where real estate was less valuable, none of these stone building were dormitories or faculty residences, although there was a central grassy commons where students crisscrossed to classes on patterned brick walks or perched on the broad rim of the fountain to eat lunch in the shade of several large oaks.

Two years earlier, Detectives Albee and Lowry had taken part in a murder investigation in Vanderlyn's art department but their activities had been confined to Van Hoeen Hall and they had never become fully oriented but a student pointed them toward Stuyvesant Hall, which was where they had arranged to meet Grace Landers and Abner Ferguson.

Inside the building, they squeezed onto a crowded elevator that let them off in front of glass double doors marked FACULTY ONLY. The doors opened onto a wide covered terrace that looked out over the river and was furnished with wrought-iron tables and chairs. On this warm June day, most of the chairs were occupied.

Lt. Harald had described to them the couple that she'd seen entering the Randolph home, so they spotted almost immediately what had to be Charlotte Randolph's niece and stepson at a table next to the railing. Both had their backs to the glare coming off the water. The woman appeared to be in her late thirties and from the gray hairs at the man's temples, he was probably early forties. They made an attractive couple and their smiles were friendly without a hint of uneasiness at being asked to meet with the police.

"Hope you don't mind if we go ahead with lunch," said Grace Landers, opening clear plastic clamshells that held green salads. She wore her light brown hair parted in the middle and tucked back behind her ears but a breeze off the river kept loosening different strands. "I hold office hours from one to three."

"And I'm teaching a graduate seminar then myself," said her husband, a slender black man with a pencil mustache who used a penknife to open their packets of dressing.

As they ate, they explained that he specialized in eighteenth-century American literature while she was the deputy chair of the math department.

"I'm afraid I can't say anything intelligent about either subject," Lowry confessed.

Dr. Abner Ferguson smiled. "Neither can a lot of our students. I hope this isn't about one of them?"

"Didn't Ms. Randolph tell you?"

Both professors gave them blank looks. "Charlotte? Tell us what?"

"Let's back up a bit," said Albee. "Ms. Randolph told us that you often bring her supper."

"Yes?" Dr. Ferguson seemed puzzled by her question.

"Did you bring her food this past week?"

They nodded. "Lasagna," said Ferguson.

"She loves pasta, but very seldom orders it for herself."

"Trying to preserve her girlish figure," said Landers with an indulgent smile as she speared a cherry tomato. "Almost eighty, but still in the game. We stop in to check on her every week or so and we usually take her something. I guess you know she's my grandmother's sister and that Gus is the son of her third husband."

"Or her fourth husband," he said, pushing aside a ring of red onion. "Charlotte claims she can't remember which."

Landers gave a rueful shake of her head. "We've never understood why she would bother with a ceremony since none of her marriages ever lasted more than eighteen months."

"The lasagna you brought her was from Giuseppone, right?"

The laughter faded from their faces at the seriousness of Lowry's tone.

"What's this about, Detective?"

"Two men were found dead on a bench on Sixth Avenue at the end of her street."

"Oh no!" said Grace Landers. "Please don't say it was gang-related. That's always been such a safe street."

"No, this looks personal. Their food was poisoned."

"Poisoned? I don't understand."

"Two takeout boxes were given to those men Tuesday evening. Warfarin was found in both boxes."

Landers, who had been frowning, immediately looked relieved. "Oh well, that lets us out. We took Charlotte's lasagna to her on Monday."

"Did you see her eat any of it?"

"Well, no. She put it in that little refrigerator in the butler's pantry to have later."

"She never ate it," said Albee. "One of those two men visited her Tuesday evening and she sent your lasagna home with him."

"Really? Who was he?"

"A man named Jack Bloss, who used to be a stage hand at the Met. He brought her a program from the night she went on for the star. He told her he'd missed lunch, so she gave him your lasagna. He stopped to eat it on that bench and next morning he was dead."

Landers seemed both shocked and bewildered. "I don't understand. How did that happen? How could someone get into Charlotte's house and — ?"

Her husband reached for her hand. "They think we did it, babe."

"Don't be silly, Gus. Why would we poison a man we never heard of?" But then she saw the looks the detectives exchanged. "That's crazy!"

"Your aunt's a wealthy woman," said Lowry. "If she dies, who inherits?"

"Juilliard," Landers answered promptly. "I may get her jewelry, but everything else has been earmarked for their scholarship programs."

"You think we'd try to kill her for *money*?" Ferguson sounded incredulous.

"Do you know who Gus is?" asked Landers, who suddenly seemed more relaxed. She nested their empty salad boxes and her husband took them over to a nearby garbage pail. "His great-grandfather was Raymond Howard. Howard Metalworks. Pipes and cables. Remind me how much your grandfather got when he sold the company, hon?"

Dr. Ferguson shrugged. "I forget. Enough to give my six cousins and me tidy nest eggs, all reinvested in blue-chip stocks. Last time I checked my portfolio, Detectives, it was a little over twenty million, so no, we wouldn't kill Charlotte for her money."

They were stunned. "But you're teachers," said Lowry.

"And pretty damn good ones, too, if I do say so."

"Not all trust fund babies lead hedonistic lives," his wife murmured.

Ferguson grinned. "In the late seventeen hundreds, John Adams wrote his wife a letter. In it, he said he had to study politics and war so that their sons might have the liberty to study mathematics and philosophy so that their *grandsons* could study painting and literature." He leaned back in his chair and gestured to the halls of learning that surrounded them. "I'm John and Abigail's black grandson, Detective Lowry."

"Did they know Matty Mutone?" Sigrid asked when Lowry and Albee finished reporting.

"They said not," Albee said.

They looked up as Tillie entered the squad room with a gray-haired woman who dabbed at her tear-swollen eyes with a wad of tissues.

"Lieutenant, this is Mrs. Woods. She's just formally identified our second victim. Jack Bloss was her brother."

Dealing with grief-stricken relatives was still the most uncomfortable part of the job for Sigrid, but she tried. "We're so sorry for your loss, Mrs. Woods." She gestured for Tillie to bring a chair. "Please sit down. Do you feel up to talking about him? Answering a few questions?"

The woman nodded tearfully and Sigrid

signaled for Hentz and Tillie to join them.

"Can we get you something?" Tillie asked. "Coffee? Water?"

Without waiting for an answer, Dinah Urbanska promptly fetched a bottle from the break room. When Lt. Harald didn't dismiss her, she slid her own chair closer to them so she could hear.

Fern Woods unscrewed the cap and took a sip of water, then set the bottle on the floor beside her. She took fresh tissues from the box that Sigrid offered and turned them over and over in her restless hands, shredding them as she talked about her brother, the shock of learning about his death, the disbelief that someone would poison him. Unlike her ex-sister-in-law, her words came hesitantly.

No, she could offer no reason why someone might want Jack dead. Were they sure it wasn't an accident? Or another heart attack? "He had a pacemaker. Maybe he took too many of his pills?"

"We're pretty sure it was in his food," Sigrid said. "Someone gave him lasagna that had Coumadin in it."

"Lasagna? Jack's last meal was lasagna?" More tears welled up in her eyes.

"Yes," Sigrid said, puzzled as to why that mattered.

"Jack liked Italian food okay, but lasagna wasn't one of his favorites. He didn't care for tomato sauce, poor guy."

"Did you ever hear him speak of Charlotte Randolph?"

Mrs. Woods nodded. "Not in years, though. Jack got me in backstage to hear her sing once when he was working at the Met, and he introduced us. Wonderful voice and not a bit snobby."

"Did they have an affair?"

"Jack wasn't married then," she said defensively. "And neither was she."

"Did it last long?"

She shook her head. "Things never lasted long with Jack, I'm afraid. My brother was a sweet man, Lieutenant, and he had many good qualities, but monogamy wasn't one of them. Their affair was long over by the time he moved down to Broadway and met Mary and —" She gave them a startled look. "Mary! His ex-wife. Does she know about Jack? Did you talk to her?"

"We did," said Tillie.

She managed a weak smile. "I can imagine what she had to say about him. But she wanted the marriage. Wanted to stop working. As I said, women never lasted long with Jack, but Mary played him like a trout. Wouldn't let him put his hand up her skirt till he'd put a ring on her finger. We were both dressers on *Skirts Ahoy,* but actors didn't like to use her if they could help it because she talked too much. It's hard to stay in character if someone's chattering in your ear like a magpie when you're trying to remember your next lines while you change costumes. She was pretty, though, and sexy and after an evening of too many martinis, they eloped. He was ready to call it quits after three months, but by then she was pregnant. They stayed together twelve years for the sake of the boy, till they were both so sick of each other that —"

Her eyes widened, then filled with tears again. "Jacky," she whispered. "Mary was ready to have his IV tubes removed a month after the accident. Now she'll get her way, won't she?"

She reached blindly for the box of tissues again. "I'm sorry. In his heart of hearts, Jack knew that Jacky was never going to open his eyes again. Never going to get up out of that bed, but he just couldn't let the boy go. Maybe it's best. Nineteen years and she barely visited him. And she certainly didn't help with the expenses. Jack had a good pension from the union, but she got part of it in the divorce settlement and after the accident, it took almost every penny he had to keep Jacky in that nursing home."

She blew her nose and gave them an apologetic smile. "But this isn't what you need to know, is it? You said Charlotte Randolph? I don't think they'd been in touch for years. Why did he go see her?"

"She said he brought her the program from the night she went on for the star after the accident."

Mrs. Woods gave a crooked smile. "Oh yes. That famous accident."

"What do you mean?" Sigrid asked.

"Nothing," said Mrs. Woods. "Nothing."

This east-facing room on the third floor had begun as a nursery. The first time Orla had seen it, fresh paper, patterned in colorful Mother Goose illustrations, covered the walls and all the trim had been painted white. The windows had white shades and sheer white curtains. The crib, rocking chair, changing table, and chest of drawers were white enamel, and although the chest held diapers and a few neutrally colored outfits, everything else was bare. No cushions, no colorful accessories.

"My wife wanted to wait until we knew which it was," Benny DelVecchio had said, pointing to two large piles of shopping bags from various Midtown department stores.

One pile held blue items, the other pink. "Send the blue things back and make this a room fit for a princess."

Although she had been hired two months in advance, Orla's first day on the job had felt like a baptism by fire. Except for a driver who shared a room in the basement with DelVecchio's bodyguard, there was no other help in the house. The cook and maid had either quit or been fired, so there was no one to tell her the lay of the land and she was too intimidated by her employer and the other two men to ask questions.

Word had gone around a few months earlier that after years of trying and now nearing forty, the wife of Benny Olds was expecting a baby and a nursemaid would be required. Someone strong and unafraid of work.

"And not pretty," the crones of their community had whispered.

The Orlano girl, they decided. She had been brought over from the old country ten years ago to nurse an elderly aunt who had never learned English. The aunt had died, the uncle had remarried, and the second wife wanted her out of the house. Almost thirty, with no dowry and no marital prospects in sight, she would make a perfect nursemaid for Sofia DelVecchio, they said.

And Sofia had agreed.

Although she had sailed through the first seven months with barely a touch of morning sickness, the last two months had been difficult, she told Orla, and the doctor had prescribed bed rest and no strenuous activity. Wrapped in a fluffy white comforter, she had interviewed Orla from the depths of a blue velvet recliner in the master bedroom on the second floor, which was where she received all her visitors now that she was no longer allowed to use the stairs.

Orla's competence had been vouched for by the crones. She was neat, and her voice did not set Sofia's nerves on edge. More to the point, she was built like a fire hydrant, her wiry dark hair did not invite a man's fingers, and those thick eyebrows could never be shaped into delicate arches.

"My husband will let you know when the baby is born," she said.

"I could start now," Orla said, eager to leave her uncle's house where she was no longer welcome.

"No! You will come when the baby is born and not a day earlier. I won't have anyone hovering over me. Your salary will start today, though. Be ready to come when he calls."

Orla's bags had been packed for a week

when Benny Olds's driver picked her up and deposited her at Number 409.

Next day, he and his wife brought their daughter home to this room that Orla had decorated with the pink things, right down to the fuzzy pink teddy bear she bought herself.

The baby, christened Aria Marie, refused Sofia's breast, so it was Orla who got up in the night, who ran down the back stairs to warm the bottle and who gave her heart so completely that her dry breasts tingled when the baby cried. Surely they would let down milk if she yielded to temptation and pressed that tiny mouth to her nipples, but she did not dare. Although Sofia usually slept through, Signor Benito would occasionally come up to the nursery in those early hours and hold out his arms to take over his daughter's feeding.

She was still fearful of the man during the day, but here in the dimly lit nursery, listening as he rocked the baby and crooned Italian lullabies, she could almost pretend that Aria was their child. She did not love him and she no longer wanted a husband, but this was a taste of what her life could have been and it made her love the baby even more.

That sweet-tempered baby had grown into

a sunny golden child, then into a happily married woman. When her own daughter was born, Aria had persuaded Sofia to let Orla come help with Laura for the first month.

Orla loved the new baby, but her breasts did not tingle when Laura cried. No warming bottles for this one, though. To Aria's delight, she suckled like a greedy little pig.

Those were happy, peaceful years. Aria came into town at least twice a month to shop, to see the latest plays, to play cards with Sofia after dinner and to help Orla tidy the kitchen after her mother went to bed.

Her death had brought so much grief that Orla was now ready to admit that having Laura here was a good thing. Already she had shaken up their routine.

On Saturday, while Orla stripped the room and Sal painted the walls — Aria had banished the Mother Goose paper when she turned eight — Laura had coaxed Sofia into shopping for new furniture. It was the first time Sofia had left the house for pleasure since the funeral and the outing seemed to have done her good.

"Spending money's always fun, isn't it, Nonna?" Laura had teased.

"Especially if it's someone else's money," Sofia had said dryly, but it was clear that she had enjoyed herself.

Fresh linens for the bed and bath had been delivered only that morning and as Orla slipped a pillow into a crisp new pillowcase, the front doorbell rang.

Orla sighed and started for the door, but Laura was halfway down the stairs by the time she reached the hall.

"I'll get it, Nonna," she called to Mrs. DelVecchio, who was in the living room, half dozing over a book.

The white-haired woman who stood on the top step was a stranger, but her smile was so warm that Laura immediately smiled back. Smiled with approval, too, at a woman who seemed comfortable with both her age and who she was. Her expensive haircut and stylish clothes flattered without trying to pretend that the body they covered was a size four and forty years younger. There was something familiar about her, though, something to do with the way she carried herself, that air of command.

Like Nonna, was Laura's subconscious thought.

"Hello," the woman said. "Is Mrs. DelVecchio in?"

"Is she expecting you?" the girl countered.

"Tell her it's Charlotte Randolph."

Laura's eyes widened in surprise, but

before she could react, she heard her grandmother say in an icy voice, "Show her in, Laura."

Laura held the door wide and the stranger passed her, then paused just inside the front room.

Mrs. DelVecchio sat like a queen in a massive chair of intricately carved wood that faced the door.

"Charlotte," she said flatly.

"Sofia," the woman answered. Impossible to flatten the music still in her voice.

"Shall I bring you some tea?" asked Laura. "Or some of Orla's lemonade?"

"No," said Mrs. DelVecchio without asking her visitor. "Nothing. Close the door, Laura, and go back upstairs."

CHAPTER 18

Sigrid leaned back in her chair and gazed at Jack Bloss's sister with such skeptical gray eyes that Fern Woods had to look away.

"Did your brother say it wasn't an accident?"

"No."

"Are you sure?"

The woman hesitated for a long moment, then gave a sigh of capitulation. "Marta Constanza didn't trip on those metal steps. Someone pushed her."

"Your brother?"

"*No!* Jack would *never* do something like that. He saw it happen, though. He was up on one of the catwalks when some guy he'd never seen before started up the steps as she was coming down. Jack said that from below, it looked like he'd missed a step accidentally. Even Constanza herself thought it was an accident, but from where Jack was standing, he thought the guy deliberately bumped her. Especially since he kept going and never stopped or looked back even though she was bleeding and people were yelling for an ambulance."

"And he didn't tell anybody at the time?"

Mrs. Woods shook her head. "His fling with Charlotte Randolph was over, but they had stayed friends and he was happy for her big break, especially when she got that great review the next day. No one else was questioning the fall and he didn't want to rain on her parade."

"So it could have been a real accident?"

"Maybe."

"But you don't think so?"

"I wasn't *there*!" she said tearfully. "I don't know! All I know's what Jack said."

"Which was?"

"She had a new boyfriend, a big-time mobster. Jack always wondered if maybe he'd sent somebody over to take out Marta Constanza since Randolph was her backup cover."

"Did he say who the mobster was?"

"Not that I remember."

Sigrid glanced at Sam Hentz, who was looking thoughtful.

"When we found your brother, he had close to five hundred dollars on him. He had just come from seeing Miss Randolph and he knew she was writing her autobiography. Would he blackmail her to keep quiet about that accident?"

"No! Jack was a good man. He wouldn't do that. I'm sure he wouldn't."

"Even though he needed money for his son?"

That made her pause.

"For Jacky?" Her eyes filled with tears again and she reached for a fresh tissue. "For Jacky, he might."

"Well, well, well," said Hentz when Tillie had escorted Mrs. Woods from the squad room. "Charlotte Randolph and Benny Olds."

"She did tell us that he used to come over and ask her to sign his opera programs," Sigrid said dryly.

"I bet he got more than a signature," said Lowry.

Elaine Albee rolled her eyes. "So that five hundred was maybe the first installment to keep Bloss from wrecking her book?"

"Or to keep him happy till he'd had a chance to eat the pasta she gave him?" asked Urbanska.

"See what you can find out," Sigrid told them.

■ ■ ■ ■

Taking the stairs two at a time, an excited Laura Edwards burst into the bedroom as Orla smoothed a final wrinkle from the bedspread.

"Charlotte Randolph, Orla! She's down there with Nonna! They know each other!"

"Who?"

"Charlotte Randolph. She used to be an opera singer. Famous!"

"*Puttana!*" Orla snarled, making a rude arm gesture.

Laura was startled. She didn't know the word, but she had seen that gesture. "Orla?"

"What does she want? Why is she here?"

"I don't know. Nonna told me to close the door and come back up here. Why? What's going on? Do you know her, too? Why don't you like her?"

"It's not my place to like or not like." She sat down on the edge of the bed. "Do this one thing for me, *cara mia.* Don't upset your nonna by asking questions."

She spoke so pleadingly that the girl said, "All right. But only if *you* tell me why."

"Will you promise not to tell?"

"I promise, Orla."

"Signor Benito loved your nonna, truly

and deeply. This you must believe. But he was a man of many appetites. Opera. Women. So —"

Laura was wide-eyed with excitement. "Charlotte Randolph was his mistress?"

"You will not speak of this."

"I won't. I promise. Poor Nonna . . . but, wow! Charlotte Randolph!"

Downstairs, Sofia watched as Charlotte walked over to the framed pictures massed on a side table and picked up a formal family portrait: Benny and Sofia with two-year-old Aria on his lap. "She had his curls, didn't she? Was that her daughter who opened the door? She's a blonde, too."

"Why are you here?" Sofia asked, reaching for the picture.

Charlotte handed it over with a smile and sat down in a nearby chair. "I'm writing a book. The story of my life."

"So?"

"My *whole* life."

Sofia leaned back in the chair and waited for the blow.

"Benny was a part of my life. You know that."

Sofia nodded wearily. "I always knew you would not keep your word."

"If you and I were the only ones left who

knew, I would have, but Jack Bloss was there and saw it all."

"Who?"

"The man who died beside your nephew."

"Godson. Matty was my godson, not my nephew."

"Whichever. Jack Bloss knew that Benny sent someone to cause that accident. He wanted money to keep quiet."

"So? This Jack Bloss? He's dead now, isn't he?"

"Yes, he's dead. But did the story die with him? I doubt it."

"So?"

"There are many stories I could tell about Benny, Sofia. I shall tell only that one. And I want something from you in return."

"You're taking everything and you want more?"

"I'm not your enemy and I don't want to hurt you."

"Ha!"

"Don't laugh. I mean it. Everyone knew that he slept with many women. He was no more faithful to me than he was to you. But you were his wife. The mother of his child. I won't write anything to hurt that. He adored you."

"And *you* bewitched him."

"The music bewitched him, not me. He

thought we were living in a Puccini opera."

"A soap opera," Sofia said scornfully.

"Possibly. Nevertheless . . ."

"Nevertheless," Sofia mimicked as she faced her old rival. "So what exactly will you write about my Benito?"

"Only the truth."

"The whole truth?"

"Certainly not."

CHAPTER 19

Built in the 1860s, the Erich Breul House was now a private museum that sat on an expensive piece of real estate in the East Twenties. According to its brochure, it contained "authentic late-Victorian furnishings and an interesting, if uneven, collection of late nineteenth-century American and European art."

"Uneven" had been a kindness, thought Dr. Dorothy Reddish, who was beginning to wonder if she'd made a serious career mistake in accepting the position of director here.

With her shiny new Ph.D. in art history and a strong major in business administration, it had seemed like such a juicy plum, a first stepping-stone to running an important museum sometime in the not-too-far future.

Now she faced the board members gathered around the mahogany dining table where the Breuls had once hosted glittering dinner parties and touched the records that lay on the table before her. One card file held an inventory of the furnishings, another listed the art works. A ledger book was devoted to finances.

She took off the gold-rimmed reading glasses that gave her youthful face a touch of gravitas and laid them atop the ledger. "Since coming here, I've gone through all the current records and I'm afraid the results are quite bleak. I know you didn't hire me to dismantle this wonderful house, but unless we sell some of the important pieces, there is simply no way it can continue. Victorian furniture isn't highly valued these days, but the Whistler portrait, for instance, would probably bring enough to keep the house limping along for another two or three years."

"Sell our Whistler?" exclaimed Mrs. Beardsley, a long-time docent and fairly recent member of the board. "But that's one of the main works that people come to see."

"Which brings me to another point," said Dr. Reddish. "Except for school groups and the occasional tour groups, the house draws less than a hundred visitors a week. If not for you and some of our hardworking docents, we couldn't afford to stay open at all. Right now, we're open from Tuesday till noon on Saturday. I propose that we cut Tuesdays from the schedule and reduce our hours on some of the other days."

"Would more advertising help?" asked one of the directors.

"It might," she agreed, "but that takes money, too."

Mrs. Beardsley heaved a great sigh. "If only we could have held that Oscar Nauman retrospective."

"Attendance did pick up after Dr. Shambley's death," said one timorous lady.

Mrs. Beardsley gave her a withering glance. "Unfortunately, Marigold, we cannot rely on having someone murdered here every week."

Not that she herself had been grief-stricken by the man's death. He had been arrogant and condescending and openly contemptuous of dear Mr. Breul, as if this collection and this jewel of a house would barely merit a footnote in any catalog of the city's cultural holdings. To tempt a scholar of his standing, though, he had been given a seat on the board that should have rightfully gone to her.

"Besides," she said, "those people were sensation seekers. The Nauman retrospective would have introduced a whole new audience to the house."

Dr. Reddish rather doubted that it would have made a permanent difference. Devotees of abstract twentieth-century art would hardly come back to examine the idiosyncratic nineteenth-century pictures that lined the walls of this mansion. Rather than be guided by knowledgeable connoisseurs, Erich Breul had followed his own taste. Happily, that taste had been eclectic enough to include several true gems like the Whistler portrait. Nevertheless, most of the art he had collected was second or third rate. From what she had read of his letters and diaries, Mr. Breul had probably been a decent man, a good husband and father, and certainly civic-minded, but he hadn't held office or swashbuckled his way to obscene wealth, so there was nothing in his personal history to excite enough interest to bring visitors flocking to his house.

The meeting ended with permission to cut Tuesday openings and a "Do the best you can" from the kindly chairman of the board, who brightly proposed that everyone give it serious thought over the summer and be ready at the fall meeting to suggest new schemes to save the house.

After seeing them out, Dr. Reddish paused at the reception desk in the great entrance hall. "They just don't get it," she said pessimistically.

Hope Ruffton, her highly efficient assistant who was in place here when she arrived, gave a sympathetic smile. "One bit of good news, though." She handed the director a letter from the morning mail. "The McAndrews Foundation is going to give us the grant you applied for."

"Really? That's grand!" But her face fell as she read the letter. "It's only for one year, not two."

"Contingent on results," said Ruffton. She hesitated. She liked her new boss. It was refreshing to work for someone who didn't automatically assume that she was basically stupid because she was female and black. The former director had barely listened when she had tried to bring something she'd noticed to his attention.

"The thing about Dr. Shambley . . ." she said.

"Yes?"

"You know that he was brought on board here to research and write a comprehensive history of the house and its contents?"

"Mrs. Beardsley told me that when I first came. I gather she disliked him."

"Understatement of the year, I'm afraid. He acted as if he was slumming to come

243

here and you know how crazy she is about this place. And how protective."

Reddish nodded encouragingly.

"Well, a week or so before he was killed, something changed. He started plundering through all the records with an intensity I hadn't seen before. Not just the papers, but opening drawers, looking in cabinets. It was almost as if he'd caught a hint about something important and wanted to chase it down."

"Important?"

"I know that sounds vague, but he had set up a sort of office in the attic where all of the Breul business papers going back to the early eighteen-hundreds are stored. I think he might have read something that set him off, because the night that he was killed, there was a reception here. He insulted one of our major donors and almost came to blows with the man who planned to underwrite the Nauman exhibit. There was a recklessness about him — as if he no longer had to care what anyone thought because he was going to be above all that and out of anyone's reach. Like he'd found the pot of gold at the end of the rainbow, you know? Smug and cocky and bursting with a secret he was dying to tell."

"Only he died without telling?"

"I guess so. The police were all over the place and I thought maybe whatever it was would come to light, but then they arrested his killer and nothing more came of it."

"So whatever excited Dr. Shambley might still be here?"

"It's probably nothing," Hope Ruffton said.

"Did he leave any notes?"

"Not that I've found. Just a briefcase that his brother took. I looked through it and through the desk he was using upstairs, but I didn't find anything."

Dr. Reddish sighed. "I saw three full file cabinets of business records from Erich Breul's shipping company up there."

She sighed again.

"Want me to go through them?" asked Ruffton.

"Thanks, but there's no point in both of us wasting time. I'll do it. Get it out of the way before I start a full hands-on, touch-everything inventory."

As two matronly ladies approached the reception desk, wallets in hand, a docent who had been reading the morning newspaper on a nearby bench put it aside and stood ready to guide them through the house once Ruffton had taken their money. The docent would also make sure that they remained behind the velvet ropes and that nothing belonging to the house left in one of those capacious handbags.

Before heading upstairs to read through bills of lading and contracts to build more barges, Dr. Reddish impulsively called the mentor who had pulled a few strings to get her this job. "I know it's short notice, Elliott, but could we possibly meet for lunch?"

To her delight, he was practically in the neighborhood. "It'll have to be a quick lunch, though. What about a picnic in your park?" he said. "I'll pick up some sushi."

"And I'll find the key. One o'clock?"

"Works for me," he said.

Denny Kapps pulled on a pair of disposable plastic gloves and took his place behind the steam table as the doors opened to let in the hungry and homeless who had been waiting on the concrete steps outside in the hot June sun. The server next to him took a second look.

"Denny? Denny Kapps? It's me, Nate Patterson. You back again? Where you been?"

Kapps shrugged. "Where you think?"

"Yeah? Bummer. They making you do the rest of your community service?"

"Yeah." He ladled soup into a bowl and passed it across the counter to a man with a thin gray beard.

"Bummer," the other man said again. "I got one more week and then I'm outta here."

"You ever see a guy named Matty something here these days?"

Patterson shrugged. "Who knows their names?"

"You mean Matty Mutone?" asked the server on the other side of Patterson. "Didn't you hear? He's the one died on that bench last week."

"Oh yeah." Patterson nodded. "The cops were here asking about him. I heard it was poison."

"Oh, shit!" said Kapps.

Promptly at one o'clock, Elliott Buntrock ambled down the brick sidewalk and met Dorothy Reddish, who had a large iron key in one hand and two bottles of water in the other.

"I always feel so ridiculously privileged whenever I'm inside one of these private gardens," he said, holding the gate open for her. "They really are urban oases, aren't they?"

He stood in the shade of a huge sycamore

tree and took a deep breath, looking more like a crane than ever as he stretched his arms wide, almost as if flexing wings. A summer breeze caught his light jacket and billowed it out from a T-shirt that advertised Browning tractors.

The small park was lovingly maintained by the residents of Sussex Square. They had lost the battle to preserve the original gas streetlights, but had been allowed to replace the gas fixtures inside the frosted globes with soft electric lights that mimicked gas flames. The wrought-iron fence and the benches inside were original, and graveled paths wound through ornamental plantings true to the period.

They were the only ones there and when they'd chosen a bench near the small fountain shaped like a trumpeter swan, Buntrock laid the sushi tray on the space between them and said, "So how's my favorite student settling in at the Breul House?"

"Except that it's probably going to close under my tenure, just fine," she said gamely, dribbling a little soy sauce over her eel and avocado morsel before popping it into her mouth. "The house has never been self-supporting and our funds will run dry next year if we don't find a new way to bring more people through the doors or something to turn on the grant fountains." She cocked her head and, with a mischievous smile that was only half-joking, said, "Are you sure you don't want to move your Nauman retrospective back to us?"

"Sorry, kid. It was never going to be here if I had anything to do with it. Besides, it would only be a temporary fix."

"I know," she sighed. "And that's what I wanted to ask you. You knew Roger Shambley, didn't you?"

"Not well, but yes."

"You say that as if you didn't like him."

Buntrock shrugged. "He was such a pompous little ass, I doubt if anyone really liked him. I doubt if he cared. Why?"

"What *would* he care about, Elliott? What would excite him?"

"Power," he said promptly. "Or fame. Why?"

She repeated what Hope Ruffton had told her, how Shambley had started rummaging through the Breul House as if hunting for something that excited him. "But if he found it, he didn't get a chance to tell anyone. Unless he got it out of the house first."

Buntrock flicked a grain of rice from his T-shirt. "Knowing Shambley, he probably wouldn't hesitate to steal something minor,

249

but something that had him that excited? Sounds more like an important piece of art that he could write a book about and go down in history as its discoverer."

He chewed thoughtfully for a moment. "Shambley's specialty was nineteenth-century art. Breul was in Europe in the eighteen-sixties, right? That's when he did most of his collecting. Millet, Manet, and Whistler, of course. Is there a Manet hanging on the walls?"

"Not that I've seen. No Millet either."

"Too early for Cezanne . . . Greek sculpture was getting quite a play then, but I doubt a big piece of marble would go unnoticed. Pompeii would have been on the Grand Tour, though. Perhaps a particularly nice little Roman bronze? Or maybe there's a piece of Etruscan gold mixed in with his wife's jewelry?"

"No. All of her good pieces were sold to endow the house and the costume things aren't worth more than a few hundred dollars."

Buntrock shook his head impatiently. "Even Etruscan gold wouldn't have made a big enough splash for Shambley. Sorry, Dot, I'm out of ideas. Hope you find whatever it is, though. If you're right about Shambley's excitement, maybe you'll get to write your own book."

CHAPTER 20

In midafternoon, Tillie turned from his computer screen with an air of accomplishment. "Listen to this, Lieutenant! The deed to Number 403 was registered to Charlotte Randolph forty-three years ago, which puts it about eighteen months after Marta Constanza's accident. Before that, the house was owned by a Matthew Littlejohn, who sold it to Benito DelVecchio."

"Who then gave it to Randolph?" Sigrid asked.

Dinah Urbanska made a face. "Poor Mrs. DelVecchio. Do you think she knew he'd moved his mistress practically next door? That was cruel."

"But convenient," said Lowry.

Hentz had been following his own trail of breadcrumbs. "I went back and pulled up some old references to Franklin McCall."

"Who?"

"The critic who just happened to be at

that performance of *La Bohème.* I cross-referenced Benito DelVecchio and got nothing, but with Benny Olds . . ."

He turned his computer screen around so that Sigrid saw black-and-white photographs from an old magazine.

"This is a historical website dedicated to the mobs of New York." He read the picture's cutline aloud. "Man about town and music critic Franklin McCall relaxing with friends at Sardi's after a performance of the New York Philharmonic." Several men in black tie and dinner jackets were seated around a table thick with cocktail glasses. "That's McCall, that's Walter Winchell, and there across the table from McCall is Benny Olds."

"Are you sure?" asked Sigrid. "The picture's not labeled."

"No, but he's mentioned in the text as hanging out with show business types. Like the way Frank Sinatra liked to hang out with mobsters in Vegas. Wait a minute and I'll show you."

A few clicks later and a mug shot of DelVecchio flashed on the screen. Hentz reduced it in size, then dropped it in next to the magazine photo.

Sigrid looked closer at the man who had employed her father's killer. Dark curly hair, hooded eyes, and a sardonic smile that probably looked sexy to any woman he aimed it at.

"Wow!" said Urbanska, looking at the first picture. "He was hot."

Albee was more dismissive. "All men look hot in a dinner jacket."

"If we're looking for motives," said Hentz, "I think we just found one. Benny not only caused the accident, I'm willing to bet he's the 'friend' who invited McCall back to another performance of *La Bohème,* saying it was to give the tenor another hearing."

"And Bloss was blackmailing her?" asked Albee.

"Why else would she give him five hundred dollars? For old times' sake?" Lowry gave a cynical snort. "Out of the kindness of her heart?"

"If the poison was meant for Jack Bloss, that makes Matty Mutone collateral damage," Sigrid said.

"About that twenty dollars Matty had," said Dinah Urbanska, who was beginning to feel she could hold her own with the others. "Jack Bloss's sister said he wasn't crazy about tomato sauce, so what if he offered Matty that money and some of his lasagna in exchange for some of Matty's fettuccine?"

"Twenty bucks for a serving of pasta?" asked Hentz.

"Why not? He was hungry and he was probably feeling flush and if this was a first payment to keep quiet, he'd be expecting that there would be more where that came from, right?"

It made a certain amount of sense, thought Sigrid. But poor sad Matty. Yes, he'd been on a path to self-destruction, but remembering the words of the woman who had comforted him after his cousin's death, she regretted that he'd found no closure.

"Tillie, take another look at that report on the hit-and-run that killed Aria Edwards. See if the driver was ever found."

The day had started with blue skies and sunshine, but by the time Sigrid and Hentz got down to Vanderbock Street in the late afternoon, the sun had disappeared behind some heavy dark clouds that were rolling in from the west. After driving around the block, Hentz gave up on finding a legal space and pulled in next to a fire hydrant. A light wind carried the smell of rain as they rang the bell at Number 403.

No response.

Hentz rang again, with the same result.

"Do we have Randolph's phone number?"

Sigrid asked.

Before he could check, she tilted her head to the left. "Never mind."

He looked in the direction of her gesture and saw Charlotte Randolph walking toward them from farther down the street, swinging an ivory cane.

She hesitated when she saw them and for a moment, looked as if she might cross the street to avoid them; then, with a visible shrug, she continued as she'd begun. She looked cool in a long gray-and-white print skirt and a loose white shirt belted at the waist. The skirt was made of a light material that brushed around her ankles as the wind picked up.

When she was close enough to be heard, she said, "I'm sorry, Lieutenant. I let the time get away from me."

The cane was evidently more for effect than necessity, because Randolph walked without using it except to help herself up the steep steps. Hentz stood aside as she unlocked her door and led the way into her sleekly modern home. She stashed her cane in a tall white umbrella stand and flicked a switch to light the crystal starbursts that hung at varying levels from the ceiling above the large open space.

"What about your attorney?" Sigrid asked.

"He wasn't able to get away today, but he told me I was probably being overly dramatic — that it was quite reasonable for you to ask for a sample of my pills."

She walked past the cluttered glass-topped dining table to the white chairs and couch near the large rear windows. "Looks as if we're going to get some rain."

Outside, the wind stirred the trees and the flowering bushes for which Sigrid, having little interest in nature, had no name.

"I'm going to have a glass of Riesling. May I pour some for you?"

"No, thank you," Sigrid said.

Randolph disappeared behind the mirrored screens that hid her butler's pantry and emerged a moment later with a crystal goblet of pale golden wine.

"My assistant looked you up, Lieutenant. You and Oscar Nauman. I have one of his pictures."

"Oh?"

"Upstairs," she added as Sigrid looked around. "Would you like to see it?"

"Perhaps another time. Right now, we'd like to hear more about your conversation with Jack Bloss last Tuesday."

"What more can I tell you, Lieutenant? It was purely innocuous. He gave me the program insert from that second night, we talked about old times, had a few drinks and he left. I'm sure that being poisoned was the furthest thing from his mind."

"Yet you gave him five hundred dollars. Why?"

She took a sip of wine, then set the goblet on the glass-and-chrome coffee table. "I'm sure that by now you know that he had a son who's been in a coma for years?"

Sigrid nodded.

"The nursing facility was raising its rates and he was strapped for money. Jack may have belonged to a good union with excellent benefits, but the boy's mother took half his pension in their divorce settlement and she balked at paying more for his care. She wanted Jack to either take him off life support or move him somewhere cheaper. I asked him what he was going to do." She reached for her wineglass as thunder rumbled outside. "He couldn't bear to do either. He said that if I'd ever had a child, I'd understand. That I would want the best I could afford and that I'd want that child to live forever." She shrugged. "I felt sorry for him."

"So you gave him money."

"So I gave him money."

"Was it a one-time thing or the first

installment for his silence?"

"His silence?"

"For not telling how Marta Constanza happened to fall that night."

Charlotte Randolph took another sip of wine and held the glass up to the light. Her hands were wrinkled and spotted with age, but her fingers were graceful as she wiped away a lipstick smudge.

When she did not speak, Sigrid said, "We spoke to his sister."

"Sister? Ah, yes. That's right. Jack did have a sister. Was she there that night?"

"No, but *he* was. He told her he was up on a catwalk and saw the whole thing. A man no one had seen before bumped Marta and kept going. He thought the accident might have been arranged by your new boyfriend. So I ask you again, Miss Randolph. Was Jack Bloss blackmailing you because of the way Benny Olds made you a star?"

"My voice made me a star," she said sharply. "My *voice*. Marta's accident just speeded it up a little." She drained the last of her wine and leaned back on the white couch with the goblet held loosely by the stem. "As for what Jack thought he saw, it would have been his word against mine. He had no proof. No photographs. No name for a man no one could describe."

"But it would raise a lot of questions. Undercut that memoir you're writing."

Randolph laughed and rose with a graceful, fluid swirl of her gray-and-white skirt. "I can't believe you're that naïve, Lieutenant. After all the things that were written about you and Oscar Nauman when he died? *'World-renowned artist leaves everything to a city cop'?* Had you rushed a book into print, I'm sure it would have been a bestseller. The public loves salacious gossip. Not that yours would have been that salacious," she added with amusement as Sigrid willed herself not to let either Hentz or Randolph see how uncomfortable that taunt made her.

The storm that had been building broke as sheets of rain pounded against the floor-to-ceiling windows. Randolph stepped behind the mirrors to refill her glass, then lingered at the windows to watch the rain for a moment before returning to her seat.

"So the five hundred dollars wasn't an attempt to buy his silence?" asked Hentz when Sigrid didn't respond to Randolph's words.

The soprano smiled at him and placed her goblet back on the low table before her. "Actually, it was, Detective Hentz. And to be quite honest, I think Jack did hope to blackmail me, but he was too decent to make a blatant demand."

"I don't understand," Hentz said.

"Not blackmail," Sigrid said. "But it really was a first installment, wasn't it? To buy his temporary silence?"

Randolph lightly clapped her hands. "Brava, Lieutenant!"

Hentz continued to look puzzled, so Randolph enlightened him. "My book will be published next April and I want it to deliver a bombshell on the day it's published, not dribble out like little firecrackers sputtering on the sidewalks for months in advance. Even my editor doesn't know the true story of how I came to sing Mimi that night. At the very last minute, I'll add one chapter and one extra picture, then *boom!*"

As if to underscore her words, a brilliant flash of lightning lit up the room, followed by an almost instant crack of thunder. Rain fell even heavier and wind whipped through Randolph's garden to plaster leaves against the glass.

"You'd destroy your own legend?" asked Hentz.

"Not destroy. To enhance it. Spice it up. Think of it: unknown singer and well-known gangster? The media will love it. Yes, if it had come out back then, I might have been harmed, lost some bookings, even been fired or blacklisted. And Marta Constanza certainly wouldn't have become my friend. But now? I think they'll find it romantic."

"What about Mrs. DelVecchio?" Sigrid asked. "Will she find it so amusingly romantic?"

"Sofia and I made a bargain years ago."

"When her husband gave you this house?"

Charlotte Randolph arched a beautifully shaped eyebrow. "You *did* do your research, didn't you?" She lifted her glass and stared into the pale golden wine. "If you wanted to be crude, you could say that this house was payment for services rendered. In return, I promised to be discreet and to keep my affair with Benny a complete secret. Living in this house so close to his helped us do that. Except in the very beginning, before anyone noticed that I wasn't his usual chorus girl, we were never seen in public together." She smiled as if remembering. "He would dress in patched overalls and a workman's cap while I wore an ugly cotton dress and bobby sox. We'd spend an afternoon at Coney Island, riding the roller coaster and eating hot dogs, then we'd come back here to drink champagne while I sang for him. Or we'd slip away for a weekend to some city where no one knew us."

"And Mrs. DelVecchio accepted this?"

"She had what she wanted," Randolph said coolly. "His name, his child, the respect of their community. I took nothing she valued and I did not publicly embarrass her. It was strictly quid pro quo."

"Did you know that Benny Olds was going to have that other singer tripped and sent to the hospital?" asked Hentz.

"Of course not!"

"Then why did he trick Franklin McCall into coming to that particular performance? The one night that you would be covering instead of Petra Savos?"

The crystal goblet slid from Randolph's fingers and splashed wine across her skirt, then bounced without breaking on the white carpet beneath her feet. White-faced, she stared at Hentz. "How on earth do you know about Petra Savos?"

"Who is Petra Savos?" asked Sigrid.

"The soprano who was supposed to be covering Marta Constanza. For some reason, she couldn't be reached that evening. Did Benny make it worth her while not to answer her phone?"

"Oh, please," said Randolph, who had recovered her poise and was now mopping her skirt with some paper cocktail napkins from a silver box on the coffee table. She retrieved her glass and put the wet napkins into it. "You credit him with planning something that complicated?"

"Benny Olds ran a large and complicated operation," said Hentz. "Until he was gunned down by the Gambinos, he was usually two or three moves ahead of the others. He probably would have made one hell of a chess player. Did he play?"

Charlotte Randolph slowly shook her head. "Not chess, Detective. Bridge. And he never lost count of the cards."

She stood and fluffed the thin material of her skirt to help it dry. "If there are no more questions?" she said, clearly ready to show them out.

Sigrid remained seated. "You make a good case for not wanting Jack Bloss dead," she conceded, "but he *is* dead. From an overdose of warfarin, so we still want to see your bottle of Coumadin."

"Oh, really, Lieutenant!"

Hentz stood. "We have a takeout box with traces of Coumadin that held lasagna from your refrigerator with your fingerprints on it, Ms. Randolph. We also have money from the dead man's pocket with your fingerprints as well. That's enough grounds for a search warrant, which would allow us to take your house apart piece by piece."

"Would you like to call your attorney?" Sigrid asked. "See if he can come after all?"

With a gesture of irritated capitulation, Charlotte Randolph stomped over to the glass-and-chrome staircase and started up. "They're in my bathroom."

Sigrid shot an amused glance at Hentz and murmured, "I thought the only usable fingerprints on the lasagna box were from our victims."

He grinned.

It was several minutes before Randolph descended the staircase, her lipstick refreshed and her chin high. "And before you ask, neither my niece nor my stepson went upstairs when they were here Monday. They dropped off the lasagna and left almost immediately."

She handed Hentz the little orange prescription bottle and he read the label aloud: "Warfarin sodium, two milligrams." The bottle had held ninety pills and would require authorization from her doctor for a refill. At the moment, it seemed to hold about ten or twelve small lavender pills.

"I suppose you feel the need to count them," she said. "I take one a day on Monday, Wednesday, and Friday, then two on the other four days. You can do the math."

"Actually," said Hentz, "it would be simpler just to see how many are missing from your new refill."

She started to protest, but Hentz showed Sigrid the date on the label. "Her druggist will have already asked for permission to refill it and I doubt if she lets herself run completely out."

"May we see your new bottle, Miss Randolph?" Sigrid asked.

With a sigh, Charlotte Randolph yielded to Hentz's logic. This time she was back much quicker than before.

"It's those wretched childproof caps," she told them. "I have a touch of arthritis in my thumbs and always have trouble getting them off. Last week, I spilled six or seven pills down the sink, so when you asked to see them, I topped off that first bottle so you wouldn't think I was the one who poisoned Jack."

"Eighty-one," said Hentz as he finished counting and poured the pills back into the bottle. "Nine missing. Eighteen milligrams."

Sigrid said, "Did you know Matty Mutone?"

"The other man that died? No. How would I?"

"He was Mrs. DelVecchio's godson. You live so close to her. Haven't you stayed in touch?"

"We were never 'in touch,' Lieutenant, except through Benny. We don't spit on each other if we pass in the street, but we could never be friends."

Hentz capped the pill bottle and left it on the table. "Did you send condolences when their daughter died last December?"

"Aria? I didn't know her. Not really. I met her a few times when she came backstage with him to get his program signed but I didn't try to charm her. So far as she knew, I was just someone her father liked to see perform at the Met or at a concert hall. She was a pretty little thing, but I've never been very good with children and we had no reason to meet after he died."

"So you wouldn't know about relationships in the DelVecchio household?"

"Absolutely not."

"Does she know that you're going to write about your affair with her husband?"

Randolph nodded. "But I don't see that this has any bearing on Jack's death, Lieutenant, so now, if you don't mind, I really am rather tired."

They all looked to the window wall, where

rain pounded against the glass.

"I'll lend you an umbrella," she said.

Chapter 21

The rain continued throughout Tuesday night as a line of thunderheads swept across the city. Roman Tramegra fretted about the baby birds in their garden until Sigrid reminded him that birds had been surviving storms since they were pterodactyls.

A two-hundred-year-old oak tree in Central Park was shattered by lightning and heavy winds sent unsecured potted plants and small signs scudding across sidewalks all over town. At Rockefeller Center, the bright summer annuals in the Channel Gardens had been beaten down, their stems broken, their fragile blossoms bruised and mangled, while the blue hydrangeas massed at one end were so waterlogged that their heavy heads touched the pavement.

At headquarters that Wednesday morning, wet shoes and dripping umbrellas had made walking across the tiled floors as slippery as dancing on ice. Jim Lowry managed to catch himself on a door frame to keep from sprawling when his feet skidded out from under him, but Dinah Urbanska went down before reaching the safety of her desk. Unwilling to watch her try to navigate the distance to the coffee urn in their break room, Sam Hentz told her to stay put and filled her mug himself. Tillie, accustomed to his children's spilled milk and juice, spread newspapers and paper towels on the floor.

Sigrid emerged — carefully — from her office with her own empty mug and Hentz said, "I heard back from Cohen about the rat bait we got from the DelVecchio garage."

"That was quick."

"Well, he says it's pretty basic chemistry. That particular brand of warfarin contains both a dye and a bittering agent that's supposed to keep children from eating it. According to Cohen, the EPA wants to make it the industry standard, but so far, that hasn't happened."

Across the room, Detective Gonzalez's head came up. "My sister's two-year-old found one of those rat baits at the babysitter's. She thought it was candy. They pumped her stomach and kept her hooked up to a heart monitor till they were sure she was going to be all right."

"Is she okay now?" asked Urbanska.

"So far as we know. She finished first grade last week and seems just fine."

"Anyhow," said Hentz, "Cohen says there was no dye and no bittering agent in the stuff that killed those two, so it didn't come out of that package."

"Did you give him the pill we got from Charlotte Randolph?"

"Yeah, but that's going to take longer and he may not be able to give us a definite answer. He'll have to send it out to a central lab. He did eliminate Mrs. DelVecchio's current prescription, though."

"That reminds me," Sigrid said. "Did we get a comparison sample of her old pills?"

"No. Miss Orlano said they were probably thrown out, remember?"

"All the same, just in case those pills weren't thrown out, call George Edwards and ask him to have Mrs. DelVecchio's doctor fax us a copy of the Coumadin prescription that was written for the first pills. Make sure it's precisely what was prescribed and not a generic or another brand. We really need to know the source of that blood thinner."

Before returning to her office, she topped off her coffee and paused at Tillie's desk. "Did you learn anything more about the driver of the car that killed Aria Edwards?"

Tillie shook his head. "The last follow-up report had a witness stating for sure that it was a white male, but no real description."

An open box sat on the floor beside his chair.

"Are those Matty's things?" Sigrid asked.

Tillie nodded. "Too bad we can't match that key he had to a car. I ran his name through DMV. No car registered in his name. His driver's license is still valid, though, and he didn't have any violations other than a couple of parking tickets, which he'd paid."

Turning to Lowry and Albee, Sigrid said, "Let's backtrack on him some more. Go back and question everyone at that soup kitchen who might have interacted with Mutone and while you're at it, try that rehab facility he was last in."

She glanced down again at the box that held the small items they'd found on Matty Mutone's body or in his grocery cart. Lying on top was that picture from the Overhold woman who'd cuddled him, a picture of Matty and Aria Edwards. Once again, she felt a wash of sadness for his wasted life. The picture currently posted on their white-board was of a methhead with sunken cheeks and dissipated eyes.

Impulsively, she picked up this picture of

Matty as a young man, laughing with his cousin, their whole lives before them. Intending to put this picture next to the other, she pulled it from the plastic sleeve and was surprised to see that instead of one picture, there were actually two similar poses that were stuck together. When she pulled them apart, something fell to the floor next to Tillie's shoe.

"Looks like a parking ticket," he said.

The printing was crisp and legible and dated the seventeenth of last December from a garage over on the East Side.

"Urbanska and I'll go," said Hentz.

Sofia DelVecchio paused at the foot of the stairs as her housekeeper closed the front door and took off her rain hat.

"Back already? Wasn't she at home?"

"I didn't go. Before I could get out the door, Laura grabbed my umbrella and snatched your envelope out of my hand. I couldn't stop her."

Sofia's lips tightened. "Couldn't or didn't."

Orla shrugged. "As soon as that woman said her name yesterday, you should have known she would find a way to go there. She wants to be a singer, too."

273

"More opera? Dear God! Is it never to stop?"

"I'll bring you an espresso," Orla said, and escaped to the kitchen.

"May I help you?" Marian Schmidt's large frame blocked the doorway of Number 403. Today, instead of Valkyrie braids, her long blond hair was tied back at the nape of her neck with a red ribbon, but she seemed as formidable as any Teutonic Valkyrie to the girl who stood there with a hopeful smile.

Rain bounced off her open umbrella and splashed on the woman's sandals, which made her take an involuntary step backward.

The girl flourished a six-by-eight envelope. "I'm here to deliver this to Ms. Randolph."

"I'll take it," said Marian Schmidt, and held out her hand.

"I was told to give it to her myself."

"And you are?"

"Laura Edwards. Tell her I'm Mrs. DelVecchio's granddaughter."

Randolph's assistant frowned. "Wait here," she said, and closed the door, leaving Laura outside in the pouring rain.

A moment or two later, the door opened again. "Come in, Miss Edwards. Let me take your umbrella. You may wipe your feet on this mat."

Laura's eyes widened as she took in the chrome and white interior, the spiky light fixtures that gleamed and sparkled overhead, the window wall at the far end. From the outside, Number 403 was of the same architectural period as her grandmother's house.

But inside?

"Oh, wow!" Laura exclaimed. "This is totally awesome!"

"Why, thank you," said the white-haired woman who sat at the grand piano that overlooked the garden where rain beat down on the flowering bushes. She half turned on the bench, which was padded in white leather. "I'm Charlotte Randolph. I believe you have something for me?"

Struck by a sudden and unaccustomed shyness, Laura nodded and walked across the long space to hand over the envelope.

Without opening it, Randolph laid it on the gleaming ebony piano top and gestured to a nearby chair. "You're Aria's daughter?"

"Did you know my mother?" she asked eagerly.

"Not really. We met when she was still a child. I was sorry to hear of her loss."

"She never mentioned you," said Laura.

"Why would she? As I said, we only met a

time or two when she was a child."

"But she knows —" The girl shook her head impatiently at her slip of tongue. "She *knew* I want to sing on stage. Not opera, of course, but still . . ."

Randolph smiled. "But still?"

She turned to face the keyboard and her fingers came down strongly on the keys. "Sing for me."

"Now?"

"Now. What shall I play? And please don't say rap."

Rather than make the long drive out to Riverhead, Elaine Albee phoned the Seaview Recovery Center. After much holding and transferring, she was eventually connected to the doctor who had overseen Matty Mutone's treatment there. He had not realized that Matty was dead. "But it doesn't surprise me, Detective. The cure rate for methamphetamine addiction is less than ten percent and the relapse time is usually within six months. I'm surprised he lasted this long."

"He only fell off in December, Doctor."

"Really?"

"And it wasn't the meth that killed him. He was poisoned. Is there anyone there who was close to him, who might have known if he had any enemies?"

"I'm looking at his file now and all that I'm seeing is that he had a cousin out here in Riverhead who visited him every week. An Aria Edwards. You might ask her."

Albee thanked the doctor and hung up. "I didn't see the point of telling him that it was the cousin's death that sent him back to meth," she told Lowry.

He jingled his car keys. "Got an umbrella?"

It was a short drive down to the soup kitchen and he even found a parking space less than half a block away, but despite Albee's large umbrella, they were both damp around the edges when they got there. The doors were soon to open for lunch and workers were busily bringing in trays of food for the steam counter.

"Yeah, he was a regular here for a while," said one, "but he didn't talk to anybody I ever saw."

"Matty? Oh, sure," said an older black woman who seemed to be in charge of the kitchen. She wiped sweat from her brow with a dishtowel tucked in her waistband. "He was a regular up to a year or so ago when he got clean. I think he had relatives that lived nearby, so he'd stop in occasionally to shoot the breeze, even help out a little if we were short-handed. A real sweetheart. We didn't see him for a while, but then he started coming in again back in — late January? Early February? As a client, not a helper. You really hate to see it, y'know? You think they're gonna make it and then *bang!*"

She called to a man carrying a tray of condiments. "Hey, Denny. You knew Matty, back last winter, didn't you?"

The stocky white man who'd paused in the doorway looked as if he'd like to deny it. "Yeah. Why?"

"These detectives are asking about him."

"Whaddya wanna ask?" he asked suspiciously. "I already told you everything I know."

"But you were friendly, right? Used to talk when you were working here last winter?"

"Yeah, we talked, but I ain't seen Matty since last December." He rested the tray on the back of a chair.

"He ever say he had enemies, someone who might've had it in for him?"

"Naw, we weren't that tight. Look, I need to get this tray out there. You want to know about him, why don't you ask the people that live across from that diner on Vanderbock Street. He said he was related to them."

■ ■ ■ ■

"So what did you think, Marian?" Charlotte Randolph said when Laura Edwards had gone and her assistant had brewed them both a cup of green tea.

"She sounded good to me, but I'm no judge. Are you going to take her on?"

"Coach her? Certainly not. In the first place, I'm phasing out the students I have. In the second place, her grandmother would never allow it. I'm surprised she even let the child bring me that envelope."

She looked around. "Where did I put it, anyhow?"

"On the piano? Yes, there it is," said Marian. "I'll get it."

The envelope was sealed.

Didn't trust her granddaughter? Charlotte wondered.

She slit it open and shook the photo inside onto the glass tabletop.

"Benny DelVecchio," she told Marian. "Four days before he was killed."

"He certainly was handsome, wasn't he?"

Oh yes, she thought. Had he lived, this picture would have been hers from the beginning. He had laughed about her wanting a formal portrait of him. "A *portrait?*

Am I so fancy now I can't just have some-body take a snapshot? I gotta have a por-trait?"

"I gave you mine," she'd said, "so it's only right I have one of you."

Hers had probably been burned the same day Sofia found it. Her cleaning woman had seen a pile of smashed records atop a bin in front of Number 409.

"All of them were yours," she'd told Charlotte.

The lab to which Marcus Livingston's secretary had sent Vincent Haas was only a five-minute walk from the Museum of Modern Art on West Fifty-Third Street, and after letting a technician swab his mouth, he decided to see for himself an example of pictures he had seen only on his computer. The admission fee was a little higher than he'd expected, but he handed over the unfamiliar bills with a growing sense of anticipation. A docent at the information desk directed him to the fourth floor.

Upon exiting the elevator, he entered a large hall and started down the nearest side, scanning the names on the placards. Half-way down, he stopped at the one that read "Oscar Nauman, American" and stepped back to take a good look at *Untitled #19*.

Compared to some of the huge canvases that covered whole walls, it was relatively small — only two feet wide by three feet tall — and had raw slashes of black and purple across an acid yellow background. By the dates on the placard beside it, Haas realized that it must have been painted about two years before his birth when Lila and Nauman were living together.

Not a study in serenity.

His eyes swept over the abstractions that surrounded him, none of which captured his interest or clamored for a closer look. They left him feeling vaguely disappointed, both in himself and in the art. He had no language for these pictures. His training had been scientific and mathematical, so it wasn't as if he'd expected to feel an electric connection, but his father had stood in front of this canvas, had worked on it while his biological mother watched from her corner of the loft.

Yet, even though he thought he felt nothing as he turned back toward the elevators, something made him stop and look a final time at that grim picture and wonder at the emotions that must have prompted it.

CHAPTER 22

Vic's Garage was located in a run-down section of Greenwich Street that would probably become gentrified once the Hudson Greenway was completed, but for now the garage was typical of the area: a shabby brick and concrete building with faded and peeling wall signs that advertised products long since discontinued. This close to the river, it was a self-parking facility with relatively low rates.

Hentz parked in the exit lane and showed his ID to Vic Leibowitz, a beefy six-footer pushing fifty, whose belly strained the bounds of his grease-stained gray T-shirt and hung over his belt like a hefty salami roll.

Before he could ask what this was about, a woman pulled in out of the rain and nudged the NO SPACES sign that blocked her entry to the ramp. She lowered her window to wave a ten-dollar bill at him.

"C'mon, Vic. Shoehorn me in, okay? I'm late for my meeting."

"Yeah, yeah, you're always late, Selma. Think this is valet parking?" But he gestured to a pimply young man to move the sign so that she could ease up to the ticket machine and take the slip of paper it spit out. When the automatic arm raised, she stopped her car on the other side of it and got out.

"You're a prince, Vic." She handed him the ten and her car keys before unfurling her umbrella and hurrying out into the rain.

When shown the ticket that had fallen from the plastic sleeve, Vic said, "Yeah, that's one of mine, but they're supposed to hand 'em back when they pay at the gate."

"So the car could still be here?" asked Detective Hentz.

Vic looked closer at the date. "Issued back in December? No way."

"You're absolutely sure? You keep track of every car that comes in?"

"No, but if it was parked here six months, I'd've noticed. Or my guys would've. Space is money, y'know? Anything left here more than ninety-six hours gets reported to the police as an unclaimed vehicle. If the title holder can't be located, and the city doesn't want it, I can sell it for scrap. Or if it's worth a little money and I feel like filling out a bunch of forms and jumping through all the hoops, I can sell it at auction. Someone did leave a sweet little BMW here a few years ago. Got a nice chunk of change for that baby. But mostly, they're junk and not worth the trouble, so I just scrap 'em."

"And how many have you scrapped since this ticket was issued?"

Vic shrugged. "I'd have to look it up. Three, or maybe four. People too lazy to dispose of their car the right way. Think it's easier just to drive it in here and walk away. I barely get enough to pay the towing fee."

He walked back to the grimy glass-fronted room that served as his office. As it turned out, Vic had actually scrapped five cars since December, one of which the city had claimed, a late-model Mercedes that had been used in a drug deal and had a bullet hole in the rear window. He had a copying machine and ran off copies of the reporting forms for them. The Mercedes had been three years old, the others were eight to ten years older than that.

Vic shook his head when asked if he could match the ticket to one of those junkers, so they would take those forms back to the station — "More fodder for the files," Hentz told Urbanska — where they would keep trying to figure out why Matty Mutone had been carrying a parking ticket for a car he didn't own and which one of those it was.

"Too bad one of them's not an Oldsmobile," she said.

The faxed prescription from Mrs. DelVecchio's doctor came through just after lunch and after showing it to a nearby druggist, Tillie broke the bad news to Sigrid.

"Sorry, Lieutenant. It's the exact same brand as Ms. Randolph's."

"So we're back at square one," she sighed.

The skies had finally cleared although there were still puddles to wet the shoes of the unwary. When Sigrid left her office shortly after five and headed for the nearest cross-town bus stop, the air felt thick and slightly sticky.

The sidewalk was crowded with commuters and walking was further impeded by construction barriers that channeled people through narrow passages no more than four feet wide in places. Just in front of her, an elderly woman stumbled on a bit of broken concrete and as Sigrid reached out to steady her, a man on the other side took the woman's arm and kept her upright.

Flustered, she thanked them both with an exasperated shake of her head. "Seventy-three years I've lived in this town and they're never going to finish building it."

The woman turned at the next corner onto a sidewalk that was smooth and barrier-free, but the man continued in step with Sigrid.

"Lieutenant Harald?" he asked.

So far as she knew, Sigrid had never met this middle-aged man before.

"Yes?"

He sidestepped a cluster of laughing teen-age girls who were barreling down on them and held out a copy of a newspaper photo, one of her that had run when Nauman died.

"I thought it was you. I've waited almost an hour for you to come out. I'm Vincent Haas."

She stopped so abruptly that someone bumped her from behind, muttered something halfway between an apology and a curse, and went around her in a huff.

"Please," said the man, and touched her arm to guide her out of the main flow of pedestrians to a place of relative calm beside a hot pretzel cart parked at the curb.

"They have told you about me?" he asked.

"Yes."

Gray eyes met blue and he was as Bunt-rock had described him: his height, his hair fast going white like Nauman's, the color of his eyes, but somehow she had expected to feel something on a psychic level that would tell her whether or not he was really Nauman's son. Instead, he was just a pleasant-faced man who could have been anybody. There was indeed something familiar about him, something she couldn't quite identify, but that probably rose from those pictures of Lila Nagy that Rudy Gottfried had shown her.

"Please," he said. "Could we go sit down somewhere. Have a drink? Talk for a few minutes? This is weird for me, too. Did they tell you? I only found out six months ago that I am not who I grew up thinking I was."

Sigrid looked around blankly. The Urban Renewal Society was only a block away. Owned and run by two former cops, the scruffy bar's smoke-stained walls were lined with autographed pictures of uniformed police officers, including four of the last six police commissioners and three mayors. Over the bar, amid a clutter of outdated handcuffs, nightsticks, and other police equipment was a wooden plaque with the names and badge numbers of former customers who had died in the line of duty. There were booths for those who wanted relative quiet with their better than average bar food, and drinks were modestly priced, but Sigrid knew that it was the precinct's favorite watering hole, which meant there might be speculative stares if she stopped in with this man.

Still, the other options ran to salad bars, Formica countertops, bright fluorescent lighting, and plastic drink cups.

"This way," she told Haas.

Chapter 23

Vincent Haas settled into the booth's brown leatherette cushion and looked around with approval, especially when he saw someone light up at the bar.

He pulled out a pack of cigarettes and offered them to Sigrid, who shook her head.

"Will it bother you if I do?" he asked.

"No, it's all right."

"I'm not a chain smoker, but not being allowed to on the plane was rather hard. I drank three beers and managed to sleep most of the way over. And now I hear that soon Americans will not be able to smoke in any restaurant."

Sigrid recognized a delaying tactic and did not rise to it. The station house had recently gone smoke free and while there had been some grousing among the uniforms, the only smoker on her team was Detective Ruben Gonzalez, who was trying to quit and looked upon the ban as a helpful crutch. She saw no need to share that with Haas.

"Did my father smoke?"

"Nauman smoked a pipe," she said carefully as their waiter approached.

"What'll it be, ma'am?" he asked Sigrid.

"Bourbon and Coke, please."

"Anything to eat?"

She shook her head.

"And for you, sir?"

Haas inquired about the brews on tap, then ordered an ale. "And a cheeseburger, medium rare. I am in love with American cheeseburgers," he confessed to Sigrid with what was probably meant to be a winning smile. "Must be in my DNA."

Which produced an awkward silence.

After a moment, Haas exhaled a stream of smoke and met it head on.

"You do not think he is my father, do you?"

"As you say," Sigrid murmured, "DNA."

"I gave a sample this morning. I want this clearly determined as much as you and Mr. Livingston."

Sigrid was surprised. "But what will they compare it with? Nauman had no close relatives."

"I don't know. Maybe they just want my

DNA in case a sample of his should turn up."

Their drinks arrived along with a dish of peanuts and sesame sticks. "And your cheeseburger will be right out," said the waiter.

"What was he like?" Haas asked.

A flood of images and memories tumbled through Sigrid's head, none of which she particularly wanted to share. But if this man was Nauman's son, it would be selfish not to.

"He liked to drive fast," she said. "He had a yellow MG and he only put the top up if it was raining."

Haas stubbed out his cigarette and took some peanuts but before they reached his mouth, his hand stopped in midair. "Yellow MG? Back home I drive a yellow Fiat Spider."

At her blank look, he said, "That's a convertible, too."

He clearly found a confirming significance to this coincidence and Sigrid felt herself sympathizing with his desire to connect with Nauman, to find a link to the man he now considered his father.

"Are you married?"

"Yes. With two daughters." Without being asked, he opened his wallet and showed her the pictures. "Anna and Maria-Louise."

She tried to see even the faintest resemblance to Nauman and failed. "They take after their mother?"

"Luckily for them, yes."

"What about your mother?" she asked as his cheeseburger and fries arrived. "Lila Nagy. Will you try to see her soon?"

"I went there first," he said, which made Sigrid think better of him. "My mother —" He hesitated and gave a helpless gesture. "For as long as I can remember, Anja and Klaus Haas were my mother and father. It is hard to think of Lila as my mother."

"I can appreciate that," Sigrid said.

"My mother did not say how often she wrote and I feared that Lila might be anxious because the letters had stopped." He took a bite of his cheeseburger with a sad smile. "I need not have worried."

"Did she know you?"

"No. I was not allowed to speak to her except through glass. That first day I held up pictures of my mother — her sister. And a picture of me when I was three. There was no spark. Nobody there. I spoke to the officials and to her doctor. I told them how far I had come and why. The doctor was very nice. He said to come back the next day and he would withhold her drugs until then. He said that she could become violent without them, but he would do this for me."

He drained his glass of ale and lifted it to signal their waiter for a refill.

"Did it make a difference?"

"Yes. She was fairly cogent at first — spoke German to me and seemed sad when I told her that Anja had died, but I don't think she fully understood who I was even though I showed her the pictures again. Then I made a mistake. I said Oscar Nauman's name and that got a string of curses. She began beating on the glass between us. She must have thought I was him. The guards had to come and take her back to her ward." He sighed. "I do not think I will go back."

The waiter set a fresh glass of ale on the table and took away the empty one.

Sigrid still had half her bourbon and she sipped it as Haas took an envelope from the inner pocket of his jacket.

"This is a picture of Lila shortly before she came to New York." He laid the photo on the table, then placed another beside it. "And this is what she looks like now."

"They let you take her picture?"

He nodded.

Sigrid picked them both up and held them side by side. The first was recognizable from the photos Rudy Gottfried had shown her. Long dark hair. Slender figure. Flashing eyes.

Except for the manic eyes, the second bore no resemblance at all. Short hair completely white. Puffy face. No trace of her former beauty.

Sigrid slid the pictures back to him.

"I'm sorry," she said. "It must be very painful for you."

"Worse if I thought I had inherited her madness. My mother had me examined by psychiatrists when I was a child and again when I was sixteen. She told me it was because she was afraid there might be some strain in the family blood and that I might become like my aunt. They assured her I was quite normal. Boringly normal, in fact. Which is probably why mathematics fascinated me."

"You're a statistician, right?"

"A *versicherungsmathematiker,* actually." He smiled. "I'm an actuary for a large insurance corporation. No artistic talent from either parent."

Which brings us back to Nauman, Sigrid thought.

"Will you be staying here long?"

"Until it can be proven one way or another if I am Oscar Nauman's son."

294

"And if you are?"

"That will depend on you, Lieutenant." He pushed the remains of his cheeseburger aside and lit another cigarette. "Some men acknowledge their bastards, others do not. I think you probably knew him better than anyone. You will know what he would do, yes?"

When she did not answer, he said, "And I think you will do whatever that is."

Sigrid drank the last of her bourbon and signaled to the waiter.

"No, no," said Haas. "Please. You must let me take care of the bill."

She thanked him and as she stood to go, she said, "My lawyer knows where you're staying?"

He nodded.

"Then I won't say goodbye."

CHAPTER 24

As she let herself into the house, Sigrid heard her housemate say, "Hold on a moment. Let me find a pencil."

She went down the short entrance hall to their kitchen and found Roman rummaging for a pencil in a drawer beneath the wall phone.

"Ah! You're back. It's a Dr. Reddish."

The name was vaguely familiar, but she couldn't think in what context.

Roman handed her the phone and went back to stirring something on the stove, something that smelled deliciously of browned garlic and a whiff of rosemary.

"Dr. Reddish? This is Sigrid Harald."

"Oh, good!" a youthful voice exclaimed. "Ms. Harald — I mean, *Lieutenant* Harald, I'm the new director at the Breul House. I hope you don't mind that I got your number from Dr. Buntrock? Did he happen to mention me?"

"Actually, he did. I believe he said you were once a student of his."

"I'm calling about Roger Shambley's murder. They tell me here that you handled the investigation."

"Yes? How can I help you?"

"I know it's a long shot, but my assistant is under the impression that Dr. Shambley might have found something significant in the house just before he was killed. Did you hear that, too?"

"It was mentioned, but I have no idea what it was." She hesitated. "Unless . . ."

"Unless?"

"I don't know if it was significant or not, but there was a docent there. A Mrs. Beardy?"

"Mrs. Beardsley?"

"That's right. She seemed to know every item in the house. An embroidered pink satin item was found in Shambley's brief-case. It looked rather like an envelope. Mrs. Beardsley said it was Mrs. Breul's glove case, but when she took us to where it was usually kept, it turned out be a duplicate. She was quite surprised that there were two. We didn't take it, so it's probably still there in the house."

"It was empty?"

"I'm afraid so. But it did look as if it had

held something long enough to leave an impression. It could have been a small book or a jeweler's box for a bracelet, who knows? It didn't come from Sophie Breul's room, though. I remember that it had a musty smell. Maybe from the attic where Shambley was working? You could ask Mrs. Beardsley."

Of course I can, thought Dorothy Reddish after she had thanked Lt. Harald and hung up. Even though it was after six o'clock, Mrs. Beardsley was probably still here in the house somewhere. She rather suspected that the woman thought of this place as her own personal life-size dollhouse.

Several years ago, someone had donated jointed manikins from a going-out-of business clothing store and Mrs. Beardsley treated them as stand-ins for the Breul family and their servants, circa 1890. A female figure stood with her hand on the bannister of the curved staircase, as if coming down to join the male figure who waited below. Erich and Sophie Breul. Mrs. Beardsley changed their clothing every month. Here in June, Sophie wore a flowery dress of cotton batiste. Erich was jaunty in a light-weight linen suit and a straw boater with a red-and-white-striped hatband, as if he were

298

about to walk out the front door for a stroll up the avenue.

The police had returned his ebony walking stick, but that was for winter. For June, Mrs. Beardsley had brought out his bamboo cane.

Upstairs in the playroom, Erich Breul Jr. would be dressed in a white sailor suit, a little boy who never grew up, a child so adored that his mother had saved all his clothes.

Reddish had to keep reminding herself that Erich Junior did, in fact, grow up. Upon finishing college in 1912, he left for a *wanderjahr* in Europe, where he was struck and killed by a team of runaway horses in a narrow Paris street. He was not quite twenty-two.

She had read the heartbroken entries in Sophie's diaries and ached for Erich Senior's grief.

But what was Shambley doing with Sophie's glove case?

She stepped out into the great hall and found Mrs. Beardsley staring at the male manikin. The older woman gave a guilty laugh, as if embarrassed to have been caught unaware.

"I know it's silly of me, but I've been trying to decide if Mr. Breul should have a buttonhole?"

"A what?"

"A boutonniere. That's what they would have called it back then. Or would it make him look too much like a dandy, which I'm quite sure he was not?"

"Oh, I don't know," Reddish said. "Maybe it was something his wife liked."

"Now that's an idea!" Mrs. Beardsley exclaimed. "I shall move Sophie closer to the railing and let her be handing him a daisy or a rosebud and he can be reaching up for it. Isn't it lucky that these manikins are so nicely jointed? Gives us so many staging possibilities."

The royal us, thought Reddish. *As if any of the other docents would dare move these two figures.*

"I wonder if you can help me," she said. "Lieutenant Harald tells me that a glove case was found in Dr. Shambley's briefcase after he was killed. Where would I find it?"

"In the attic," the woman replied promptly, and immediately started up the stairs. "We were all so surprised to learn that there were two glove cases and we surmised that Mr. Breul must have used it to keep some private reminder of his wife after her death, so rather than leave it with

300

Sophie's other things, I put it back in the attic."

Reddish dutifully followed her up the several flights to the attic, where she herself had begun going through the records of Erich Breul's shipping company.

"We gave Dr. Shambley the use of Erich Junior's desk that was stored up here when we redid the playroom. *You,* of course, are using the desk Erich Senior used."

She made it sound as if she hoped Reddish appreciated the privilege.

Slightly panting as they entered the fourth-floor attic, she opened a lower drawer of this smaller oak desk and brought out a flat cardboard gift box. Inside, now carefully wrapped in tissue paper, was the embroidered pink satin glove case that Lt. Harald had described. It was faded and discolored on the edges.

"I wanted to have it cleaned and restored," said Mrs. Beardsley, "but then I thought that perhaps it was best to leave it as it was in case we ever found whatever it was that it used to hold."

With her fingers, Reddish traced the outlines of the impression. Something about two inches thick that measured approximately nine by four inches. "And you have no idea what that might be?"

"Not at all." True regret lay in Mrs. Beardsley's voice. "But it was so chaotic back then, with police all over the house from attic to basement and making wicked accusations."

Reddish looked around. Here near the stairs, space had been cleared for the desk, a swivel chair, and a floor lamp. Two file cabinets stood nearby. Stretching far back under the rafters were bulky shapes draped in dust cloths, pieces of furniture unwanted and no longer needed downstairs.

"Has all that furniture been catalogued and evaluated?" she asked.

"I'm afraid so, Dr. Reddish. Like you, our former director hoped to find something that could be sold without diminishing the holdings of the house. Unfortunately . . ."

"And this is where Dr. Shambley worked while updating his history of the house?"

"He was everywhere," said Mrs. Beardsley with remembered annoyance. "Not to speak ill of the dead, but he was such an unpleasant little man. He'd wave his hand for you to get out of his way and then push right past you if you didn't move fast enough to suit him. Nobody here mourned him, I can tell you. But yes, this is where he worked. We have no idea where he found that second glove case. It certainly wasn't in the desk.

Maybe in the file cabinets?"

Dorothy Reddish sighed as she opened one of the drawers. Although each folder was neatly labeled in some long-dead secretary's Spenserian script, the files that she had examined all had to do with the early founding of the Breul fortune, which began with three leaky river barges and the opening of the Erie Canal back in the 1820s. A second fortune came from running blockades during the Civil War. From there, the Breuls had moved into banking and investments, and the bulk of those records had probably gone with the company when it was sold after Erich Senior's death. The documents here seemed to be from that simpler beginning and may have been kept for sentimental reasons. They tracked the transport of manufactured products like tools and yard goods going west, and raw materials like lumber and barrels of apples coming east.

It wasn't quite her field, thought Reddish, but it might be possible to put together an exhibit showing the contributions made to American industry and westward expansion by the Breuls.

Assuming she could keep the house open that long.

CHAPTER 25

Tillie had spent most of Wednesday afternoon cross-checking with the DMV to identify the last known owners of the abandoned cars that Vic's Garage had sold for scrap. He posted a list on the whiteboard the next morning, hoping to spark new lines of inquiry.

"Let's try their last addresses," Sigrid said. "Split up the list and see if you can find any neighbors to interview. There has to be a link back to Matty Mutone. Detective Hentz and I will see if any of these names ring a bell at the DelVecchio house."

Once again, Miss Orlano answered the door of Number 409 and once again, it was with a scowl. But she grudgingly showed them into the front parlor, where Sofia DelVecchio sat with a young and very attractive blonde who introduced herself as Laura Edwards and who became protective when

Sigrid explained that they were there with a couple of simple questions.

"I think my dad wanted to be here if you needed to question my grandmother again."

"Yes," Sigrid said, speaking to Mrs. DelVecchio, "and if you would rather call him and ask him to meet you at my office, we can certainly do that. Our questions are the same for Miss Orlano and Mr. Salvador, so they will have to come as well."

Mrs. DelVecchio gave an annoyed sigh. "Ask your questions."

Sam Hentz handed her the list that Tillie had drawn up. "Do you recognize any of these names?"

Mrs. DelVecchio's reading glasses hung from her neck by a slender gold chain and as she put them on, her granddaughter leaned forward to read the list over her shoulder.

"Who *are* these people and why am I supposed to know them?"

"We think one of them knew your godson. He had a car key and a parking ticket for a car that might have belonged to one of these names. It would simplify things if you recognized which name that might be."

The older woman shook her head and handed the list to her housekeeper, who had joined them. "Orla?"

Those bushy eyebrows seemed to bristle and came together in an annoyed V as she squinted at the list. "No, I don't know any of these."

"Are you sure?"

The young woman laughed and jumped to her feet. "Stop faking it, Orla! You know you can't read fine print without your glasses. Where are they? In the kitchen?"

She was back a moment later with a pair of bifocals.

Rolling her eyes, Miss Orlano lifted the paper and made an exaggerated show of reading the names aloud. She paused at one. "Toby Quaranto. I knew a Tobia Quaranto once, but he's been gone ten years, rest his soul. Besides, he lived in Brooklyn and this one says Queens."

Sigrid took the list back and said, "Where will we find Mr. Salvador?"

"I saw him through the kitchen window," Laura Edwards volunteered. "He's cleaning the koi pond. Shall I call him?"

"If you'll tell him we're here, we can meet him downstairs."

Mrs. DelVecchio gave an autocratic wave of her thin hand. "Orla? Show Lieutenant Harald through to the garden."

"You sit, Orla," said Laura Edwards, jumping to her feet again. "I'll do it,

306

Nonna."

Sigrid and Hentz followed her down the wood-paneled hallway to the kitchen and from there, out to the deck, where she called, "Sal? These people want to ask you something about Matty."

"Yeah?" He scooped a final dead leaf from the surface of the koi pond as the two detectives, trailed by the girl, joined him at the garden bench.

Once again he was dressed in green coveralls, and with his shaggy gray head and slightly stooped shoulders, he reminded Hentz more strongly than ever of the dwarf in Wagner's *Ring* cycle — a good-natured Alberich, who propped his net against the bench and gave them a friendly smile of recognition.

They explained why they were there and gave him the list but he began shaking his head even before he read it. "Matty was okay, but me and him weren't tight. He was family. I was just help. We didn't hang out together and I never heard him mention any friends by name. You, Miss Laura?"

She shook her head, too. "I'm afraid not, Sal. Just Mother. Poor Matty."

"Did you see him often?" asked Hentz.

"He came to Mother's wake. That was the last time. I'm afraid he was on drugs and incoherent, so Nonna told him to stay away from the funeral. That he dishonored her memory by showing up like that."

"And before that?"

She brushed a lock of long blond hair from her face and squinted in the sunlight as she considered the question. "I forget. Maybe fall break? He'd been clean for several months then and Mother was so happy for him. Happy, but always worried that he was going to fall off the tracks again. I think they were about the same age, but he was like a kid brother that never quite grew up."

"And neither of you ever heard him mention a friend's name?"

"I think he used to volunteer at that soup kitchen around on Sixth," said Salvador. "Martha's Table. They might know."

Sigrid thanked them, and although Laura Edwards offered to take them back through the house, she said, "No, we'll go out through the garage."

Carrying his net, Sal walked ahead to open the door. As they passed the vintage Oldsmobile draped in its tarpaulin, Hentz patted the fender. "I bet it's still a sweet ride."

"You better believe it. They just don't make 'em like this anymore. The clutch is starting to slip a little, but we don't take it out enough to make it worth getting fixed yet."

"Did Matty drive it much?"

"Matty?" Sal laughed. "Naw. He learned to drive on an automatic and never got good at shifting gears. He drove Mrs. D to a charity thing once and stalled it out three times. After that, she told me never to give him the keys again."

CHAPTER 26

"So what did you think?" asked Sigrid as she clicked her seat belt and opened her notepad. "Were they telling the truth?"

"Hard to say," said Hentz, who was driving. "I didn't notice any obvious tells, did you?"

Sigrid smiled. "Widening eyes, gasps of recognition? If only." She jotted a few notes on their interview at the DelVecchio house.

"Want to swing by that soup kitchen?" asked Hentz.

"Not much point, is there? Lowry and Albee didn't learn anything when they tried again yesterday. What are we missing here, Hentz? Who's not telling us what we need to know? Two men dead. Takeouts that came from two houses. But which one killed them? Charlotte Randolph had a prescription for the right kind of Coumadin but no reason to kill Jack Bloss if she really is going to tell the whole story of her big break in her book. I'm willing to believe Mrs. DelVecchio still has some of her old pills, but where's her motive for killing her godson?"

"If anyone's not telling the whole truth, my money would be on her, though," said Hentz as he braked for a red light. Beyond the light, cabs and buses were trying to make four lanes out of three and horns blared impatiently as pedestrians in the crosswalk threaded around turning cars. "That woman could be the snow queen."

"But her granddaughter and son-in-law seem fond of her. And don't forget that she lost her daughter only six months ago. She's probably still grieving."

"Yeah, well, everyone says Matty blamed himself for not driving Aria Edwards that day. Maybe she blamed him, too."

Sigrid was unconvinced. "I'm not saying she couldn't have done it, and poison is classically a woman's choice of method. I just don't think she would have waited six months if that were the case. So why now? What triggered this?"

As they neared the station, she spotted a Sabrett's yellow-and-blue umbrella on the corner. "Let me out here. I'm getting a hot dog for lunch. You want one?"

"Mustard and onions," he said.

■ ■ ■ ■

Although most of her team were still out running down the owners of the abandoned cars that had been scrapped, Sigrid and Hentz were not the only two who had opted for a lunch of street food. When they reached the office, Tillie was working on an enormous turkey wrap and Gonzalez had only been back long enough to unwrap a couple of egg rolls.

He dipped one end into a container of plum sauce and reported that he had come up dry on the first owner he tried to find, a Winston James Goldman. The other name on his list belonged to an elderly man who was afraid that he was going to get socked with the parking fees. "He had a bad case of pneumonia in January and was in the hospital for so long that he decided the fee was going to be more than the car was worth. His kids had been after him to quit driving anyhow. He still had his ticket, though, so it wasn't Matty's car."

Tillie had been waiting with barely concealed eagerness for Gonzalez to finish his report so that he could talk. "I think we can now say for sure which car it was, Lieutenant. A full copy of the report on the Aria

Edwards hit-and-run came in while you were out."

"And?"

"Wait'll you hear!" He wiped his mouth and fingers on a paper napkin. "It happened December sixteenth, at a few minutes past three, and the circumstances are pretty much like what we heard. Mrs. Edwards stepped off the curb at Madison and East Fifty-Third right in front of a car that was driven by a white male. It knocked her down, ran over her, and just kept going. Ran a red light and was gone. Witnesses say it was an older white sedan — either a Toyota or a Honda. No license number, although one witness thought the end number was either an eight or a six."

He handed Sigrid the report and paged through another file. "Now look at this. The parking ticket for Vic's garage is time-stamped December sixteenth at three-forty. Only thirty minutes after the incident. *And* one of those abandoned cars was a white Honda Civic with a license number ending in a three. A three could be mistaken for a six or eight, right?"

Sigrid nodded and looked at the list of the former owners that he had compiled earlier. "This Elton Denver Kapps may have been responsible for Aria Edwards's death,

313

but what was Matty doing with his parking ticket?"

There were blank looks all around.

"Who's trying to find Kapps?"

Tillie consulted his list. "That would be Urbanska."

It had been a busy morning for Detective Dinah Urbanska. The DMV's last address for Elton Denver Kapps was above a store on the Bowery that sold light fixtures.

The door that led upstairs stood open, so she stepped into the vestibule to read the names on the mailboxes.

No Kapps.

The manager and owner of Lee's Lighting was a small Chinese American woman with glossy black hair and a bright friendly smile. "Elton Kapps? And he lived here? Ah! You must mean Denny Kapps. He moved out almost eighteen months ago."

"What can you tell me about him?" Urbanska asked.

The manager shrugged her thin shoulders. "Not much. He rented one of the rooms here for less than two years. Always late with the rent. Didn't seem to have a regular job. I got tired of dunning him and asked him to leave."

"Do you know where he went?"

"Little Italy," she said promptly. "Off Delancey. He gave me the address so I could mail him back his security deposit after I'd had a chance to see if he'd done any damage. He hadn't, so I did. Let me see if I kept it."

She disappeared through a door in the back and while she was gone, Urbanska looked around the store. Dozens of fixtures hung from the ceiling. All shapes and sizes. Everything from crystal chandeliers to hammered brass and black iron. Crowding the tables and counters were lamp bases of carved wood, shiny chrome, frosted glass, and blocky ceramics that were as colorful as a box of kindergarten crayons. A forest of floor lamps were massed in one corner and at the back were shelves stacked with shades of all shapes. Ever since moving into the apartment she shared with two friends, she had wanted a lamp for reading in bed. Her room was small, though, and so was the bedside table, but here was a wall lamp with an adjustable arm that would give the necessary light without taking up any table space.

The manager returned with the address for Denny Kapps and her dark eyes alertly followed Urbanska's. "I can give you a good price on that wall lamp."

"How good?"

It was a very good price indeed and as Urbanska pulled out her credit card, the woman said, "You'll probably want a narrow rectangular shade so you can push the arm up against the wall out of your way when the lamp's not in use. Let me show you what we have."

Jim Lowry and Elaine Albee each returned empty-handed shortly before one o'clock.

"The Mercedes' owner of record died last year," said Lowry, "and his widow gave the car to her grandson. He told her someone had stolen it, but she didn't seem surprised to hear it had been involved in a drug deal. She says she never heard of Matty Mutone and she has no idea where her grandson is."

Albee had a similar report. "The Pinto's owner got married several months ago and took her husband's name, which is why her new address didn't show up in DMV's records. She said the car was a total lemon and she just wanted to be rid of it. Leaving it at a garage seemed as good a way as any. That was around Hanukkah, she said, which would be about a week before the date on the ticket, so there wouldn't be a connection with Mutone."

Detective Urbanska joined them a few

minutes later carrying a large white plastic bag in one hand and a fruit salad in the other. Several strands of golden brown hair had come loose from their clips. Before she could reach her desk, the corner of her bag sent the open container of Gonzalez's plum sauce into his lap.

"Dammit, Urbanska!" he said, trying to wipe the sticky mess off his khaki slacks before heading to the lavatory.

"Sorry, sorry, sorry!" she wailed.

Hentz deflected the bag from his coffee cup as she passed and the others watched as she stowed it in the kneehole of her own desk without doing further damage.

"Any luck?" Hentz asked.

"The owner of the white Honda wasn't at home," she said, "but I did get the name of his parole officer."

"Parole officer?" asked Sigrid.

"Yes, ma'am. The super at his building said he got out about two weeks ago."

She flipped open her notepad and passed it to Tillie. "Maybe you can contact him?"

Gonzalez returned with a large wet spot on the upper leg of his pants.

While they finished eating lunch and batted the known facts of the case back and forth, Tillie was listening on the phone and making notes as he ate. When he hung up, he was shaking his head in wonder. "Elton Denver Kapps was sentenced to eighteen months for aggravated assault. He was paroled, but then violated his parole and was picked up last December — December seventeenth, the day *after* the hit-and-run, to be exact — and sent back to prison. He got out about ten days ago and is currently doing community service as a condition of his early release. Guess where?"

"Oh, my God!" Elaine Albee exclaimed. "Martha's Table?"

"That Denny we talked to yesterday was Elton Denver Kapps?" asked Jim Lowry.

"Go bring him in," said Sigrid, tossing the remains of her hot dog into the nearest wastebasket.

CHAPTER 27

Denny Kapps sat at the table in the interview room and stared at the two-way mirror as if he could see the officers on the other side. Even though Urbanska knew he couldn't, it was still a bit unnerving to the young detective when he looked straight at her and grinned.

"How long's this cat-and-mouse game gonna go on till somebody tells me why I'm here?" he asked.

His eyes were a clear bright blue and a cowlick at the upper right edge of his hairline gave his thin face an appealing boyishness even though his rap sheet put his age at twenty-six. "And don't be fooled by his wide-eyed look of innocence," his parole officer had warned them. "He'll trade on his good looks if you let him."

Small chance of that working with Lt. Harald, thought Hentz as they entered the interview room and took seats across the table from Kapps.

She came straight to the point with him. "You're the owner of a white 1980 Honda Civic?"

"Yeah. Hey! You found it?"

"Found it?"

"I reported it a week ago."

"When did you last see it?" Hentz asked.

"Well, to be honest, not since back in December. See, what happened is that I lent it to a guy I met at Martha's Table, one of those guys you people found dead on that bench on Sixth. Matty Somebody. He needed a car in a hurry, but before he could give me the key back, I got picked up and sent back to prison. When I got out last week, I went looking for him. They hadn't seen him for a while at the soup kitchen, and then next thing I heard, he was dead, so I figured somebody stole my car."

"Yeah? Why would you lend your car to somebody you barely knew?"

"Because I was behind on my rent and he paid me forty dollars."

"When was this?"

"December sixteenth. I know because I got picked up on the seventeenth."

"So why didn't you tell us this when we questioned you at the soup kitchen?"

"I just got out of prison and you come

320

asking about a guy who's just been murdered? I didn't want to get mixed up in it, okay?"

Hentz exchanged a skeptical look with Sigrid, who said, "On December the sixteenth, your car was involved in a hit-and-run on Madison Avenue. You want to tell us about that?"

"Huh?"

"You ran over a woman and then fled the scene."

"What? No, that wasn't me! I told you. I lent my car to Matty."

As Denny Kapps sat there, vigorously shaking his head in denial, Sigrid realized that they had it all wrong. If Denny had stashed his car in that garage, why would Matty have the parking ticket? And why would he have the car key?

"You're sure you didn't see Matty after you got out of prison?"

"Positive. No one knew where he was. They said he was living on the street, that he was into meth pretty heavy, but I couldn't seem to catch up with him. If it really was my car that hit somebody, he was the one driving. Not me. Honest."

Sigrid stood up abruptly. "Thank you for your help, Mr. Kapps. That will be all. You're free to go."

"Wait a minute! That's it? You hauled me in just for this? Where's my car? You guys impound it?"

"Sorry," Hentz said, and explained what had happened to the Honda.

"They *scrapped* it? Why? It ran like a top. I kept it tuned myself. Who the hell told that guy he could scrap it? I'll sue the bastard."

"I don't understand," said Dinah Urbanska. "Why would Matty kill his cousin? Everybody says he was crazy about her. And why borrow a car to do it?"

"Do we know for certain that the DelVecchio car really did break down that day?" asked Tillie. "Or was it so he could drive a different car that might not get connected to him?"

With his penchant for details, he had added the pertinent December dates to the timeline on their whiteboard.

"We've been told Aria Edwards came into the city to spend a few days with Mrs. DelVecchio and do some Christmas shopping," Sigrid said. "Did she spend any time with Matty?"

"Maybe something happened between them," said Elaine Albee. She frowned at the timeline. "He supposedly went off the rails and started using speed the day after the accident because he was so torn up over her death. What if he actually started the day *before* and they fought so that he ran her down in some drug-induced rage?"

Sigrid listened as they batted theories back and forth, but none of them felt right to her. "Let's not overthink this," she said. "Maybe Aria Edwards's death really was an accident. Matty was supposed to pick her up that afternoon but the car was out of commission. So he borrows Kapps's car. That model — a 1980 Honda Civic. Would that be a manual drive or an automatic?"

"Probably a manual," Tillie said promptly.

"Well, damn!" said Hentz, who saw where she was going. "Sal told us he wasn't allowed to drive that Oldsmobile because he couldn't shift gears without stalling out every time."

Like the others, Elaine Albee was suddenly picturing the scene in her head. "He could have called her. Told her what car he'd be driving. It was snowing, though. The streets would've been slippery."

"So when she saw him, she stepped off the curb," said Lowry, "and instead of clutching and braking, he hit the gas instead and ran over her. Then panicked and ran."

"No wonder he started using meth again,"

Urbanska said softly.

Sigrid nodded. "Everyone says he blamed himself for Aria's death. What if he was telling the truth? But that was six months ago. So who killed Matty? And why now?"

It was the one question she wound up asking herself in every homicide that wasn't a slam dunk open-and-shut. Why now? Why not yesterday? Why not last week or tomorrow?

Murder in the heat of the moment seldom gave them problems. It was the dish served cold that sent them running down blind alleys.

There must have been a catalyst that provoked this murder.

Of course, she thought, looking at the timeline on their whiteboard. "Gonzalez, see if you can catch Kapps and bring him back. And, Tillie, get us a search warrant for the DelVecchio house. Let's find out if Mrs. DelVecchio's old Coumadin pills really did get thrown out last December."

In the attic of the Breul House, Dorothy Reddish pushed back her chair and stood up to stretch and bend. Her joints felt stiff after sitting so long. Determined to try and figure out what Dr. Shambley might have hoped to find, she had gone through the first file cabinet with no success. Nor had the top two drawers of the second one yielded anything. But when she sat down and opened the drawer that was in easy reach of the chair Shambley had used, she immediately saw that something had been crammed into one of the folders. Instead of single sheets of papers listing invoices and inventories and bills of lading, there were more than a dozen thick envelopes. All had "E. Breul" in the return address but with different European cities.

She laid them on the desk before her and a frisson of excitement ran through her as she realized that this blocked stack might have left that impression on the second embroidered glove case that had turned up around the time of Shambley's death. Letters from Erich Breul, Junior? Why had Shambley hidden them here in a file cabinet instead of taking them to the director who preceded her here?

Hardly daring to breathe, she took the pink satin case out of the drawer, freed it from the tissue paper in which Mrs. Beardsley had so carefully wrapped it, and slipped the envelopes inside.

A perfect fit!

The fourteen envelopes had European stamps and the 1912 postmarks were consistent with Erich Junior's *wanderjahr* after he finished college. His handwriting was quite legible and Reddish skimmed through them until she was stopped dead in her tracks by a letter written in August of that year. That was when the dutiful Erich Junior finally seemed to have strayed from the list of activities set out by Erich Senior. He had bought a bicycle, somehow acquired a monkey, and was cycling along the Rhone River when an enormous white dog popped up of nowhere, barking so ferociously that he had crashed his bicycle into the nearest tree. And who should come to his rescue but two impoverished artists who were spending the summer there. One was French, a cyclist himself and most apologetic about Erich Junior's twisted front wheel. The other was the dog's owner, a Spanish animal lover who coaxed the frightened monkey down from the tree.

Georges Braque and Pablo Picasso.

When the village blacksmith said he would have to send to Orange for the parts needed to repair the bicycle, they insisted that Erich Junior come home with them. Upon hearing that it was his birthday, they toasted him with a bottle of wine, then set about creating a portrait of him and the monkey, using what they called *papier collé.* Dinner that evening sounded like a raucous wine-filled celebration when they presented him with the finished collage. In return, he gave his bicycle to Braque, his monkey to Picasso, and caught the morning train to Lyons with the collage tied up in brown paper.

Instead of returning to the conventional paths his father had prescribed, however, he seemed to have spent as much time among the artists of Montmartre as in the venerable Louvre.

Wow! thought Reddish. *Could that collage be what Shambley had searched for? Perhaps even found?*

She put the letters back in the satin glove case and went looking for Mrs. Beardsley.

Sofia DelVecchio looked around the sleek uncluttered great room of the house her husband had given his mistress all those years ago. So much chrome and glass and shiny surfaces, the neutral whites broken only by pots of greenery and the large colorful abstract canvases that hung on the walls. A rear wall of glass flooded the space with natural light and brought the garden into the room.

She was thrown off balance by the contrast between the traditional middle-class home she had shared with her unfaithful husband

and this theatrical setting his mistress had created. "Benito *liked* this?"

"He never saw it," said Charlotte Randolph. "I didn't tear out the walls and redecorate until after he was gone. But you're right. He would have hated it. When I painted over the dark wood paneling, he wanted to put it back the way it was." She gave Sofia a wry smile. "You smashed my records, I smashed your walls."

"And you think that makes us even?"

"Oh, for God's sake, Sofia, can't we let it go? Benny's been dead more than twenty-five years —"

"Thirty years," the other woman snapped.

"Is it that long?"

"You don't know? Oh, but then you took another woman's husband before the year was out, didn't you?"

"You were the widow, Sofia, not me. You could follow his hearse to the cemetery and wear black for a year. I had to sing two nights later."

"The voice again," Sofia sneered, stung by the undeniable truth that she had never earned a single penny in her whole eighty-two years, while Charlotte had enjoyed a career that brought her both fame and wealth. More wealth than she herself now enjoyed.

Money had flowed when Benito was alive and he had lavished it on his wife and daughter, but he had also lavished it on his women and his lieutenants. *Those damned Oldsmobiles to ensure their loyalty!* Even though she had cut back on servants after his death, very little remained by the time Aria was grown. She'd had to sell some of her jewelry to pay for Aria's wedding. Without her son-in-law's sound financial advice, the house would have had to go years ago and she might now be living in an in-law apartment in his and Aria's house. In Riverhead of all places, not here in Manhattan.

"Why did you come, Sofia?" Charlotte asked abruptly. They were both still standing. Sofia had refused to sit and Charlotte did not intend to let the other woman tower over her. "Surely it wasn't just to insult me?"

"Laura wants me to ask you to give her voice lessons."

"What? *You* ask *me*? That's absurd."

"She's under the impression that we're friends."

"Why on earth would she think that?"

"You came to the house. She brought you something from me. You had her sing for you."

"She said she wanted to sing on stage. I

329

was curious to hear if she had a voice."

"Does she?"

Charlotte gave a noncommittal shrug. "It's on the thin side, but she can carry a tune and could probably learn how to project. She's a pretty child and with a little luck, she might well have a stage career. Not opera, but maybe musical comedy."

"And you're just the one to help her, aren't you?"

Charlotte stared at her old rival in dawning comprehension. "Don't tell me you're afraid I'm going to take her from you."

"You're the glamorous one," Sofia said bitterly. "You'll charm her the way you charmed Benito. You'll wave your magic voice and give her a career."

"Wrong, wrong, *wrong!*" Charlotte stamped her small foot for emphasis. "Yes, I could probably get a casting director to give her an audition, but a career takes talent and the willingness to work for it. If you think I want to take her on as a protégée, think again. She's your granddaughter, not mine, and it's time you got over thinking I'm your enemy. Yes, Benny and I had three or four good years. Yes, he liked to come to the Met and hear me sing. In the end, though, he was just as unfaithful to me as he was to you." Her voice softened. "And

330

from the very beginning, I knew that you were the one he would have grown old with if he'd had the chance. I was so jealous of you."

"Jealous of *me*? Really?"

"Yes, really." Charlotte's blue eyes were steady and unwavering and tinged with such sorrow and regret that Sofia felt something loosen in her heart. All these years, she had hated this woman, but now — ? She could almost pity her because her words were true — Benito *had* always come back to her. To *her,* not to Charlotte.

"Tell your granddaughter that you tried, but I wouldn't budge," Charlotte said. "And that I don't want to be bothered again."

"As you wish."

Wrapped in a mantle of proud dignity, Sofia turned to go with the hint of a smug smile on her lips.

Afterward, Charlotte mixed herself a martini, propped Benny's picture on a stack of books, and lifted her glass to him. Critics had always praised her acting as warmly as her singing and it was gratifying to know that she could still fake sincerity so convincingly.

How would it benefit Sofia to know that she had become rather tired of Benny as their first passions cooled? That it had not overly grieved her when he was killed? Kinder to let Sofia believe that she had won the battle. He really had been a handsome devil, though, and in the beginning, knowing that he controlled such dark forces only added spice to their affair. Later, her voice and her growing reputation made him jealous and his possessiveness smothered her. It had been too dangerous to look elsewhere here in the city, but those European tours! *Tomás, Andre, Kallistos.* Their faces tumbled through her memory. *But what was the name of that musical director in Vienna? Whose were those long fingers that caressed my body?*

She could see his face, but what was his name?

"A collage?" Mrs. Beardsley turned from changing Erich Senior's cufflinks.

"Early cubism," Dr. Reddish said encouragingly. "It would have looked something like a human figure and maybe a monkey somewhere. Perhaps on his shoulder or in his lap."

"No, it was a monkey face," said Mrs. Beardsley. "One of Pascal's posters."

"Who's Pascal?"

"He was our caretaker here. Such a sweet boy." The older woman's voice was indulgent. "His mind stopped growing when he was ten or eleven, but he was a very competent caretaker and janitor. Much more willing and helpful than that Jeb we have now. Just yesterday, I asked him to —"

"Posters," Reddish reminded her gently.

"Yes. Dr. Kimmelshue. Two directors before you. There's a box of rolled-up posters in the basement. Museums and art galleries used to send them to us all the time. Dr. Kimmelshue told Pascal that he could take any he wanted to tack up on his wall. Most of the ones he chose were representational, but that one must have appealed to him because of the monkey."

"Where is it now?" Reddish asked. "Did he take it with him when he left?"

"I don't think so. He was moving to Louisiana and he didn't have much luggage, so when I told him to leave his room exactly as he found it, I think he put all the posters back in that box. He was very literal-minded. Shall I look?"

"No, I'll do it," said Reddish, and headed downstairs to the basement that was surprisingly cool and dry.

Despite Mrs. Beardsley's criticism of the current caretaker, this warren of rooms was also quite clean. No musty smell of mildew either.

Nearest the stairs were Jeb's quarters: a bedroom, bath, and tiny kitchen galley for making coffee or warming up takeout meals. Except for a laundry room, the rest of the extensive basement was used for storage. Pictures that earlier directors had decided were not of the same quality as the ones selected to hang upstairs were covered in dust cloths. She had examined each one when she first came and was in complete agreement with those directors. Erich Breul had been an ardent collector, but his tastes could, to put it charitably, lead him astray. Too, several of the largest and most bathetic canvases, handsomely framed in gilt and gold leaf, had come from his wife's childhood home in Zurich and were meant to edify in the most saccharine way possible.

A large cardboard carton held more than a dozen rolled-up posters from some of the city's major museums. They stood on end and Dorothy Reddish quickly verified that each one was modern. She was puzzled to find two identical posters of a Léger that hung in the Guggenheim. One of them was still shrink-wrapped and had the Guggenheim's price sticker attached. No monkeyheaded poster, though.

"Can I help you, Dr. Reddish?"

She turned to see Jeb Paracha standing in

334

the doorway of his room with a vacuum cleaner in his strong brown hands. "I don't suppose there are any cubist posters hanging on your walls, are there?"

"Cubist posters?" He was clearly puzzled, but he stepped back so that she could enter.

Except for a large landscape with snow-covered mountains, the walls were bare. She described the poster she was seeking and received only a blank look.

As she turned to continue her search, he held out the vacuum cleaner. "This thing's pretty much had it. No suction. Any chance we could get a new one?"

"Speak to Miss Ruffton or Mrs. Beardsley," she said. "Maybe there's a little wiggle room left in the housekeeping budget."

Steamer trunks, large suitcases, several leather-bound wardrobe trunks along with a couple of hat trunks were stacked in a side room. No flying off to Europe with only one carry-on and a tote bag for the Breuls. Not with such long bulky dresses and all those petticoats.

According to Hope Ruffton, the luggage stored here held extra clothes and oddments from past Breuls. "Mrs. Beardsley went through them and took out anything worth using upstairs."

With rapidly diminishing hope, Dr. Reddish opened the nearest trunk and saw articles of feminine clothing, but the contents of a large steamer trunk took her breath away once she removed the upper tray that held masculine gloves, collars, ties, and socks. Underneath, the first things that hit her eye were four canvases loosely rolled together. Whoever had put them there had rolled them surface side out so to reduce the chance of cracking the paint. With trembling fingers, she laid them flat atop the nearby trunks and read the signatures: three Matisses and a pair of Légers.

In the letters, Erich Junior had described to his father some of the exhibitions he'd attended before his fatal accident. "I am sure that you, with your deep love and knowledge of pure art, would agree that these *Fauves* as they are called truly are 'wild beasts,' but I find them strangely compelling."

Oh, Junior! Reddish thought. *If only you could have known.*

These five paintings the son had collected would more than ensure the financial safety of the father's house for years to come.

Returning to the trunk, she carefully removed the books and clothes that someone had shipped back to New York after the young man's death. At the very bottom were two large sheets of white paper. Sandwiched between them so that it lay flat on the floor of the trunk was a third sheet, a collage of papers pasted onto a sheet of drawing paper. Torn pieces of newsprint, wallpaper, and even a wine label formed a roughly human shape, topped with the cubistic face of a monkey.

It was signed in charcoal on the back in two clearly different hands: *"A notre petit singe américain — Picasso et G. Braque."*

Her first happiness was for the house. Her second was the memory of Elliott Buntrock saying, "Maybe you'll get to write your own book."

She couldn't wait to tell him how right he was.

CHAPTER 28

While Tillie went to get a search warrant, Detective Gonzalez sprinted after Denny Kapps.

"He used the restroom and then he asked where the nearest bus stop was, so maybe I can still catch him," he said.

Ten minutes later, he was back with a thoroughly pissed Kapps in tow.

"He was in line at the Sabrett's wagon," Gonzalez said triumphantly.

"What's with you people?" Kapps complained. "You dragged me down here before I could eat lunch at Martha's, and now you haul me in again before I can get a hot dog?"

"We'll buy you two hot dogs," Sigrid said, reaching into the pocket of her white slacks.

Into her empty pocket.

Hentz grinned and handed her a ten.

"Just a few more questions, Mr. Kapps. Your car. Was it an automatic or a manual?"

"Manual," he answered promptly. "The

gears might've started to slip a little, but there was nothing wrong with it and that asshole shouldn't have scrapped it."

"Tell us again how you happened to lend your car to Matty Mutone."

Kapps rolled his eyes. "What else is there to tell? He came into Martha's about noon that day. Said he needed a car in a hurry and offered me forty bucks to lend him mine. I gave him the keys and told him where it was parked. He was supposed to bring it back next day, but then, like I said, I got picked up and sent to Rikers."

"Did he say why he needed a car in such a hurry?"

"I dunno. Something about having to pick somebody up in Midtown. He didn't say who. I thought maybe his girlfriend?"

Sigrid looked down at her notes. "You told us that you got out Saturday before last and went looking for Matty. Where did you look and who did you talk to?"

He shrugged. "I asked around. They told me at the soup kitchen that he was back on the street, back on speed, and that he'd come in to eat there off and on. They also said that he had people up on Vanderbock across from that diner."

"Did you go to the house on Vander-bock?"

"Didn't know which one it was, did I? But I asked about him at the diner and one of the guys there said he knew Matty. I asked him if he'd seen him with my car."

"Get his name?" asked Hentz.

"I don't remember. Al, maybe?"

"Could it be Sal?"

"Sal? Yeah! That's it! Little short guy, big head of hair. Said Matty didn't have a car, though."

"Did you describe it to him?"

"Yeah. A 1980 white Honda Civic. Said he hadn't seen it. Hey! That why you asked if it was a manual?"

"What do you mean?"

" 'Cause that's what that Sal asked. Said Matty wasn't good with manuals."

Sigrid glanced at the timeline again. "What day was this?"

"Last Tuesday morning. I stopped in for coffee."

"Did you go to the house then? Talk to the housekeeper or the woman who was Matty's godmother?"

"Godmother?" He shook his head. "When this Sal said Matty didn't have my car and he hadn't seen him in a couple of weeks, I decided to wait till he showed up at Martha's Table again."

"Thank you, Mr. Kapps," Sigrid said, and

handed him Hentz's ten. "Enjoy your lunch."

"I'm sorry, Dr. Bohr," said Mrs. Bayles, "but Mr. Livingston's at lunch right now. May I take a message?"

"Well, he seemed in such a rush that I shepherded the DNA samples through the testing myself. Tell him there's no doubt in my mind that we have a perfect match."

"So Vincent Haas really is Oscar Nauman's natural son?"

There was a long silence.

"Perhaps you should have Mr. Livingston call me," said Dr. Bohr, and gave her his personal number.

The first thing Sofia DelVecchio noticed upon leaving Charlotte Randolph's house were two police cars parked in front of her own house and a small knot of curious onlookers across the street. The second was her granddaughter Laura, who broke into a run toward her as soon as she saw Sofia, her pretty young face twisted in a mixture of fear and anger.

"Nonna! Where were you? Come quick!"

"What's wrong?" she asked, alarmed.

"The police are tearing the house apart. I tried to make them wait till I could call

341

Dad, but they wouldn't. He's on his way but it'll be another thirty minutes before he can get here."

"What are they looking for?"

"They won't say and they're going to arrest Orla if she doesn't get out of the way so they can search your room."

"Cretina!" Sofia murmured, and hurried down the sidewalk.

As she entered her house, a uniformed officer came down the stairs with a firm hold on Miss Orlano's arm. Her housekeeper was struggling and cursing him in Italian.

"Basta, Orla!" Sofia said sternly.

"Signora!" Orla cried, and burst into tearful Italian.

"In English, Orla."

"They're going through your room! Opening drawers, touching your things. How can they do this? Can't Mr. George make them go away?"

Sofia looked up the stairs and saw Sigrid on the landing. "Lieutenant Harald. What's happening?"

"I'm sorry," she said, "but we do have a search warrant."

"Then tell me what you're looking for so we can end this."

"That bottle of Coumadin you stopped

taking last winter." Sigrid motioned for the officer to let go of Miss Orlano. "It's the same formulation that killed your godson and the other man."

Released, the old woman hobbled over to her employer. "It's not here. I have remembered for sure. I *did* throw it away, just after Christmas."

"Then there's nothing to worry about, is there?" Sigrid said.

Number 409 was a three-story house. Even with her whole team searching, there were so many places in which to conceal a small pill bottle that George Edwards made it in from Riverhead about ten minutes before they found it.

Empty.

"Where was it?" Sigrid asked when Dina Urbanska brought her the little orange plastic bottle.

"In the toe of a shoe in her closet."

"Whose closet?"

Urbanska nodded toward the housekeeper. "Miss Orlano's."

"Orla?" said George Edwards.

The elderly woman shook her head and tears streamed down her wrinkled face, her bushy gray eyebrows drawn together in misery.

"It was still in her medicine cabinet when

you came asking for it last week," she told Sigrid. "I hid it so you would not think she was the one who poisoned Matty's food."

"Why would I think that, Miss Orlano?"

"Because of Aria."

George Edwards's head swung around sharply. "What?" His acne-scarred face was furrowed with surprise.

His daughter seemed equally bewildered. "Orla? What do you mean? How does Mother have anything to do with this?"

"Orla!" Sofia DelVecchio's voice cut through the other voices like a whiplash. *"Dimmi la verità!"*

"La verità?" Orla whimpered. *"La verità es Matty. Lui l'ha uccisa. Quando —"*

"In English, Orla. Now!"

"Wait a minute, Sofia," said George Edwards. "Orla, as your attorney, I'm advising you to say nothing more."

"As you wish," Sigrid said. "Where's Mr. Salvador?"

"Sal? Why do you want him?"

"He and Miss Orlano were, by their own statements, the only two to touch the takeout carton from Giuseppone's. She served herself and Mrs. DelVecchio from it out here in the kitchen and Mr. Salvador was the one who took it to Matty. I'd like to hear what he has to say."

"I think he's in the kitchen," said Laura Edwards.

"I'll get him," said Detective Hentz, and went down the hallway.

Sigrid followed. "We'll question him out there."

"I'll come, too," said Edwards.

"Are you representing him as well?"

"And anybody else in this house who needs me, Lieutenant."

Sofia DelVecchio, Laura Edwards, and a distraught Orla were told to wait in the living room under Dinah Urbanska's watchful eyes.

The handyman sat at the kitchen table and looked up apprehensively as Sigrid and her team entered and closed the door to the hallway. He had been weeding the flowerbeds when Orla warned him that the police were there. His shaggy pepper-and-salt hair was damp from the heat and sweat dampened the back of his dark green coveralls as well. His grass-stained hands left dirty marks on the glass of ice water on the table before him.

"What's going on, Mr. George?"

"They have more questions, Sal, but if it's something you shouldn't answer, I'll tell you."

Sigrid took the chair across from him and

Hentz sat down next to her with his note-pad and tape recorder.

"Mr. Salvador, we were told that when you were in the diner last week, someone came in looking for Matty and you said you knew him. Is that correct?"

"Yes," he admitted cautiously. "Why?"

"Did you two talk?"

"Yeah. Why?"

"What about?"

"He said he'd let Matty use his car back before Christmas and did I know where it was?"

"And did you?"

"No. Last time I saw Matty, he was push-ing a grocery cart. No car. Then when the guy told me what kind of car it was, I said Matty wouldn't keep it. He never really got the hang of a stick shift. Stalled it out every time. As for where the car was, I told him Matty'd been back on drugs for the last six months and probably couldn't remember that far back."

"And then?"

Sal shrugged. "Then nothing. The guy said he'd try to catch up with Matty at the soup kitchen and left." He pulled a paper napkin from the holder on the table and wiped the mud from his glass.

"Did you repeat that conversation to

anybody else?"

Sal shook his head and finished drinking his ice water.

"You're sure?"

"Come to think of it, I might've told Orla. It was funny that Matty would borrow a car he'd have a lot of trouble driving."

"And when did you tell her this?"

"Last Tuesday. Around lunchtime. I remember because she said she'd run into Matty that morning. When he saw her, he started crying again. Still blaming himself for Miss Aria." He gave the lawyer a sympathetic look. "Sorry, Mr. George, but you know how he was always going on about how he should've been driving her that day."

"Yes, Sal." Edwards had loosened his tie and now ran a handkerchief across his homely pockmarked face. His voice was sad. "I know."

"And what did she say when you told her about the car?" Sigrid asked.

Sal shrugged. "Nothing. She was unloading the dishwasher and all of a sudden a plate slipped out of her hand and smashed all over the floor, so after that, we were cleaning up glass. First time I ever saw her break anything."

"That evening, you were the one who went to Giuseppone's for takeouts, right?"

He nodded. "Just like every Tuesday. Chicken or veal for me and a double order of some sort of pasta for Mrs. D and Orla, so that there'd be enough to send down for Matty, too. I had the chicken parmigiana last Tuesday and they had fettuccine."

"Did you eat your supper here in the kitchen?"

"No, I took it downstairs to watch television. I didn't come back up till Orla called me. She was supposed to take the carton down to Matty, but her arthritis was bothering her so much she asked me to do it and I did. But like I told you people, Matty wasn't there yet. Just the other guy. Eating lasagna. So I left the box with him."

"And?"

"And what? That was it. I came back here."

"Did you look back before you turned the corner?"

"Oh yeah, that's right. I saw him opening our box."

"Even though you'd made it clear that the food was for Matty?"

"I didn't think it really mattered. A lot of times, Matty never even came."

"Thank you, Mr. Salvador. One of my officers will transcribe this conversation and we'll need you to stop by and sign it tomorrow."

Sal looked up at the lawyer. "Okay for me to do that, Mr. George?"

"Yes, Sal." He exhaled deeply, almost as if he hadn't breathed for the last five minutes. "I suppose you'll want to question Orla now, Lieutenant?"

Sigrid nodded. "And I suppose you'll advise her not to answer?"

But they were too late.

"I tried to tell her not to speak," Urbanska said, "but she wasn't under arrest and I couldn't Mirandize her and once she started talking, she wouldn't stop."

All three of the women seemed traumatized. Mrs. DelVecchio was white-faced, Miss Orlano looked shattered, and Laura Edward burst into tears as she rushed to her father's arms.

"Matty was the one who ran over Mother!" she sobbed. "And Orla poisoned him for it."

"She should have told me," said Mrs. DelVecchio, "and I would have done it myself. I don't care what it takes, George. You *cannot* let Orla go to prison."

"We'll start with bail and go from there," he said as Lowry stepped forward with

349

handcuffs. "Are those really necessary?"

Lowry looked at Sigrid. "Lieutenant?"

"No handcuffs," she said. "Just read her her rights."

CHAPTER 29

"So your killer's a seventy-five year-old arthritic woman?" Captain McKinnon asked when Sigrid briefed him that afternoon.

"Her attorney's already posted bail and will probably be filing continuances or appeals until we all die of old age, but that's the DA's problem, not ours."

"Are you sorry it wasn't Benny Olds's widow?"

"Not really. Sofia DelVecchio may be living on the last of his dirty money, but she wasn't the one who ran his organization and it can't have been easy for her. Giving his glamorous mistress a house only a few doors from them? How humiliating is that?"

"She was pretty glamorous herself," Mac reminded her. "Although a beautiful blond, full-fledged opera star must've been pretty stiff competition."

Sigrid nodded. "Their daughter was her

hole card. Everyone says Benny was crazy about her from the moment she was born. They all were, especially Miss Orlano. She was the nursemaid, the one who got up to give the baby a bottle every night because she wouldn't nurse . . ."

Her voice trailed off and her eyes held a faraway look.

"What?" said Mac.

She came back with a start. "Sir?"

"You seemed to be remembering something."

Sigrid shook her head and smiled. "Just thinking about the baby birds my housemate found in our bushes. Did Mother tell you about them?"

"And how one of the eggs was from a different bird?" He chuckled. "Like bringing home an extra baby from the hospital. You'd think the parents could tell."

"Not if there's enough similarity," Sigrid said, remembering how Sofia DelVecchio's hair had started off light brown, yet became spun gold before it turned white.

Strictly speaking, it was none of the department's business, but on her way home, Sigrid yielded to curiosity and detoured to Number 403 Vanderbock. Charlotte Randolph herself answered the doorbell.

"I should have called," Sigrid apologized, "but I thought you might like to know that we've arrested someone for poisoning the pasta that killed your friend."

"I saw the police cars in front of the DelVecchio house," said Randolph, gesturing for Sigrid to enter. "Was it Sofia?"

"No. Her housekeeper. A Miss Orlano."

Sigrid followed her across the wide airy space and took a seat on one of the white couches.

"So Jack wasn't the intended victim?"

"No. It was the other one, Mrs. DelVecchio's godson."

"I want to hear all the details, Lieutenant, but first I want a glass of wine. I don't suppose there's any point in offering you a glass?"

"I'm off duty now."

Charlotte Randolph disappeared behind the mirrored screen. There was a clink of glassware and the woman returned with two wine goblets and a bottle of Riesling.

"Did you know Miss Orlano?" Sigrid asked.

"Orla? I knew who she was, of course. Benny hired her when his daughter was born and I saw her pushing the baby carriage occasionally. She knew about Benny and me and she still gives me the evil eye if we pass on the sidewalk. Very loyal to Sofia. I didn't let it bother me then and I don't now, but I shan't miss her. So what was the other man to her? Why poison his food?"

"He was Mrs. DelVecchio's godson," Sigrid said, and gave her an encapsulated account of how Matty Mutone had been responsible for Aria Edwards's death last December.

"Poor man," Randolph said. "And poor Orla. Benny used to say she idolized Aria."

They sipped their wine in silent contemplation until Sigrid said, "Will you write about this in your book?"

"I don't think so. It's not a part of my story."

"Really? Wasn't Aria your baby?"

Randolph had set her empty glass on the table and was reaching for the bottle, so even though Sigrid had clearly startled her, nothing was spilled or broken. "Why on earth would you think that?"

"Benny Olds named his daughter Aria. You said this house was a *quid pro quo* and that he gave it to you around the time she was born. Miss Orlano told me that when she came to Number 409, all the servants had quit or been fired and no new ones were hired until after the baby was born. She also said that the baby refused to nurse and had to be bottle-fed. It made me wonder if the servants had been let go earlier so that they couldn't talk and that the reason the baby didn't nurse was because Sofia wasn't her mother."

"Is this something you'll put in your report?"

Sigrid shook her head. "No."

"I have your word on that?"

"You have my word."

Charlotte Randolph topped off both their glasses and leaned back onto the white cushions with a deep sigh. "We never told. Even Orla doesn't know."

She paused and took a swallow of the pale golden wine.

"When I realized that I was pregnant, I wanted to get an abortion but Benny and Sofia had tried to have a baby for years, with no success. Benny said he'd make all the arrangements and give me this house if I'd carry it to term and then let them have the baby. I certainly didn't want a child. Not then and not now. I told my agent that I had polyps on my vocal cords and that the top specialist was in Rome. My sister and I stayed over there till I was near term. Then we flew home to this house. Sofia pretended to be having a difficult pregnancy and had stayed in her room the last two months. If she had to come down, she wore a small round pillow under her maternity smock. No one saw her except when she was wrapped up in a comforter. Benny even fired all the servants in case they suspected something. When the time came, my sister called Benny and he and Sofia took me to the hospital. They checked me in under Sofia's name and she kept out of sight until it was time to bring the baby home. Sofia was a good mother and she loved the child."

"You never regretted your decision?"

"Not for one single moment."

"You don't want to tell Laura Edwards that you're her grandmother?"

"Good God, no!"

CHAPTER 30

With an arrest made and mellowed by the wine she'd drunk, Sigrid was looking forward to a quiet evening with that new book of poetry she'd picked up at BookExpo on Saturday.

Upon unlocking her front door, though, she walked into a noisy, smoke-filled hall. Roman Tramegra stood on a stepstool to silence the smoke alarm on the ceiling.

"What happened?" she asked, leaving the door open to help the smoke dissipate.

"I always do this," her housemate fumed. "I mean to leave the kitchen just for a minute and the next thing I know . . . I'm so sorry, my dear. It was going to be Cornish game hens *en croute* with asparagus puree tonight. Now, I'm afraid it'll have to be takeout. Would you like Italian, Mexican, or Chinese?"

Before she could answer, the phone rang and it was Marcus Livingston, who invited her to join him for dinner. "Vincent Haas is flying back to Austria day after tomorrow and I thought a bon voyage party might not be amiss. At Madigan's. Let him taste the best steak in the city before he leaves."

"Does this mean he's not Nauman's son?"

"It does."

For a moment, Sigrid couldn't decide if she was pleased or sorry. "You said *party*. Who else is coming?"

"Just Elliott Buntrock and Rudy Gottfried."

"May I bring a friend with me? Elliott knows him."

"By all means."

On the walk over to the restaurant, which was just a few blocks south of them on the river, Sigrid told Roman about Vincent Haas and his claim to be Nauman's son.

"My dear Sigrid. No wonder you've seemed so distracted. How very distressing for you this must have been," Roman said. "Will tonight be a wake?"

"What do you mean?"

"That poor man must have thought he'd be going home a millionaire and now, not only is he *not* Oscar's son, he may never learn who his real father is."

■ ■ ■ ■

Madigan's was a turn-of-the-century tavern and chophouse with absolutely no pretensions of trendiness. Back in the days of sailing ships, laboring dockworkers had eaten and drunk here and its clientele was still more blue collar than white. Dirty sawdust soaked up any spilled beverages and the air was thick with the smells of beer, cigarettes, and grilled meat. The high-backed wooden booths were slightly sticky but more than roomy enough to hold six people. How it could pass a sanitary inspection was anyone's guess, but when she mentioned this to Marcus once, he had laughed and said, "If they ever get cited, I'll defend them pro bono."

Like Marcus, Sigrid had been introduced to this relic of old New York by Oscar Nauman. Indeed, this was where they'd first eaten. In their short time together, he had taken her everywhere from four-star restaurants in midtown to dim sum places in Chinatown and a gyro stand in Times Square, but he'd had a special fondness for this scruffy old restaurant and it did serve the best steaks she'd ever tasted. She had avoided it since his death, but somehow it felt right to come here tonight to say good-bye to the man who wasn't his son, but could have been.

Roman, of course, was enchanted. He stepped inside, took a deep breath, and immediately exclaimed in his deep bass voice, "What atmosphere! What *ambience*! I had no idea such a place still existed."

Women could no longer be legally excluded, but neither were they encouraged, so Sigrid was the only female there that night.

She and Roman were the last to arrive and the other four slid over to make room for them. She introduced Roman and gave Vincent Haas a look of sympathy. "Are you very disappointed about the DNA results?"

"A little," he admitted. "Once I met you, I knew you would do what was fair if things turned out that way, but I meant it when I said it wasn't just about money. I really did think my birth certificate was true. Now I'll never know who my biological father is. Lila certainly can't tell me." He gave a fatalistic shrug. "Oh well."

A waiter arrived with thick glass mugs of beer and a basket of rolls. His apron was stained, but the rolls were warm and crusty. They were ready to order by the time he brought beers for Sigrid and Roman. She opted for chargrilled lamb chops while the others wanted varying cuts of steak with baked potatoes.

As the meal progressed, talk turned to other subjects: the things Haas had seen and done on this trip, suggestions for how to spend his final day, the souvenirs he had bought for his daughters, and the long flight back to Austria that was facing him.

It was almost nine as the meal drew to a close, but Marcus Livingston seemed in no hurry to leave. He signaled the waiter for another round of drinks.

"None for me," said Vincent Haas. "I thought I was over my jet lag, but for some reason, I'm really tired."

"I'll help you get a cab," Rudy Gottfried said. "Don't let them take my beer. I'll be back."

Haas stood and they exchanged the usual parting pleasantries of people who did not know each other well and did not expect to meet again.

"I really do appreciate your kindness," he told Sigrid.

"He seems like a decent man," she said, watching him leave with Gottfried. "Did he want to challenge the test?"

"No," said her lawyer.

"Where did you get a sample of Nauman's

DNA? I thought Mrs. Bayles had cleared everything from the Connecticut house."

"She did." He speared a final morsel of steak with his fork. "You do know that Oscar willed his body to science?"

Sigrid nodded.

He reached across the table and squeezed her hand. "Science gave a little bit of it back."

Rudy Gottfried rejoined them a few minutes later and downed his beer in one long swallow.

"Another?" asked Livingston, who was eyeing him closely.

"Yeah, what the hell."

Roman exchanged a look of curiosity with Sigrid.

"Is something going on here?" asked Buntrock, who had also picked up on the sudden tension.

Livingston said nothing, just signaled the waiter with Gottfried's empty glass.

"I didn't tell him," Rudy said.

"Tell him what?" Sigrid asked while Roman sat silently for once and did not chime in with a dozen questions.

"I gave the lab a sample of my DNA, too. It matched."

"You and Lila Nagy?" Sigrid was stunned.

He gave her a shame-faced nod. "You're

362

going to think I betrayed Oscar, but it wasn't like that. He and Lila had a huge fight. They both said it was over. Oscar meant it. She didn't. He was gone for three days. When he came back to the loft, she tried every trick in her bag to get him back in her bed again, but none of them worked. Took her another month to face the facts and move out. I'm not proud of what happened. It was just rebound sex, though. She thought it would hurt him, but he really wouldn't have given a damn at that point. It never occurred to either of us that she was pregnant when she left New York. Maybe she really believed Oscar was the father, or maybe it was wishful thinking. Who knows?"

The waiter set a fresh beer in front of him and he drank half of it, then pushed the rest aside.

"Will you see Haas again?" Sigrid asked.

Rudy shook his head. "It's a little late to be his daddy."

"Not too late to be a grandfather to his daughters," said Buntrock.

"No, the past is past . . ." His voice trailed off into silence. "He gave me his card, but I won't write. It really is too late."

"Keep the card," Livingston advised him. "You never know."

■ ■ ■ ■

Only the brightest stars make it through Manhattan's light pollution, but the moon was nearly full and it shone brightly in the western sky as Sigrid and Roman walked home through nearly deserted streets.

"Do you ever wish you had children?" Roman asked.

Sigrid shook her head. "I like my work too much. Besides, I can't see myself as a single mother."

"You're still young. You might find someone new."

"Trying to get rid of me, Roman?"

"No!" He stopped and looked down at her earnestly. "Never that. Remember how we first met? When you thought I was a thief who had broken into Anne's apartment?"

She smiled and started to walk on but he stayed where he was.

"Then we found Tante Ophelia's house and you agreed to rent it with me?"

"Yes?"

"I don't wish to sound maudlin, my dear, but these last years have been the happiest of my entire life. I would never have written a book without you."

"It hasn't been a one-way street, Roman."

"Really?"

"Really," she said, and impulsively tucked her arm in his as they walked on.

She would always miss Nauman but that cold lump of grief she had carried around for so long was almost completely melted. Without Roman to nag and prod, to ask endless questions about police procedure, to bombard her with quirky facts about science and nature, not to mention his forays into culinary wonders, she might still be in bed with the covers over her head.

They turned west at Christopher Street and the moon met them full on, casting long shadows behind them and lighting their way ahead.

ACKNOWLEDGMENTS

Luci Zahray, aka "The Poison Lady," briefed me on the effects of blood thinners and Roy Harris told me about stage hands and their unions. I thank them both.

Thanks also to Jamie Raab, my publisher and longtime friend from the old Warner Books days, for giving me warm support and advocacy within the corporation.

To Lindsey Rose, huge gratitude. Finally! The editor I've yearned for ever since Sara Ann Freed died. I wish I had another dozen books for you.

To Vicky Bijur, my nurturing agent for more than thirty years — what absolute luck that I reviewed Jack Early's *A Creative Kind of Killer,* which led to my becoming your first client. Pure serendipity.

AUTHOR'S NOTE

I had not intended to write a final Sigrid Harald book, but those pictures that had been left stashed in the basement of the Breul House (*Corpus Christmas*) kept begging to be taken out of that trunk. And many readers wanted reassurance that Sigrid would find true peace of mind in the end. So here we are.

While each book can be read as a stand-alone, there is an arc to them as a whole. I read Dorothy L. Sayers's Lord Peter series completely out of order and can remember how delighted I was to see the dowager duchess appear for the chronologically first time when I had already met her in later books. Perhaps readers familiar with Elliott Buntrock will be similarly amused to meet him for the first time in *Corpus Christmas*.

Lila Nagy was initially mentioned in *Corpus Christmas* as well. Her story is dealt with more fully in *Fugitive Colors*.

Although the first eight books in this series were written in what was the current "now" at the time and with absolutely no regard to aging my characters, this book takes place in the 1990s, a year after *Fugitive Colors* but before *Three-Day Town.* Sigrid and Judge Deborah Knott have not met and Anne Harald has not yet married Captain McKinnon. People could still smoke in restaurants, subways still took tokens, and getting online required a dial-up service. No Google, no Facebook.

ABOUT THE AUTHOR

Margaret Maron grew up in the country near Raleigh, North Carolina. After three years in Italy and several more in Brooklyn, New York, she and her artist husband returned to the farm that has been in her family for over a hundred years and she began writing a series based on her own background. The first book, *Bootlegger's Daughter,* became a *Washington Post* bestseller that swept the major mystery awards for its year — winning the Edgar, Agatha, Anthony, and Macavity Awards for Best Novel — and is among the 100 Favorite Mysteries of the Century as selected by the Independent Mystery Booksellers Association. She is also the author of nine Sigrid Harald detective novels. In 2008, Maron received the North Carolina Award for Literature, the highest civilian honor the state bestows on its authors. In 2013, the Mystery Writers of America celebrated Maron's contributions to the mystery genre by naming her a Grand Master — an honor first bestowed on Agatha Christie; and in 2016, she was inducted into the North Carolina Literary Hall of Fame. To find out more about her, visit MargaretMaron.com.

The employees of Thorndike Press hope you have enjoyed this Large Print book. All our Thorndike, Wheeler, and Kennebec Large Print titles are designed for easy reading, and all our books are made to last. Other Thorndike Press Large Print books are available at your library, through selected bookstores, or directly from us.

For information about titles, please call:
(800) 223-1244

or visit our website at:
gale.com/thorndike

To share your comments, please write:
Publisher
Thorndike Press
10 Water St., Suite 310
Waterville, ME 04901